"A DARK, STRIKINGLY ORIGINAL BOOK . . . WORTHY OF COMPARISON WITH . . . *RIDDLE-MASTER OF HED* TRILOGY."

—Peter S. Beagle

"A wonderful, magical novel, ripe with mythology and magic—I haven't read anything like it before. . . . It's beautiful—I loved it!"

—Marion Zimmer Bradley

"**YEARWOOD** is a rich, strange, heady mixture, filled with the scents and tastes and sounds of magic. . . . I look forward with great interest to the rest of the story."

—Elizabeth A. Lynn

"His skilled blending of elements from Celtic and Nordic myths is highly unusual. . . . I, for one, shall be most eager to see the next volume in the series."

—Andre Norton

"**YEARWOOD** is a fine book . . . late at night, when the wind is making curious noises outside the windows, and you know that someone—or something—from legend will stride out of the shadows in the next minute or two."

—Robin McKinley

YEARWOOD

Paul Hazel

A TIMESCAPE BOOK
PUBLISHED BY POCKET BOOKS NEW YORK

A Timescape Book published by
POCKET BOOKS, a Simon & Schuster division of
GULF & WESTERN CORPORATION
1230 Avenue of the Americas, New York, N.Y. 10020

ISBN: 0-671-41605-7

First Timescape Books printing April, 1981

10 9 8 7 6 5 4 3 2 1

POCKET and colophon are trademarks of Simon & Schuster.

Printed in the U.S.A.

For Karen,
for Sara and for Tom

Acknowledgments

I would like to express my thanks to Barbara Cizik, who deciphered the manuscript and typed it; to my editor, Natalie Greenberg, for her enthusiasm and guidance; and to my copyeditor, Elisabeth Gleason Humez, for her good counsel. Whatever confusion and error remain are at my insistence.

Contents

I.
The Winter Brood

1.

My mother and her women are of the bitter lineage of the Selchie, the spawn of sealmen and shore folk. In their blood the memory of the undersea kingdoms still rages. In their dreams they still lust for the whiskered and webfooted men who mounted their long dead grandmothers on the shores around Hren and at Weeds in the broad days at the world's beginning. Or so it was whispered in kitchens and halls, a song to keep time with the churning, the pitchers upended, the sour loaves rising like summer mold in the pans. The words floated up to the bedlofts. The eager girls listened and gazed remotely at shapes in the straw.

I thought it foolishness. But there were women enough in those years, crones with their crows' looks, maids with wet eyes, who against hope and all reason still set out from our hill kingdoms and made the hard journey to the coast. There they sat on the shore; the black waves rolled in on them. But if the sealmen ever returned, I had not heard of it. Yet Yllvere—my mother as the servants tell it—settled down at first more readily than Urien's other women. Urien—who was not my father—took her to his bed when she had barely begun her courses.

At the start he was pleased with her and her proud looks, her hair yellow as beer. He married her the next year on the Eve of Teimhne, defying the auguries. Teimhne, according to the old Kell reckoning, was the first night of winter and, with the last loss of light, a time of dread. But Urien hated the women's gods. He scoffed at their mysteries. He had spent his youth in the South, where a man's word was foremost and kings held the law. He had only scorn for the Northmen. When even his housethralls complained to him, huddling before the hall fire on his wedding night, sulking and afraid behind their shields, he laughed at them. They begged him to reconsider. He puffed his hairy cheeks and swore. Though a

12

soldier, he was not unlearned. He had kept watch of the stars and understood the progress of seasons. The Kell cannot count, he said. He would have left it at that had they let him.

Yllvere was his third wife and his last. The others had died soon after their weddings though the wise Kell had held those days to be blessed. The first wife collapsed from fever, the second from a fit which came upon her soon after the birth of the one true heir of the house. The boy was a winter child and sickly, with a birthmark the shape of a horn on his shoulder. The women howled when they saw it and scattered like geese to the hall.

In the evening his mother strangled him. When the servants came to the chamber, her eyes showed only the whites and her mouth foamed. Urien sent the corpse back to her people without guard or ceremony. He had her driven in a plain farmer's cart down to the coast. He refused to pay the price of the burial. Little else was talked of that winter. When Yllvere entered the house, she feared him. She did what he asked and bore him three daughters in as many years. Quickly and silently she bore them, as the aurochs calve in their stalls, her arms folded and nothing in her eyes. But, by all accounts, the wildness in her was merely waiting.

Our house was Morrigan, a seat between the twin peaks of Géar Finn—the highest point in the West. To the east one could look down on a broad plain scattered with river towns and, if one's eyes were keen, to the place where rivers met. There the High King raised Tinkern, the last of godshrines, and Ormkill, the great hall from which, in better days, he ruled. That was a gentle country, worn smooth by its rivers. There the yews grew thick and the furze bloomed golden in April. There, at the river's edge, it was said, every field swelled ripe with barley. On those hillsides the bees were no longer wild but lived, content, in wicker houses set out by men whose dogs, both winter and summer, slept indoors and underfoot. When I was young, such tales seemed strange to me.

Ours was a harder, more ancient land—its rough peaks broken by storms. Our roads, such as they were, had come down from kingdoms now vanished. They were old and narrow. The passes cut through the hills were treacherous, for the stonework was crude and rockslides frequent. Since their making they had never been mended.

The guard towers that lined the cliffs had not been manned in the memory of our people. Even Urien's books despaired of true knowledge of them. They spoke of their builders as giants and their fashioning as sorcery. But to my mind such talk was foolishness. Magicians would have built better roads.

To the west were the sea lands which were so often on the tongues of the women. But they were many days' journey from Morrigan. From the battlements, looking out between the teeth of stone or higher up in the house from Urien's walk, where—an old man in the years I knew him—he read in good light and bad from the books of the wars, one could never see the rolling ocean nor the islands off the coast. But from Géar Finn, from the dark wood on the mountainside, Grieve, my sister, said one might truly see them and the ruined towers at the river's mouth and, if the day were clear, the masts of dragon ships that floated in the harbor. I never doubted this, though I knew soon enough that her thin legs had never carried her into the wood nor that she had ever seen such sights with her own eyes.

"Tell me how you know this?" I asked her. But she would only watch me blankly.

But if I asked, "What is it like there?" Then she would smile, her eyes removed as though they haunted that far place. "In the broad world," she would say to me, "there is nothing to compare with it unless it were the fair realm undersea. There the Selchie first came to land. And, though they are gone, their magic still clings to it. For where they walked, the very sand is emerald and the sea that thunders on the headlands blazes green as fire." Her voice would quiver then and she would go off into herself. But it was the ships I thought of—the bright ships and the bold men who rode them, free of the land, out in the whirling gulf where only stars watched. There would be silence then, long and unchallenged in the hall.

In those years there were none to argue it. So the years followed, one upon another, much as the Kell had counted them, each one chasing round the next as hawks drive sparrows and are driven forth by eagles in their turn.

I had by then grown tall and could, I judged, compete in matters of strength and cunning with many older than myself. Though I was shy a winter of my fourteenth year, the servants were already wary of me. Lately even my aunts and sisters had begun to treat me with caution.

There are advantages to being born the only son and a bastard in a house of women—but not many. Still, for good or ill, in most things I had my way. By then the housethralls, the bearded men with their battle gear strapped to their horses—they who had come in the years Urien had covered himself with glory—now in his disgrace deserted him. He was too old and plagued with sores. Two servants were needed to lift him from his bed. He could not keep me in rein. The women, being witchfolk, kept their own counsel and left me much to mine.

Nonetheless, I did not tell Yllvere my mind was fixed on climbing to the mountain wood, to the high place where Grieve had promised I could look out on the sea. Yllvere would have forbidden that, if nothing else. She would have set her grim servant to lock me in the stable and kept him there to stand guard by the door. Though I suspected it was little more than a nesting place for crows, the wood was holy to the Kell. For the Kell, who believed their grandfathers were sealmen, swore as well that not a few of their grandmothers had been changed into trees. No matter what I thought of that, I was of no mind to court unneeded trouble and for the sake of prudence determined to go armed.

Before dawn I rose and dressed. Stealthily I crept down the dim backstairs and passed the upper kitchen. Neither the cook nor any of her women was as yet about. If I surprised, as I must have, a gray mouse on the stone, I met with nothing else alive.

The armory ran parallel to the guest hall, along the length of the inner wall. In those years the armory had a gray and empty look. It had had, ever since the thralls rode off. Much of the battle gear was gone, the hooks that held it empty. What little remained was rusted for want of use. Tabak, my mother's servant and the one man under sixty in the house, kept his arms apart, even to the point of sleeping with his ax. But it was none of his I wanted.

The longroom twisted toward the back. In its farthest corner, too removed to be of service if need came suddenly, hung Urien's sword. It was a thick two-handed blade. With it he had killed twelve men. My eyes went to it. Even in the bad light its pommel gleamed. Time had barely touched the metal. But the belt and scabbard were rotted. When I pulled it out, the leather parted, giving off

15

a stench like vile old flesh. My lip curled. I thought, just such a ruin has Urien come to. But I did not much care to dwell on him. The sword settled in my belt, I turned quickly, hastening my steps to get out once more into the air.

In the yard I breathed again. The hens fluttered from my path. I threw a stone at the cook's red dog, who came poking out to bark, and drove him back. I might have used the gate. Instead I climbed the palisade. It was more trouble, but it was nearer the mountain. Perhaps I thought myself a thief and meant to act like one. I found the handholds in the stone with ease. With no great effort I made the ledge. A moment later I was bounding up the mountain.

As I remember, it was April, already two months past the thaw and by chance the sign month of my birth. This was an oddity within the house, for all the women were of the winter brood. But in those days I gave no thought to it. The high fields were green and steamed with morning vapor. As I walked, the mist about me broke. Over the hillside there were flowers, their petals still folded in the raw light before sunrise. Many I knew—sorrel, mullein root, and asphodel—such as the aunts gathered, bent over and chanting beneath their breaths. Late and early I had seen them, moving speculatively across the fields. Now those fields were empty, and I ran. When, panting, I looked back, the house was still asleep below me. The day dawned cloudless, the air chilled. Even now I cannot remember a time when I felt more alone in all the world nor liked it better.

In my eagerness I went straight for the wood, leaving a darkened track in the grass behind me like a wake. At the border of the upper meadow the ground rose steeply. Out of the grass, I clambered over gray outcroppings of stone. By then, had anyone wished to follow, my destination would have seemed plain enough. I gave no thought to that. I walked west along the rim of the house lands. Tall spires of ash and elm rose like a wall, dividing what was Urien's—the order of orchards, fields and windrows where the sun, like clockwork, rose and set—from the deep wood of the Kell, where daylight dwindled under interwoven boughs, where morning and evening were scarcely set apart and had no meaning.

At the edge of the wood, like gateposts a dozen feet apart, stood two great trees. Their trunks were gray and more massive than pillars. But their branches were thin and spidery, hung thick with moss. In truth they were no gate at all. Nothing entered here. No path penetrated the gloom. In this place woodcutters were forbidden. Even Yllvere and her sisters, though daughters of the Kell, did not visit here but held it in awe, a place apart from men. The wood was old beyond telling. Yet unlike the great forests—Anhornim in the North and Isenveld in the West, whose peoples are numbered in the books of the wars—it had no name. The women, if they spoke of it at all, called it simply the wood upon the mountain.

I was young. What was there to fear, I thought, of a place that is not even worthy of a name? So I brought upon myself the wound that ever since has marked me. But then I did not know it but thought only that presently I would look out on the sea.

I pushed my way in through a screen of brambles. Even as I entered I did not forget the guest prayer. I spoke aloud although it sounded strangely in my ears. When I had done I added, "Dagda, Lord, I pray for you, if this is Anu's wood, keep harm from me." All else was silent. A gray dusk lay about me. I rubbed my eyes.

I stood within an immense, shaded hall. The floor was carpeted with drifts of leaves, brown and blackened and smelling of mold. The ceiling high above my head was raftered all across with boughs. Between was emptiness. Nothing grew in that bad light. No wind stirred.

I scaled the nearer limbs with both my eyes but found no place to climb. I would have done better with a good rope than a borrowed sword. But I had given no thought to that beforehand, only that the wood was ill rumored and that I had best go armed.

Well, I thought, there is sure to be a good perch farther on. So I lumbered through the drifts of leaves, pleased at least that there was no small bracken to scratch my eyes. Yet, however long I looked, no limb drooped down for me. In all directions there were only the great gray trunks, pale and corpselike, as useless as greased poles. My heart sank. I had come seeking the sea and meant to look on it. Having come this far, I was of no mind to return unsatisfied to Morrigan, to meet, with nothing more to show for it, the questions of my sisters and my aunts. The house rose up again within my thoughts. Angrily, I looked back the way I had come.

He stood there, huge in the tracks that I had made, his broad ax slung upon his shoulder. I gaped at him.

"The boundaries of this place are clear," he said. "You have two good eyes. Surely you have seen that none have walked here."

He could see the anger in my face. The frown he was used to. He knew it at least as well as I knew his own. We were familiar enemies. Though it could not always have been so, it seemed that Tabak had always been about the house. The first of my memories are of him. I was not quite three when a great storm had wrapped itself about the house. Shaken from my bed and blubbering, I had run the dark length of the hall to Yllvere's chamber. He it was who met me outside her door. Each night she would set him there like some tethered animal. His shoulders filled the door frame. He barred the way to her. I remember even his words before he sent me back. "No, my lordling," he had said, "you will find no comfort here." The house shook in the wind. It was as though the thunder itself had spoken. That memory was with me when I answered him.

"Has she called you from your den to haul me back?" I said. Like a stick thrown to her hound, I thought, and swore. "You know I will not gladly go with you."

His eyes were steady. But though his voice was low, yet something of that remembered storm had darkened it.

"It serves little to quarrel with you, lord," he answered evenly. "Whether you come or stay, it is on your head, not on mine."

Still I could not believe that I would be let go so easily.

"Has she not sent you?" I demanded.

He shook his head. "I saw you climb the wall, bearing a sword that was none of yours. That was enough." He remained where he was, too far away to take hold of me. I watched him carefully and yet I did not want to meet his eyes.

"And when you do not bring me back?" I said. "And when she turns her icy stare on you, how will you answer?"

The long, still look of his did not alter. "Lord, it is no more than you are heir to. She knows it. Like any of the Kell, it is the sea you long for." His voice was soft but like a curse he uttered it. Of all the household he was

18

the only one who called me lord. I always thought it mockery. But no smile broke his lips. He simply stood and spoke. And yet the words were like a hiss, like a sea wave sucked back upon itself. The sound unnerved me. I would not listen. "Begone!" I cried and ran myself.

I fled through the aisles of trees. Panting, I drank the dark air down in gulps. The trees grew thicker. Still I ran. Winded, when at last I turned to see how near he came, I found him gone.

Good riddance to that goblin then, I thought. For so I thought of him—a goblin or some great winter bear, a thing that drags its huge shape through ice caves in the dark. Though, in truth, I was alone in that. To the women he was a handsome man, though it seemed they never liked him better for it. For all their craft there was something deep and old in him they could not manage or outwit.

It troubled me to think he had followed me, more so if Yllvere had not sent him searching. My mother's servant, he had no leave for actions of his own. He was Yllvere's alone. Whether Urien's sword was gone or not should have made no difference to him. But more it troubled me how easily, for all his dark looks and his warning, he had let me go. Still I could make little of it and, though puzzled, I drove his cold eyes from my mind.

Thereafter I went more slowly. The black leaves whispered above my head, though now I rarely saw them. A grayness smothered everything so that I felt rather than saw the trees' far summits. Yet, it seemed, they frowned on me. Cautiously, I climbed into a ravine and up the rock face at its northern edge. Even above the rock there was no break in the trees. The air felt heavy. I strained my eyes to see. Away to the left the slope mounted up again. I went on. It was the wood then that beckoned me. I wandered. In time I forgot to look for a low branch I might climb. Almost idly I walked beneath the trees. The grayness filled my sight. Like cool deep water it flowed over me.

My feet were well along the road before I noticed it. As long as the road ran straight, the drifting leaves had masked it. But when the slope grew steep, much like a stair, the road climbed and then the heavy blocks of polished stone shone through. It was an ancient road and yet no rents or breaches tore it. The seams, where they were visible beneath the leaves, were fitted with skill and in a manner now long out of use. I knew it was not the broken work of the quarriers of our old kingdoms but a craft far older. The pride and art that fashioned such stone had faded.

Mournfully, I thought of the great age of the world. I was young then and unaccustomed to such thoughts. In the years that came the *filidh* would say of me that I walked deftly in time, at ease in it as man might ford a river. For as the long years passed I came to know its deep currents and its sandy places. In truth, it started there. Much that would befall me, both the blessing and the curse, began in that deep wood as I gazed upon a road shaped in another age, of which neither we nor the Kell had memory nor so much as one whispered name.

Upward the strange road wound. Looping forward and back, it coiled across the land like the spine of a serpent. I wondered how many ages had come and gone since last a man had walked here. I went more quickly then, curious, spurred on by it. After a while the drifted leaves were fewer. Looking back, I found I had left the last of the trees behind. Yet as before the arch of boughs spread black and impenetrable overhead. It puzzled me. Either the leaves did not fall or else an army came, nightly out of the ground, to sweep the debris away. No less than an army could have cleared the vastness of the country along the road. Either way it was foolishness. I went on doggedly. I meant to discover the reason for such a road. Perhaps, I thought, it rises to one pinnacle or the other of Géar Finn. I remembered the sea again. Upon the summit I knew I might look out over all the West, even to holy Hren itself, whose shore, Grieve said, was emerald.

The stair road climbed along steep featureless walls. Well-hidden from the sun, not even moss or lichen grew there. When, for a moment, I leaned my shoulder, slumped, to rest against the wall, the damp cold bit into it. Surprised, I pulled away. With unaccustomed fierceness I remembered the warmth of the house, the hall fire and the oven rooms on the floor beneath. The bright world, Morrigan, its fields and pastures, seemed far away. I wondered if it were still morning there or if the day had passed already into afternoon. Indeed the light, poor as it had been, had faded more. But whether the sun were draining away from the world beyond or whether the tangled canopy had merely thickened I could not guess. No longer seeing where I went, I should have feared to lose my way and circle, unknowing, back upon myself, had I not felt the road, tier on tier, rising steadily through the lake of darkness.

One foot followed another. Only the stair road, it seemed, had gradually altered underfoot. I had been thinking that for sime time, weighing the difference, half-unconsciously changing my stride.

Something fled past me on the stair. Although I could not see it, I heard a squeak, felt a small furred body rush by my legs, heard for an instant the scrape of claws on stone trail off below. Startled, I grabbed for the wall to hold my balance. But the cold stone I had expected now was gone. In its place was a dry roughness. I scratched it with my nails. One ragged piece came away in my hand.

I turned it over in my palm. It had the feel of bark. Amazement took me. Then with both hands flat against it, I eased my way along the wall, counting the steps, thirty, then a hundred. Everywhere I touched, the wall was bark, extending immeasurably, ever higher than my reach.

Fearing I knew not what, I edged to the other side. Cautiously, I stretched out my hand. But reaching to my fingers' ends I touched only air. My heart leapt high against my ribs.

I stood at the brink, looking out at a chasm I could not see. One misstep and I would have walked, unknowing, into the gulf of air. A tremor ran through me. I hugged the wall. For the first time in my life I feared the Kell, those subtle women and their spider ways. I had come unbidden to this place, their wood where no men came. For an awful moment, I clung to the bark, afraid to move.

Then indeed I might have fallen. For the darkness filled me and blacker than darkness was my own fear. Yet I had not come courting death. Slowly I raised my head, forcing my eyes to search the great vault overhead. I felt a whirling in my brain. I made myself still.

They were no more than sparks, silver holes torn in the blackness—vague and far away, filtered and recast by the darkness. Yet I saw them, like a sprinkling of stars. I raised myself up and followed them, rung upon rung of the stair road until the darkness turned ashen and shapes appeared as out of a mist.

I had climbed to a high place in a tree whose size was beyond telling. Around me were branches broad as avenues where six men might have walked abreast. About

21

the bole of the tree the stair road curled. Now the ragged bark shone silver. It was evening. The long day I had climbed, tireless, like one under an enchantment. But now the vastness took my breath. I could not close my eyes, for the great sight filled it. I stiffened my limbs and made the last steps to the summit of the stair.

I came out among the ebony leaves at the tree's height. The moonlight fell about me and cast a long shadow at my back.

Then at last my eyes leapt out across the jagged wood, out beyond the mountain wall, across the headlands, tumbling seaward. It was the moment I had come for. Yet even in that moment, the line of the dark-rimmed sea already in my eyes, I shuddered. For in that moment I understood why far below me no leaf fell.

Gwen Gildrun, the name shocked through my blood. It took my breath.

Gwen Gildrun.

From the beginning of the world this tree had grown. I was not unlearned. Though not such a marvel as my aunts would freely speak of, I had looked into the books of lore and taken such instruction as could be found when the *filidh* came riding in in winter, trading their songs for a horn of ale.

Gwen Gildrun they called it, the God-Tree. Its roots, they said, sank far beneath the roots of mountains. Old it was as the land upon whose back it stood, a colossus, age after age adding girth and limb until, formless and ever widening, it spanned many leagues. And from the beginning not one leaf fell nor would until the day of doom when the world cracked and the very moon above me fell and darkness once more swallowed up the mountains and the sea. Yet where it grew the *filidh,* for all their learning, could not tell nor, they said, could any man. In that they erred. In their cold hearts the Kell had kept it.

In that moment I ceased to fear the Kell. This was deeper than any magic of shore folk. Though guardians of the place, they were its servants only. Filled with holy dread, they kept away. Better to crawl among the fields below, searching out rats' teeth and henbane, better to hide indoors boiling cats' bones on the kitchen fires. I was alone in this. I stood at the world's height, alone where none had followed, in a place like unto that where creatures first drew breath. I have done a great thing, I thought. Surely, all folk shall talk of this.

I climbed, wondering, through the maze of ancient wood. The undying branches spread in all directions. Indolent they seemed as basking snakes, here smooth and serpentine, but elsewhere curled and knotted, their rough spikes poking up like spears. The tree had no end, no shape. So huge it was that whole great cities might have sunk unseen beneath the humps and swells of shining leaves.

I made a twisted path. In the upper wind the black leaves sighed, the cold air pouring out of the deepest sky. Yet even such a wind could not fill up the quiet. Unmoved and huge, older than the world, the stillness lay beneath the scratch of limbs. The wind sucked at it vainly and was lost. I listened. Something hissed at my back. I turned.

In a nest of vines, still when I looked on them as figures carved in stone, two fledging crows, their eyes like glittering amber, peered back at me. Frozen and unblinking, they met my gaze.

Suddenly the heart within me laughed. Here was a prize to dazzle even Yllvere and the aunts and proof unchallengeable of my climb. The crows of Gwen Gildrun! The glory of it filled my mind.

I meant to have them. Slowly I slid my hand into the nest and dug among the shards of lizard skulls and cracked fish bones. Their cold still eyes, curious but unmoved, stared back at me. Cautiously I put my hands on them. All bone and down they were. Then all at once afraid, they pecked my thumbs. I cuffed them smartly and wound them in my cloak. They did not cry out. And yet, I should have thought.

Over me the immense dark wings had opened with a crack. For an instant only I saw her, the harsh old head disfigured, ruined with scars. She fell too quickly. When I felt the iron claws rake my shoulder, I had only just lifted my borrowed sword. The blood splashed down along my arm.

That moment we both shrieked, she hot with victory, I with searing pain. I covered myself as best I could with both my arms. Her black shadow passed over me. For a breath's space, I was free of her. I set my teeth, knowing I must find a way to make the stair and make it quickly.

I ducked beneath a limb and ran. The rest happened

faster than I thought. I did not see her. She plummeted out of the darkness, from some space invisible between the branches and the moon. Her iron claws grabbed my hair.

With one cruel motion the cold beak thrust itself into my eye. The pain exploded in my skull. I screamed and flailed my arms. Yet I made the opening and plunged back down. The branches caught her. She screeched in anguish, bewailing the loss of her children. Long afterward I heard her, the way barred by the twisted limbs, battering the wood with her vast wings.

Gwen Gildrun covered me. So I escaped the worst of her hatred. But blood poured down my cheek. Weakened, I fell as much as ran. Perhaps the god was with me on the stair. Of the time that followed I have little memory.

2.

YLLVERE AND HER WOMEN FOUND ME. I LAY AT the edge of the wood between the gate trees. She looked into my face. She saw the small life fluttering within my cloak. Sadly, she sent her women back and made them stand across the wall in the next field.

When the women were gone, she knelt beside me. With her own dress linen and a drop from a vial that hung from a silver chain about her waist, she washed my eye, soaking and scouring the rent flesh beneath it where the blood had dried. Her red-gold hair fell before her face and shaded her saucer eyes. Though not quite three-and-thirty, she was mistress of Urien's house and much besides. Because of his sores, his age and shame, she was mistress in truth of the fields and stables and each of the villages about our holding. The pale leaden roof of the forge and the stone walls of the grainery, the houses, sheds and kaleyards and all that was within and without them were in her keeping. The men of the villages, the women and their young, bound to the land, were bound the more to do her bidding. In truth, from the ridge on the high ground wherever it pleased her to look she ruled. And yet those few times in my life that she was gentle with me she seemed shy as a maid.

"I came each day," she said.

I stared at her uncomprehendingly. "How long?" I asked.

"Many days."

I stirred then and moaned. I did not understand. "It is just this morning at sunrise that I went." I spoke with difficulty; my thoughts were frayed. I was dizzy and felt that I would faint. She touched my hair and spoke the name she had for me.

"How long?" I pleaded.

She took my head and laid it in her lap. She smiled. "There is no time within the wood." Her voice was soft but there was hardness at the edge of it. "Without we counted, watching the moon pare down and then grow fat again. We did not know when you would return. We waited." She watched me carefully even as she spoke. So a potter watches, whirling on the wheel the clay beneath his hand, to know that instant when the shape he seeks is made. It gave me pause.

"Why have you sent the women back?" I asked.

She moved and for an instant in the fold of her dress I saw the silver glitter of a knife. She knew that I had seen it and drew back.

"It is a holy place," she said. "No man goes there." There was impatience in her voice but no alarm. "All that is there is as it was at the world's beginning. The power of fashioning out of fire and air has never gone from it." She looked at my ruined eye. "That which makes may unmake, child," she said. "I feared the wood would eat your soul and return to me a man's shape from which the man had gone."

Whatever thoughts then moved across her face I could not read them. She lifted the knife and fastened it securely within her belt.

She said, "I was prepared for what might have come here in your stead." I stared. In those years I lived with her I barely knew the mysteries that claimed her moods. For what child does? But beyond others a strange blood ruled her heart. She was, like all her women, winter born. In her blood seethed memories of the witch kingdoms that were gone. Yet they but gave the outer shape to her grim will. Within their shadow moved another, deeper, more fiercely held, like a knotted fist upon a jewel. I felt its coldness rub against my life. My wits were numb. At the same time her words had shamed me and I burned.

"Mother," I said, "it was not death but life I brought back from the wood." With what strength I had I spread the cloak. The crows in their nesting down began to squawk.

I saw the sharp breath she took then. Her hands slipped back beside her waist. She would not touch them. Presently she said, "You have gone where no man has gone since the first age and yet you are a child. In this especially. These are not the wild crows of the fields. They are Gwen Gildrun's and in that neither Death's nor Life's. The matter is not fixed. It may be they are both." I meant to question her, but already she had waved her women near.

Vydd came, Yllvere's sister, wrapped in a blue robe, her face like a withered apple. She walked barefoot, leaning on her staff. Even in those days the sea longing troubled her. She lived not in Morrigan but in a small hut on the mountain. The walls of the great house frightened her, she said—indoors, among so many women, she could not smell the sea. All knew she was mad. But her eyes, if they were wild, were sometimes tender. She smiled at me. They let her come first. Behind her came the attendant women. Of these only a few were from the villages in our holding. Mostly they came from the river town, out of Laudd and Hwawl, to serve Yllvere, to sit at her feet and learn her craft. Among them were my sisters—Sanngion, Ryth and Grieve, the youngest after me, whom I loved. Only she and mad Vydd smiled on me. When she had seen the crows, Grieve laughed. Then the crows too were comforted and tucked their small heads beneath their stubby wings. The women did not speak to me but bore me on a litter to the house.

This happened in my thirteenth year, in the month of my birth sign, which is April. In the dark of the next moon, when I regained my strength, they held the rite that proclaimed my manhood. I suffered the ceremony silently. All knew I had proved myself beyond their brief mystery on the stable floor. The rite itself was no more than a sham. There were no warriors to share it with me. Urien summoned the millwright out of the village and a few old men from the towns. He offered me neither a sword nor armor. He did not make me his heir. The mill-wright, who had known him many years, rebuked him for his lack of courtesy. Urien only spat in the dust. "What good is a one-eyed man?" he said. He was old then and bitter. The dead child was often in his thoughts.

Urien was not a king, nor even a great lord, though the lands he held had grown to rival the most splendid in the North. As a young man in the service of the High King he had killed twelve men that mattered, eleven in the field—enemies, but men like himself, fond of women and hunting and a drink among friends. He knocked them from their horses. Whacking at them long enough to find a hole between the leather and the iron, he drove his thick sword into their flesh. Somewhere, it is written who they were—what wives were widowed, which sons took their place—but little came of it. The eleven earned him many wounds but small fame. The twelfth was Lot, a man in the king's own following, whom Urien slew at the very feet of the king when the court came down on its yearly pilgrimage to the island of Hren. Lot was drunk that day and in a bad temper, which is to say, he was his usual self. He was not beloved, even among his own kindred. Nor do the *filidh* flatter him. He was a man without luck. While drunk near the holy place where the sea narrows between Hren and the mainland, he insulted the king. Nowhere is it written what was said. When in the years that came I heard the words, it was only to me it mattered. But the offense was fresh then. Because of it Urien slit Lot's throat. In the sight of the soldiers he did it and the High King, who had his own reasons, rewarded him with the house and lands of Morrigan, a gift worthy of kings, ceded to Urien and his descendants forever.

Morrigan was not the first house in the North to be founded on murder. It would not be the last. But like all that is ill gotten, it did him no good. Fate left him only the corpse of a son, his thin neck broken. Such children as Yllvere bore him he could have done without, myself among them. Yet I often wondered whether I would have loved him had I known his company when he was master of Morrigan and his sword arm strong.

There were even times when I wished him my father, since I had none. Sometimes I would wait for hours out-side the locked doors of the tower room beneath the mountain, listening to him pace the floor or to the rustle of pages as he read the great books of the wars. Often I heard him curse and call out the names of the house gods or, sadly, remembering the old wars in the South, the names of the dead he knew.

In the winter, when the light was poor, he would summon Grieve to the tower to read to him. I climbed the long stairs after her and she would let me crouch in behind. Hidden in a corner, far from the fire, I would hear the tales of the old wars, of the bold men and burnt towns, or, best of all, of the far green seas where the heathen fleets, dragon-prowed and heavy with gold, rode the foam like serpents themselves. To these tales I owe what knowledge I had of the outer world, of the genealogies of the northern kingdoms, of their histories and statecraft and such practical matters as the mounting of seiges and the marshaling of assaults. They were good teachers, more patient and less trouble than human tutors would have been. If I had no word of praise from them nor any kindness, neither did I suffer the needless cruelty and disapproval for minor and imagined wrongs nor thrashings when I fell into error.

· I learned quickly. As Grieve read, her voice thin and plaintive in the cold tower room, I memorized the words. Later, when Urien had gone to his bed, I intoned the lockspell she had shown me and, going in once more, took down the books in their heavy leather sheaths and matched my memory to the words until I had learned to make out the figures on my own. It was a cleric's, not a warrior's, training; yet it served me. It filled the empty places in my longing. It gave me dreams. If it left me unsatisfied with the familiar world of Morrigan, it could not be helped. A youth who has heard of the far sea kingdoms and of their ruin and of the frenzy of dragonkind in their nests of blood at Weeds, he will not willingly content himself with idling befroe the kitchen fires with only the dark mumbling of his aunts for company. So from the first my mind was fixed on journeying; and, feeling little wanted where I was, I determined early to try me luck in the world. However slow I was in going, the thought was seldom far from me.

One day I had gone out in the fields with Grieve, bearing the crows, one on each shoulder. I meant to teach them to circle above me, scouting the land, and to return at my command.

"Ninguh, go forth," I cried, lifting my arm and sending

28

the first soaring. "Ninmir, follow." She gave me a haughty look over her shoulder. She spread her wings in the bright air and in a moment she was also gone. Then Grieve and I were alone on the hill.

"So I shall go," I said. "As easily as a crow soars, so I shall leave this house."

Her chin dropped down. She would not meet my eye. "To what place?" she asked.

I answered quickly. "To Ormkill," I said, "to the seat of the High King." For a moment I closed my one good eye, trying to form a picture of the great oak hall that I had never seen, under whose roofbeams it was said a hundred spearmen might gather and a score of serving-women at their call.

Grieve frowned. She was but two years older, yet more a mother to me than Yllvere had been. "Poor boy," she sighed. "You live in dreams. It is not as it is written in the books of the wars. The glory of that hall is broken. Fifteen winters are now gone since the High King vanished. The Steward, Thigg, rules in his place, and badly. Once more the riverlands are in arms. The fields are not tended and the farmers starve."

"Yet I will see it."

She watched me sadly and did not answer all at once but waited as though she debated with herself. "And if you should not find him there?" she said at last.

Bitterly I turned aside. I knew she meant my father. A blush crept slowly across my face. Some things are best not spoken.

"Why are you angry?" she asked.

I looked to see if she were mocking me. Her face was still. Yet a shudder went through me. All my life my father had lain beneath a silence in the house. He was a weight upon our tongues that none dared lift. From the servants I understood I was a bastard. They had their ways of seeing that I knew. But though I spied on them and listened unseen to their gossip, beyond this they themselves knew little more. Yllvere never spoke of it. My early questions she met with cold annoyance. I learned quickly to let the matter be. Yet it twisted in me.

Softly, she circled my waist with her thin arm. Then, as through all those first years, Grieve set herself before the void and kept the dark at bay. Already I was taller by four hands. Any who would have seen us walking together across the field would have thought she was the child. Yet her thoughts were deep and as many-channeled as the mines beneath our mountains. At once I regretted my anger.

"I wonder who he is," I told her simply, "whether he is a great lord or a man like any other. I have thought of this often and have no answer." I paused a moment, then went on. "It is said your father beat her when Yllvere would not give up the name."

Her lips were parted but she did not speak.

We had reached the huge plate of stone which lay in the eastern meadow. The walls of Morrigan had been quarried here. In places there were still scars from the scoring of the rock. But storms had dulled the lines and left the boulders rounded. A wide track led away from it, along which the heavy blocks that made the palisades had been drawn on sledges. Even this was overgrown. In places it had become indistinguishable from the field. We turned back along it.

My mind still burdened, I had spoken more than I intended. Though, in truth, once started, I had expected no more than the chance to share my mood and so to ease it. A little way on she stopped and took my hand.

"I know the time will come when you will leave," she said. "Sorely I will miss you then. But that time is not yet. Deeper than words I know this. Above us, even as I heard her, the crows were circling, high up in the mountain wind.

"How is it that you know?" I asked.

She made a witch sign in the air between us so I would not continue. Yet I pressed her. She looked at me out of her deep, troubled eyes. Though she was dearer to me than any in the house, something in her look reminded me that she was as much like the others as surely she was apart. In many things their ways were hers. The Kell blood flooded her veins and one might never know for certain whether she or it was master of her thoughts.

"I have watched and counted," she said thickly. So the Kell have always answered when they meant to keep their secrets to themselves.

I shook my head. She saw then how I hated it.

"Is this all you can say to me?" I shouted.

The sun above the mountain flickered like two mirrored flames within her eyes. She did not blink.

"You must speak with Vydd," she answered hotly. This told me nothing but I saw how much the words had cost her. I made no more of it. The rest of the way we went in silence. Before the house I called the crows down from the wind.

Ninmir, whose name in the old tongue means Memory, came first. Then Ninguh, whose name means Thought. Fierce with sight, their eyes, like Grieve's, shone red-gold in the sun.

3.

THERE WERE TWO VILLAGES NEAR THE HOUSE of Morrigan, but the people feared us. Though the times were poor enough, there were no village women willing to nurse a young bastard for a few copper coins. Thus it happened that the first years of my childhood were spent unavoidably in the company of my aunts and sisters. I learned to walk on the hard bakery floor. For toys I had neither a sword nor arrows but a sow's clavicle and ointment jars. It fell to Grieve to teach me to speak. My first words were the names of plants and medicinal herbs. The men's language I had to master on my own, piecing it together from the chronicles of Gedd, the records of wars, which Urien kept under lock in his tower. This also I owe to Grieve. She taught me the lockspells that unsealed the iron doors. With her only I have no quarrel.

The women were foragers, collectors of fungus, foxbane and crows' ankles. Roots and stalks hung from the rafters. Black pots hissed on the open fires. Morning and evening the House of Morrigan smelled of musk, seared oil and burflour cakes baking past midnight in earthen ovens. But their lives, like their bodies, were thin. There was no strength in their food; the wine they made in the press was bitter and the color of water.

Vydd was the oldest. She had come when Yllvere called her, to tutor Sanngion, the first living born, and stayed on for the others, Ryth and Grieve. Yllvere gave them names of her own design, without so much as asking the leave of her lord. Yllvere grew stronger with the birth of each daughter, as Urien grew less. When his liegemen deserted him, she took hold of the house, kept accounts and managed the holding. Yet after their naming she left my sisters to Vydd.

Yllvere had no talent for mothering. She became in its place a mistress of earth magic, which was the legacy of the Kell, and not only the lesser skills of healing but also those more subtle matters of the binding of wills of men and of beasts. With the years she drew into her art. In the day she ordered the planting and spinning and set the hour for the ingathering of the grain. In the evening she withdrew to her cell at the bottom of the house. A long stair went down to it, a place behind the ovens where the floor was so hot it burned the soles of her feet. There she whispered and sang in the old tongue until long after the women had crawled off to their beds. The rest was Vydd's —what my sisters ate and wore, the games played and lore mastered. That much I learned from the servants in the years when they spoke freely before me, a child waddling between their knees. Their eyes filled with mirth at the odd ways of their mistress, before they saw that I understood. Vydd lived in the house then. The walls of Morrigan had not yet begun to fill her with dread nor had she begun to look for the smell of the sea. That time would come.

A month after I had come down from the quarry with Grieve I had still not gone to Vydd's hut on the mountain. Yet the thought deviled me. I sucked on it daily like a sore tooth. When I rolled over in my sleep I saw her withered face in the cracks of the wall. The wind blew under the eaves and I heard the low moan of her voice. Once when I had gone out on the mountain to clear the weeds from the cistern which held the water for the house I saw her against the side of a hill. She was leaning on her stick and looking across to me. She called out the name she had for me. I heard it clearly. I pretended not to notice and went down the long way to the house before I had finished. The truth was, I had been too long alone with my thoughts. But for that day with Grieve and my childhood questions of Yllvere, I had spoken of my father to no living man.

Yet I brooded over him. When I was younger, I had built him into a great lord. In my mind I saw him, wronged by some enemy, rise up in his war gear and full of righteous anger cut an armed man down in his place so that the man twisted like a spider, the cold metal stuck in his chest. In those moments, my own heart racing, we seemed as one. His foes were mine and also his glory. I killed a hundred men in my imagining, all in his service. When I was older I saw the folly of so much gore. Then, though I saw him stern and brave, I hoped there was more to him than a string of murders. Any fool, I reasoned, can poke another man's belly with a knife. I wished him better than that, perhaps because I wished myself more as well. In time I also hated him because he never rode within the walls of Morrigan, his retinue behind him, to acknowledge me. Then I thought, perhaps he is only a tinker or a harper or even a rude farmer from Tyre, a riverman, a make of fish weirs. But neither lord nor sailor came to claim me. One season rolled on to another. From one month to the next I made ready to set out seeking him, since he had not come. Time passed. Yet I did not go up to Vydd on the mountain. At heart I feared knowing and kept my thoughts to myself.

It was nearly winter when the millwright came up alone from his village. I was in the yard and saw him. He wore a clean longshirt and had brushed his beard. Under his arm he carried a sheaf of tables bound in aurochs' hide. By that I knew he had come on the matter of the service his village owed us. His name was Jjared. Like all men of our mountains he was small, the gray wool of his head barely reaching to the middle of my chest. He grinned when he saw me and came to my side. Despite his holiday dress, he smelled of barley as he had since the months of the harvest.

"Come, lad," he said cheerfully, "show me in to Urien. For I have brought the book and come to settle our accounts." He laughed but there was no mockery in him. Yet between us we both knew he lied. He went to Urien out of their old friendship. In truth, it was Yllvere who had set the service. I knew that when he had finished in the tower, he would follow the long stair down to the oven rooms to meet with my mother and settle the matter in earnest. It has been so as long as I remembered. Still I went with him. That too was for show. He knew the way as well as I.

At the top of the stairs I knocked upon the heavy door. It was cast in one thick slab of iron and drank the sound of my rapping. But Urien had heard it.

"Who comes to me?" he shouted from within, his voice like an echo out of stone.

I started to speak, but Jjared hushed me. Though one of our carls, he was a man well thought of. So I gave him his way in this.

"It is Jjared, my lord," he answered, "come to reckon the service."

"It is well," Urien said. His voice was softer now. It may be there was even pleasure in it. But before he bade him enter, he added, an old man mumbling to himself, "See, all is not forgotten. It is the proper day. The winter stars hover at the rim of the horizon. There is a coldness in the ground. I feel it even here."

A silence followed. I heard the chair scrape and his labored walk across the floor. But on the other side of the door he stopped. Perhaps I moved. There was some uncertainty in his hand upon the latch.

"There is another with you," he spat accusingly.

My back stiffened. I moved to speak. Once more Jjared placed his hand before his lips and in my stead he answered evenly, "I met the lad in the yard and bade him bring me to you."

"Whose lad is that?" he thundered.

Jjared motioned me to silence. But a fire burned in me and I would not have more of it.

"It is Herawd," I said plainly, using the name Grieve called me. For a moment there was no sound. When he broke the silence, the voice behind the door was cold and stern.

"Send Yllvere's bastard back to her," he said.

Jjared looked at me. Though it pained me, I was too proud to look away. To this day what interest he had in me I do not know for certain, only that he was a man well schooled in courtesy. It may be that he thought he served us both. Like other men he had no love for the women's gods. It may be he saw in me a hand to strengthen Urien against the Kell. Who is to say? If that were his purpose, it failed him utterly. For that monent I knew I would go at last to Vydd and soon be done with the house and its lord together.

Halfway down the stair I heard the iron door open. I did not stop to listen. No longer was it a concern of mine.

I went first to the mews at the north end of the stable. No hawks had been cooped there since Lot went off on his unlucky pilgrimage with the High King and Urien came back in his place. But there, tucked back from the narrow windows, on a shelf out of the wind, I kept my crows. I meant to gather what was mine, little as it was. My thoughts on Vydd and what I would say to her, I toyed absently with a mole I had in my pocket. I had found it squeaking by the door, a cat's plaything, and brought it up for them.

"Ninguh," I called out softly before I had quite reached the place. No voice answered me. I forged into the small passage between the stable and the mews, turned a corner and came before the perch. The shelf was empty. The leather straps with which I had bound the crows were cut. My head swam with astonishment. "Who would dare this?" I cried aloud. But there were none to answer it. I went out angry, nursing all that wronged me.

The clouds were low over Géar Finn, its twin horns hidden. The wind came down from there, sailing over the walls. Already there were a few brown leaves swirling in the yard, the first carrion of autumn. The air was heavy, gray enough for snow, but there was none.

I went over the wall to avoid the servants and my sisters. I was of no mind for prying eyes and questions. For some time I followed the track north and west, then parted from it. Vydd's hut was away from the land we tilled, in a patch of rubble that barely suited goats. The grass was scarce and the ground littered with mounds of stone. The hut, when I came upon it on the hillside, seemed little more than a slightly larger mound with rough holes scratched into the sides for a door and windows. Flaps of deerhide covered the openings. Rag ends of smoke escaped around the edges. But if Vydd were mad, she was also the eldest witch born. So I had not come this way often. Yet once or twice she had smiled at me, a smile so unlooked-for that it had followed me for days.

I stepped down into the hole and peered inside. Vydd was hunched over a crude table with her back to me, intent on some work of hers I could not see. The hut was dingy with smoke. It was difficult to see much clearly. Yet I recognized at the level of my forehead the herbs of her art, which she had hanging from the roofbeams. The hut smelled of mullein root, dried snakeskin and smoke. The rest seemed to be pots and bowls, loose on the floor or piled one on another along the wall. In one corner I could make out a low bed with just a rag of a blanket.

Without turning, she poked at the fire with her stick. Her arm was thin.

I tugged at the flap to let her know someone was there. "Aunt," I said, "I have come to see you." I ducked inside.

She glanced around without surprise and winked at me. "Agravaine," she said, for she had her own name for me, "I am pleased . . . as they are." She pulled herself back from her work.

Just above the table a vaporous wing unfolded in the gloom. The dark shape coughed. A second black thing shook its sly head and glared at me. They were my crows and Vydd was the thief. It was in my mouth to rail at her, but something caught my words.

Vydd steadied herself with her crooked stick and stood before me. "My child," she said, "I have had a dream about them. So I went and brought them here to watch them and to see if the dream were true." This nonsense untied my tongue. I said, "Had I dreamed of a dragon, I would not stick it in my pocket and run home with it."

"You may have already," she answered, laughing. "Or something very like." I grew impatient. "These are mine," I told her. "I mean to have them."

"And so, my fox, you shall. When I am done with them. First I must teach them manspeech. See, already I have cut their tongues. The blood stopped quickly. It is a good sign." A curl of smoke came from her parted lips. I stared at her angrily. She held in her hand a short pipe, which she put back then between her small mouse teeth. She drew at the stem as though she thought. Then she said, "You must be patient. It is not such advice as the young take easily. But you will have to make do with it. We old women are like the earth; we give our secrets grudgingly. Still you will learn and we shall give you what is needful as we must." At that she laughed, a small chirping laugh like a cricket's, and pulled my arm. "Come, sit with me," she said. "Let it rest between us. The crows are only borrowed. Soon enough you will have them back."

But I stayed by the door so that she was at my arm again. "Come," she said in a voice grown softer but with the laughter drained from it. "An old women needs company." I watched her face, a nest of fine wrinkles, her small ragged mouth like a hole in a spider's web. It saddened me. For that I followed her, tucking my head down and stooping my shoulders to keep from bumping the roofbeams. She watched my progress with careful eyes.

"My house was not made for giants," she said when I found a place, snug between the table and the wall.

I answered without thinking. "I am a man like any other."

She said nothing but made a low murmur in her throat. For some time she appeared to busy herself, shifting bowls of meal and powder without particular purpose between the table and the floor. Perhaps it gave her time to think. I do not know.

"When the liegemen fled the house, you were not born," she said afterward. "Such as stayed with him are withered, bent with their years. I doubt that you have seen a proper man."

"There are men in the villages" I answered. "I have talked with the millwright, Jjared, and seen the rest."

"Then you know what I mean."

"Truly, they are small," I said, puzzled. "They come, it is said, from the folk that tunneled in the mines beneath Géar Finn. They are small as all miners are. I have thought of this, Aunt, and such is my answer. I see nothing more in it."

She rocked gently as she sat on her stool and listened to me. She was full of tiny movements. She sucked her pipe or bit her thumbs. Yet her eyes were on me like a baited trap. "Why is it you have turned your mind to this?" she asked when I had done.

I shook my head. "As I have said, for they are small. Truly, I have seen how the world is."

"Just so," she answered chuckling. "What lad would think himself apart from other men? Yet for this you turn your reason from yourself." All at once she threw back her small head and gazed at me with dancing eyes. "Shall I tell you what no others will?"

I had come with questions. So I nodded.

She smiled, but there was sadness in her face as well. She said, "The village men are as other men, no smaller. Had you been elsewhere you would have known this."

My skin prickled. "But you said I had seen no proper man."

"There are men and there are men," she said.

I could make nothing of this and glared at her. "My mother has a servant," I protested. "Tabak, the one she keeps to herself to do her bidding."

"I know of him."

"Then you have seen there is not an inch between us."

"He is very like you," she answered, but I saw she had some other meaning to it.

"I do not follow you," I said.

She paused a long moment to reprove me. "Then let it be. I will bring you some broth. Perhaps you will drink a little wisdom down with it. Afterward we will talk about that which brings you."

I wanted another word, but she was busy muttering among the bowls and ladling water from a crock. When I talked to her, she would not listen, but went on poking the fire. She settled an iron pot on the coals, then lay back to watch it. Rocking gently on her stool, her pipe back between her teeth, she sang. The song was old. Half the words I did not know. There was a part about the lost kingdoms undersea and another meant, I thought, to be the wail of sealmen heard among the rocks. The rest was gibberish, but I felt the longing in it. Ninmir came out of the corner where she had crouched and pranced across the table until she stood before Vydd's knees. The young crow seemed to study my aunt, cocking her black head as though she listened. The song lingered in the air when she had done.

When I found my voice, I said, "I came to ask about my father."

She brought me a cup of broth before she spoke. She put it in my hands. "What have they told you, child?" she asked.

"Nothing, but that I am not Urien's."

"It is fitting," she replied gravely. "For that is all they know."

"Then you must tell me."

"First drink what I have given you."

So that she would go on, I drank. It tasted of brine. "This is bitter," I said.

"Truly," she answered, "it is that. Now hold your tongue." Then she drew her stick into her lap and began to measure lengths along it with her thumb until I saw that she was counting. When she came to a certain place, she stopped. When she began to speak, her voice, it seemed, was drawn up from that same far place wherein she had found her song.

"Two winters before your birth," she said, "when your mother was just seventeen, she quit Urien's bed at last.

38

Grieve was born then. Thereafter she no longer went to him. The snow was high that year. When it grew dark and the roofbeams groaned beneath the drifts, the whole house slept on the floor in front of the ovens. Even Urien came down despite his pride. Only Yllvere stayed in the upper house. For she could not bear the sight of the world's men. Agravaine, you know we are the Kell. That at least was never hid from you. And though we have never seen them, still we remember the men of old—how once they came from their fair kingdoms undersea and walked as bold as life upon the shore. In our dreams we feel their breath and see their steaming hair, black as pitch and wet upon their necks. The hollows of our bellies feel the loss. When we awaken in the night, the cold leather of their arms still chills our backs. Whether late or early, in time all yield to it.

"So, child, it came to her as well. Nightly we heard her groaning from her bed. She took to chanting spells and weeping and calling out great oaths. Once a house-thrall, who had gone out on the mountain to gather wood, discovered her wandering over the hills without her cloak or even a sheath to cover her. Fearing the worst, I brewed burdock and candlewick in a broth and set it hot before her. She would not drink. When they had got her to her bed, we stationed guards before the doors. In their boots, to keep themselves awake, the guards placed stones. Yet in spite of vigilance, one morning, yawning and brushing the spellwebs from their eyes, they found her gone.

"Urien shaved his head and wept. He was a man then and she had been his favorite. He forgot his hunting companions. When in the hall they drank and hung on each other's arms, joking about the women in the river towns, he had them beaten. They only sneered at him. Once, when the rage was hottest in his blood, he cut a man with his knife. So one by one they left him, cursing his weakness, his anger and his tears. He did not plead to keep them. But nightly he went to the wall that ringed the yards, each night facing a new direction, first west to the great sea, that being the most likely, then east toward Ormkill. When he saw no sign of her, he turned north to the kingdoms of his own people and when the horizon remained empty, south toward Weeds, where once the dragons came ashore despoiling the godshrine at Reon. What remained of the household waited with him, the women keeping close to the windows, the dog boy on the roof of his kennel, all night under the stars, till all grew weary of the watch.

"One year yielded to the next. It was deep in the second winter when she came back. She rode a fine mare. At her side, leading the horse, was Tabak. He was much larger than Urien or any of the earls, a colossus with a barrel chest and long brown arms. The eyes in his sun-blackened face were deep and strange, the color of almonds. He was dressed, as she was, in embroidered cloth far richer than the hillspun which was then the custom of the house. Yet he was no lord, but her servant only. He wore a huge ax strapped to his back and at his side a stout two-handed sword. Still, for all his weaponry, he was gentle with her. He helped her down from her mount that day with care. The servants crowded into the yard. All saw at once the reason for his gentleness. Neither her robes nor belts of leather and silver could hide the thick swelling she carried beneath. We lowered our eyes so none would see her shame. We thought, having shown herself, she would mount her mare again and ride out through the gates, back to her new-found lord, to the place of his dwelling in some far place. We waited, none daring to speak.

"Your mother stared at us. She called us each by name, her sisters and her daughters and all the servants one by one. Yet there was a majesty in her bearing and we feared her. Grieve hid behind my skirts. She would not go out to her. A fierce glow patched your mother's cheeks. 'Tell Urien,' she commanded, 'that I have brought the house an heir.' No one moved. Finally, one old woman, Branwen, the last of Urien's own servants, taking a long glance over her shoulder, disappeared into the house. After a time Urien came to his tower window. His beard was tangled. In two years his hair had gone white. Even the women felt sorry for him. Knowing he was there, Yllvere did not need to look at him. Unclasping her costly cloak and handing it to her servant, she passed calmly over the threshold.

"That spring you were born. A dozen lamps were set by her bedside. There were as many women to attend her. But at the end there was only myself alone with her. The birth was hard. Although she had eased many another into the world before you, you were far larger. Your head and shoulders seemed too broad to pass from her. I took the knife myself. If it were not for the working of the goddess and such skill as I had, you both would have perished. As it was, she lost much blood and kept long to her bed.

"Urien did not come to her. It was I who brought the news. I found him in his tower before the fire. 'The thing is done,' he said with assurance when he saw me at the door. 'It is a manchild,' I answered boldly. His look was sullen, but there was craft in his eyes. In his lap he held the book of wars. He closed it quickly. Yet I saw that it was the Red Branch which marks the names and heraldry of the great houses back to the first age. 'Well, woman, what is it that she calls him?' he asked me softly. He tried to sweeten his voice, but it did no good. I saw he meant to track it in the book, for all true names follow, root and branch, back to their beginnings. So I was silent.

" 'Be not too long, at it,' he said.

" 'There was no naming,' I answered finally and in that I told the truth. Then I said, 'At the moment of birth she fainted. I called the women and they took the child.'

"At this his breath came from him in a hiss. 'See to it that when she gives the name I know it,' he warned me harshly. I nodded and went out greatly troubled. But from that time I saw to it that no true name was given you. And this was easier than I had thought.

"I have told you she lost much blood. From the dark of one moon to the dark of another, her mind was addled. She forgot the names of her servingwomen and remained indifferent to her own. All the while you fed at her milk-hard breasts, she took no more note of you than would a viper its young. It was I who held you when you cried. When the weakness left her, she returned to her magic and took up as before. There were the house to manage and the fields. Thereafter you were left to me, and when the fevered dreams burned in my head, it fell to your sisters. They took you as readily as they would take a new doll and tired as easily when you squirmed and vomited. Each named you in her turn. For Sanngion you were Elbrim, for Ryth, Hwyll. They say Grieve calls you Herawd now. She kept you longest, so perhaps that name is best. Yet it is as meaningless as the one I gave you. Still, there was ever someone in the house to do Urien's bidding. I have no doubt that each name was tiptoed up the tower stairs to him nor that he traced them as they came, night after night folding back the pages of the great book in the

41

bad light of the fire until his eyes began to fail. No good it did him."

Then Vydd laughed and laid her stick against the wall. The pipe was dead in her hand. Once more she filled it and, plucking a live coal from the fire, she puffed her shallow cheeks till it was lit. The blue smoke curled past her forehead and mingled in her hair. Presently she said, "This much I know of your beginning." My face fell.

At last I said, "Some I knew, though much was strange to me. Yet nothing touches on my father, either who he is or where I must go to find him."

Vydd saw my disappointment. She smiled thinly. "That hour must come, my child, though it is not yet. Give thanks for that. It is more a blessing than you know. Rather be still and sit with me."

But I saw only her want of company. So I frowned and stood, crouching beneath the roof. I had my own thoughts and my longing. So I forgot myself. "When I open your riddles there is only dust inside," I told her harshly. Her eyes went queer. She was old and witchborn. It was difficult to remember that she was also a woman. She wept before me. She leaned against the wall, frail as her old stick, and trembled.

"For a time you may keep the crows to teach them," I said awkwardly, for I sought a way to please her. But truly I knew not how to comfort her.

"The fault is mine that you are cruel," she said. Her voice was soft as though it came from far off. There was music and sadness in it like a young woman's. "I feared that Urien would discover what you were and kill you. For that I did not let you have a name. Without a name you have no heart, as no man has until he knows himself. Yet surely your name would give your heart to you and break it all at once."

I caught her fiercely by the shoulders then. I lifted her. Light as a child she was. "By the god," I cried, "damn hearts and breaking! Just tell me who I am!"

She shivered at my touch. Her eyes burned strangely. For an instant she had laid her head against my chest. A great roar drummed against my ears, a sound so huge I thought it filled the earth. Yet I could not tell what it was. Then, it seemed reluctantly, she pulled herself away. The sound went with her, retreating like a great rain going, like a cloud that drifts far off upon the mountain.

"Put me down, child," she commanded coldly. Startled,

42

I found an old woman in my arms. She smelled of smoke and salt. My flesh crawled. At once I let her touch the floor. She hobbled back to her stool, then turned to look at me.

She said, "For years beyond telling, the Kell have watched and counted, child. This only I will tell you. That for which you wait is near. But it goes ever as it must. It will not be hurried. Still, your part will not be hidden longer than you can bear."

My blood rushed through me and I cried, "You tell me nothing!"

She turned her face to the wall, drawing her small feet up beneath her like a child. "Go then to Yllvere," she murmured thickly. "Ask her where her servant went the night you were born."

"You give me but another nut to crack," I said. "Better to ask her outright my father's name."

She hissed at me. Her tongue flickered in her mouth, black like a swan's. A fever took her. Her tangled hair stood out from her head like silver wire. "You are neither child nor man," she screamed at me, "but a fool only. She is greater than all the daughters of the Kell. What was given her has not been given since the world was young. You who share our blood, how is it you are blind to this?"

"I have feared her, but I shall no longer," I answered when I thought. "Now I shall not ask, but make her answer."

Her gray eyes smoldered in her head. She whispered darkly, sucking at her lips. "She will not answer. The oath that binds her she dares not break. Do only as I bid you. Seek her in her cell when the house sleeps and she is by herself. Then, though it shame you, grab hold of her robe. If you do this, she cannot turn from you. Then she will tell you what she can. Only do not look overlong into her fires. Such was not made for men."

She ceased. There was a weariness in her face, and pain. Her fury had eaten all my thoughts. I had no word to say to her. So I went out on the hillside. The wind was cold. The bank of clouds had drifted farther down the mountain. In the gray weather a few hard kernels of first snow sped past my eye. Yllvere will be in her cell tonight, I thought. For it was the Eve of Teimhne, when men fear darkness more than other times and stay indoors. Even then I saw how swiftly the light was draining from the world. Already the owls were out hunting. The river lands were dark, the shoulders of the mountain deep in shadow. I went quickly then until at last I saw the walls of Morrigan, its roofs and chimneys pricking into the last light like thorns. For a moment I watched it. There all the years of my life were numbered. But for the villages in our holding and the wood upon the mountain I knew no other place. As I watched, the windows stared back at me, bleak and empty, like the eyes of a man whose soul has left him.

After a time I went down to it. I shunned the back lanes and side doors, that led into the yard, and went instead to the high front gate that opened in the wall. There I entered, much as a stranger would, toiling up the steep road from the east, begging bread and a place indoors before the fire, on this the year's long night.

4.

THOUGH I SELDOM DID, I WENT THAT NIGHT INto the hall for company. The meal was done and the servants clearing. By some mischance the dogs got in. Yelping for the smell of meat and snapping at the bones, they toppled a table and had to be driven from the hall. Sanngion, who had put on a new robe only to see a greasy platter overturned upon it, sent word to have the dog boy beaten. She was a woman of middle height, seventeen then, yellow-haired and spare, with the gray eyes of the Kell but with a wide unthinking mouth that was hers only. Like that of all my sisters her skin was fair, almost to whiteness. Yet Yllvere was fairer still, even beyond the race. In the village I had sometimes heard her called the ice witch, though not to my face. But my mother had already gone from the hall, leaving Sanngion to order the women. I saw by the way she sent them scurrying that this pleased her. She held her head tilted slightly, as I had seen my mother do a thousand times, only Sanngion had not her grace. I turned from watching her and stopped a serving girl to take a horn of beer. It may be Sanngion felt my eye had left her. She called out loudly to be certain that I heard, "Elbrim grows fearless lately. See, sisters, how tardily he came into the hall, the Great Night already fallen."

"I see not where it is a concern of yours," I said.

"Our dark brother grows surly too," she answered without faltering. Yet I saw she glanced sidelong at Ryth to be certain that the other shared her sport. Ryth smiled absently into her cup. Sanngion went on, "You should not be offended. Indeed it is a pleasure to have you dine with us, so rarely it is you do."

Ryth giggled. Wiping the wine stain from her upper lip, she said, "Yes, tell us why you honor us. From what I've seen, you prize the damp mews and nursing wormy crows above our company."

"No," said Sanngion. "It is the dark he prizes, being half in it already."

Ryth laughed outright then, but nervously. Only Grieve sat silent at her place.

"Truly that is something that I wonder," Ryth said, joining in. "As you are, can you both see and dream at once?" She looked around to see what I would say.

Sanngion's smile had widened. She crossed her thin arms upon her breasts. "Yes, brother, I am curious to hear this also."

They knew I had no answer for them.

Ryth pouted. "His love for his crows is more." Slyly, she began to whine.

"The crows are gone," I said. Then all at once I rose up from the table. Standing over them, I let them feel my height. "Today," I said, "I gave them to Vydd's keeping."

Grieve whipped around me. Her breath came sharply. There was wonder in her look, and fear, and, just as I turned to find the door, at the very corner of her lips, a smile.

I went up the stairs that bent around the watchtower. It was opposite to Urien's and smaller, with space for but a single guard. On the stair a lamp was burning. It made a patch of oily soot above the flame. Throughout the house this night the lamps were bright. In the hall and in the kitchen, fires had been built high to last past midnight, when the servants would roll out new logs to keep the fires till morning. Such was the custom on Teimhne. I took the stair lamp down and smothered it.

The guard post was unmanned. Urien had none to watch for him. But Yllvere's fame, her women told each other boldly, had spread among the river lords and kept their spearmen from our mountain. In truth none came. But then Morrigan was always on the edges of the world. I climbed out on the roof, holding to a spike to keep my balance. Here I meant to wait until the housethralls pulled the last logs on the hearths and crawled, weary and relieved, into the safety of their beds. Above the walls I could look out across the night. The smudged light of the nearest village leapt red against the winter clouds. There, alone before the barred doors of his kin, one man would keep a huge fire burning through the night. That also was the custom.

A chill wind drove down from the mountain. I heard the deathless leaves of Gwen Gildrun whisper on it. I closed my mind and would not listen. Instead I thought of Yllvere. Soon, I thought, she will go down the long stair to her cell beneath the house. Yet I knew the rest must sleep before I followed. I pulled the wool of my cloak closer about my shoulders. Still I shivered.

Beyond the wall the world lay silent, hushed but for the wind, and hidden. Only the red light of the village fire was with me. It watched me like an eye. I wished it gone, blinded like my own. I closed the one that saw and sat, waiting for the night to fill my head with darkness, the wind to chill the heart I did not have until it stopped. There are places in the soul a man would hide from, times a man might rather die than see too clearly his own face. I was a long time alone. Then something nudged me. I turned and found Grieve sitting down beside me, the red light of the distant fire curling like a worm in each of her eyes.

"Herawd?" she said.

"It is not my name."

"She told you, then."

"Nothing."

"She spoke with you."

"She told me a long story which did not have my father's name. For this I was angry with her. So she took away my own."

"Not then," she said. "When you were born."

"It is the same."

"No."

"I do not have it."

46

"My father would have killed you had he known."

"He is too old."

"Not in the beginning. It was his searching that sucked his life."

"In the books you read him."

"Yes."

"And you knew then what he looked for?"

"Yes."

"And still you read to him."

She smiled. "Only what I pleased, not what he sought." She looked at me hopefully. "Come in to the fire," she said.

It had begun to snow. Huge flakes like wheels of crystal swirled above the roof and filled our sight. I thought of the man upon the mountain whose work it was to feed the fire. I pitied him. The farmers say on Teimhne that even the dead fear this long night, that it will never end. For the dead are the earth's as well and keep her seasons. Drawn, they crawl from their deep shadows. Their faces, the color of iron, hang at the edges of the light. He that keeps the fire must look on them, even on the faces of those he loved.

"Go down to bed," I told her. She stared at me. Then her face twisted and she broke away. I did not follow her. I heard her footsteps vanish on the stair. A long time after, I went down.

The fire burned high in the empty hall, throwing the shadows back into corners. A wide passage led past the kitchens. Many doors and openings branched off along the way, the rooms empty but filled with light—here with lamps and there with candles. Everywhere beneath the roof the hot air smelled of wax and oil. The kitchen opened under a broad stone arch. There in the large round chamber the ovens roared with flame. The knives were put away. But on the flat square tables the rising bowls lay abandoned where the cook had left them, unscrubbed and sour. From the scullery there came a sound. I peered in but it was only a pair of eels, still alive and rolling over one another in a pail.

Across the room by the side of the ovens there was a door. It was small and windowless. Its hinges were gray metal. No device marked it. It might have led into the yard or out to the cold pantry where the meat hung in coats of fat and the stone floors were sticky with blood.

But it did not. Even in its plainness it was Yllvere's. All the house knew it and let it be.

The latch came easily. It opened with my touch upon the ring. Inside, a narrow stair dropped into the dark. I went a few steps. On one side, cut within the wall, there was a ledge where once, I judged, torches had been kept. Nothing remained but a clay vessel cracked along one side and a black stain where the tar had hardened on the stone. She also is at home in the dark, I thought, and so went on.

At first there was light from above, a wavering glow from the oven fires. Then the narrow stairs turned a corner and the weak light faded. After that I had only the sound of my own breath for company, though once I thought I heard the faint trickle of unseen water dripping on the rock. Gradually the air grew cooler. I felt my way along the wall. The stone was rough and crudely set, older work than the house above. In places there were fissures—some wide enough to hold my fist. I thought of snakes and dared not thrust my hand in them.

It was not the same dark underground. Here daylight never entered. Changeless, with no seasons, the dark had settled ever farther down within itself, bloated yet never satisfied, sucking at the upper world. All my life I had heard whispers, servants' talk, that the stair was deeply delved, cut into the heart of the mountain rock, or that it joined, after twisting through a maze of many tunnels and vaulted rooms, the great mines that lay beneath Géar Finn. I had thought it only women's talk. Now I wondered.

The Kell say that at the beginning, in a place that no man knows, the dark, in the anguish of her labor, waited to devour the sun and moon, her children, as they sprang from her side. Cold she was and hungry, coiled like a serpent about the well from which the waters of time flow into the world. It was the god Duinn, it is said, who tricked her, filling her belly with great stones. I pondered this but could not laugh. Who is to say whether such talk is truth or lies? I knew only that the darkness weighed on me. It stole my sight and blew dust into my mouth. Although I had wished for darkness alone upon the roof, I grew to fear it underground. For a moment I wanted no more of it and wished for light. But then I shook myself, finding courage in my own flesh. Have I not climbed

48

their sacred tree? I thought. Like Duinn, have I not stolen from their dark mother the children of the air?

I went more quickly after that. The passage that had been almost cold grew warmer by degrees. A whisper of parched air blew against my cheek. As suddenly it was gone. But soon it came in scalding waves that buffeted my chest and arms. Deep within the stone something beat and thundered. Then around a corner a red glare leapt up along the wall. I crept down to it. Softly, like a thief, I slipped within my mother's cell.

All at once a sheet of flame took all my sight. Shielding my face, I shuddered and fell back. Intent upon the fire, Yllvere did not notice me. Her arms were raised, her robe dropped to her elbows so that the pale skin took on the color of the fire. The hot wind lifted her long hair, red-gold and gleaming, like a flame itself. Her eyes were fierce, her small mouth twisted, the eldest words of Kell speech in her throat.

"Sí man i yulma nin enquantuva?" she asked the fire. Then in some sadness of her own she turned away, plucking a bowl from her table. She drew a small claw from it. The nails were red-silver and scattered light. I saw she meant to toss it to the flames. Already she had lifted it. But in that motion, out of the sides of her eyes, she saw me.

"Go back!" she hissed, her clear brows arched, caught up in some half-finished spell. Her look was dangerous. In that moment I took hold of her robe. The thick cloth seemed to sear my hands. This put me in a rage, and I held more tightly till I saw the skin of all my fingers blacken and peel away. The bright blood foamed; stubs of bone poked through my boiling flesh. Then at once the pain and burning passed and I knew it for the spell it was. The cloth was only warm. In anger I let out my breath.

"What am I that you toy with me?" I said. Even as I spoke the firelight darkened a little and the roar of flames grew less.

She studied me out of her deep eyes. "So man comes here," she warned and turned again to watch the fire.

I pulled her back.

"None came into your holy wood. And yet I went to it," I said. She moved fretfully, but I would not let her go.

"I must tend the fire," she answered quickly, watching

it. "It is my duty. Not even you and your fool's bravery could do it in my place. Not you nor anyone unless I choose."

I turned my eye to the thing in her hand. "Surely," I mocked her, "you do not feed your fire with lizards' claws. Who is it brings wood down these stairs for you?"

"No one comes here but myself."

With that I laughed.

She drew her hair back from her face, where it had flown before her eyes. She answered softly, gentle all at once. "Come to the fire," she said. "Gaze into it and see yourself what burns."

"I have cut enough wood on the mountain to know the look of it," I answered curtly, for I had not forgotten what Vydd told me and would not look into the flames.

Her pale brows drew together. "I remember you so small," she said. "Your child's hands could not hurt me then." She shook her head. "Now let me go."

"Tell me my father's name," I said

A sound came out of her, such as I have heard a hoar-pig make when I had cornered it against a rock. A death sound. She could not hide it. She looked at me as one compelled against her will. Then something altered in her face. "It is not the world's wood I burn," she said. "If you would only look at it."

"I did not come to watch your fire."

"It is more and greater than you think," she said. "Here a root of Gwen Gildrun breaks the earth." Her bright eyes swept across my face.

"No," I said. "It is too far."

"Hear me," she whispered. Her eyes were gray and fire-gold as she spoke. "On the day I came from the bed in which I bore you I found it here, one bent twig growing small up through the stones. I broke it off. I wanted only a little light. And when I had set a flame to it, it passed completely from my thoughts. But on the next night I found it grown again and burned it and so the next. But always there was more than there had been."

She stopped to draw a breath and loosed it. I saw the weariness in the lines of her throat and wondered. I felt the firelight flicker. She held herself, tightening her fingers on her arms.

"Nightly these fourteen years," she said, "I have come to this deep place to clear the maze of wood. Nightly I cast it in the fire. For should I stop, the root of that great tree would drive its hard fingers between the stones that bear the house and it would fall." Her voice shook slightly and she stopped.

My thoughts came in a swarm, wildly as thoughts had come to me in dreams. I saw the towers tumbled and the walls in ruin. A cold wind whined above the broken stone. Then I thought, what if she lies? Her face was turned back toward the fire. I could not see it.

"Please," she cried. "It fades!"

I felt my hand upon her robe. "Tell me what I ask," I said.

Her lips had parted but her voice stopped, clenched between her teeth. I had seen Grieve do this and knew at last where she had got it from. She stood a moment, wordless before me.

"Does it require such thought?" I asked harshly.

The tired lines of her mouth drew back. "Do you think you catch me unprepared in this?" she said. "I have seen that look in you a thousand times. When you could scarcely talk, your eyes would ask it. When you were older and too proud to ask, then you would hide your face when I would pass and so I knew."

"Then be done with it!" I shouted. "Say my father's name and I will let you go."

"No," she whispered. "I will not barter it like a herring wife." Her voice was shrill. "I swore it to your father on the day I left him. I swore it by the kingdoms undersea, by all we lost, by our last hope of its return. He made me swear it. It was no choice of mine. But I will live it and so you must."

I shook my head from side to side and cursed. I crushed her robe between my hands. "What sort of man commands so black a promise?"

She drew back a little. "When you come to him at last, then you must ask him."

"And will you say where I will find him?"

"No."

"Or, if ever I saw him, how I would know his face?"

The skin below her eyes was patched with grief. "I would tell you if I knew," she answered sadly. "It was long ago. He will have changed. Men do."

My hot breath sprang from me. The sharp words tore my throat. "You leave me nothing, then!" I cried. "No, less than nothing. Not even my own name to give him."

Her voice was small, thin as a thread of silver. It bound

me before I knew. "This I will give you," she whispered softly. "From the beginning I have saved it." She looked at my long face as one would watch a child. "You know," she said, "that it was given out I fainted before I gave the name. But for the instant I saw you, huge and bawling, my blood still on your face, I knew what it would be. If I fainted, I did so smiling. And I was myself again long before any but Vydd knew. I have kept it since, whispering it in my thoughts." She paused and smiled at me. She touched my face and smoothed my hair. I felt the robe cloth move, loose, in my lax fingers. Unthinking I let it fall. Even as she saw it she sprang away. At the edge of her low voice was laughter. "As you were mountain-born," she said. "I called you Finn."

I stared at her in disbelief. "It is but half a name," I cried. Already she stood before the fire. Just as she threw it, I saw the silver glitter of the claw as it tumbled toward the hearth. My breath caught. I meant to jerk my head away. Too soon the hot flames reared before my eyes.

"Poor Finn," she sighed within the roar. "There was another born that night. I clove the name that you might share it. The other Tabak took away, even before I looked on it or touched its face. Whatever the women thought of Tabak, he was not mine. If he served me, it was service to his lord. And when he took the child, he did his own lord's bidding. I bartered then, one life to ransom one. I paid that price for you, to keep a promise the Kell made when long ago they walked the shores of Hren. There to see the Selchie, their black eyes shining, come walking once more from the sea."

She finished but I did not look at her. A sickness ate at me and sucked my life. My shoulders slumped. I felt my head fill up with flame.

5.

THE SNOW LAY DEEP UPON GÉAR FINN. I SAW IT one day to the next. When I woke to see the women un-fastening the skins from the windows to break the ice and let air in, I saw it. Its two horns stood out white and distant against the winter sky. But in the evening the mountain flung its long arms out at me across the ice fields and the walls. It welled huge and unsatisfied within the yard. Four-handed, it clawed the casement and came in. Restless, it waited in the room, leering from the foot of my bed with both its heads, its mouths unhinged, creaking and moaning like old trees in a gale. Yet it did not frighten me. I knew it for the riddle, unanswered, that raked my mind.

Each night I waited for it, coiled in myself, as cats wait for their prey. But more often, when they remembered and against the cold, the women would rebind the skins. Then if I stirred within the bed, they said it was a fever. Sometimes I tried to speak to them, for I wished the windows clear and open, free to let the mountain in. "See," they would whisper among themselves, "he dreams." So they would creep out softly, deaf to the mountain, banging with its arms and hands against the wall.

I slept.

Grieve came in the evenings, bearing a lantern and a tray. Without a word she knelt beside the bed. I saw her pale hands take the cup and lift the hot wine to my lips. Perhaps I drank. But it was only her hands that I remembered, her fingers gray with cold. Sometimes there was another, but not in that place. A tree spread over us and the wind was warm. I took hold of her bare arms. Her skin, I remember, was white as ivory. The hair that fell about her shoulders was thick and full, dark as the holes between the stars. Its blackness troubled me. It was like no other I knew except my own. When we kissed, her black eyes did not leave my face. "Finn," she murmured once and held me half away. Though I knew it was a dream, it hurt me. I had not dreamed of women so before. I felt an emptiness in the hollow of my palm where her small breast had been. When she was gone, I wept. Perhaps all men know this. Yet it was new to me and I did not understand my grief. In the dream I called after her, a name I could not remember when I awoke.

The sound came softly. Rapping. I sat up in my bed. Blinking, I looked around. A log was sputtering in the grate. I closed my eye and leaned back once more, waiting for sleep to take me and the dream to come. Instead I listened to the wind nuzzling the chimneys like a wolf. The snow hissed on the stones below. In time I nodded and almost slept. Something rapped again. I stirred. My

53

eye went to the door. The servants had left it open. A single torch was flickering in its wall iron, casting a sullen yellow light across the floor. I turned my head, the sound still in my ears, until I knew the place from which it came.

I got up slowly. My knees were stiff and it was hard to stand. To cover my nakedness I dragged the great fur blanket after me. A sharp pain started in my legs and did not stop until it branched all through me like a tree of ice. I hobbled more than walked, dizzy from standing and the cold. When at last I found the window, I tore away the leather strings and pried off the skins where they had frozen to the wood. The snow blew in, a cold gust that stung my face and thatched my brows.

Shaking the dusting of snow from her black wings, the crow hopped quickly from the ledge. She was twice the size she had been and yet I knew her. Her fierce eyes glared at me. She flew up past my face. My wits still wild, I thought she meant to peck my eye. I heard my breath shake faintly from my lips. Instead she perched upon a rafter near my head. She saw me wince.

"I am fed and not on human meat," she rasped. Her voice was like the rattling of loose stones. Numbly I stared at her. If I had begun to tremble in the cold, I did not feel it.

"What do you want of me?" I said. The sound of my own voice was strange in my ears.

"I am yours and so I came."

"I did not send for you."

"No matter; it is time."

"To what purpose?"

"Twelve days past, the New Year came and went," she croaked. "You have slept long enough. I came to wake you."

I reached for her. My cold fingers scratched the empty air. Then I remember only the coldness where I lay and the hard whine of the wind blowing off the mountain. Later there were voices. The sound of quick feet on the stone. They came and went away. After a while I heard a heavier tread. The door was pulled back wide to let some huge thing pass. Thick arms dug beneath my back. Something pulled, then lifted me. Above my face the dark head loomed, the deep eyes looking down. For a moment I saw the wolfish grin through the twisted matter of his beard. He knelt and put me gently on the bed.

"Tabak," I whispered in surprise.

Heedless, the voices went back and forth among themselves.

"—there by the window—"

"—his arms stretched out, the fingers frozen shut—"

"—beating?—"

"—Yes—"

"—the straps. Pulled out, the window—"

"—Why?—"

"To live," the stern voice said. I saw him go, more like a bear than a man, the great shoulders edging sideways through the door, filling it so that the light from the hall torch faltered and then came back when he had passed. I meant to call to him. It was on my lips.

Her hands were in her lap. Encircled by her gray fingers was a cup of wine. Later I felt the liquid hot within my throat and coughed. Grieve's gray eyes had opened wide.

"Herawd," she whispered.

"I must teach you my true name," I said. She did not pay the least attention but flung her thin arms about my shoulders, burying her head against my chest. "I so feared—," she sobbed, her fingers tight in the tangle of my hair.

"You have spilled the wine," I laughed. I moved to lift her so I might see her face. I found I could. She was startled and pleased at once to see my strength. Her lashes stuck together with her tears. I put her down.

"I had thought—I—" She tried to speak. She stopped, looking at me suddenly, as though for the first time. "Mother said—that you—would surely—die," she said slowly, each word by itself as though she tested every one to see if it were counterfeit. "You were so cold, she said, that she sould barely touch you. When Tabak carried you from the roof—"

"No," I interrupted her. "You are mistaken. It was here. I remember it. I had gone to the window."

"Yes, of course," she said and smiled, relieved. "That too, but the first time. That night, on Teimhne, when we had talked and the snow was falling. Then Tabak came into the hall with you."

But already I had stopped her. "This you saw?"

"No," she said, though it made no difference. "I had not come down. It was Mother, as I told you."

Again I stopped her. "Who else saw it?"

"No one. For it was early."

"But did you touch me?"

She shook her head. "I came here. I pleaded with her. Still she would not let me in. It was two days before she would unbolt the door. I cried when I saw you. I could not stop. It was my fault I left you in your black mood. But I swear I did not know you meant to stay, the snow already falling."

"You told her this?"

"Yes." But she was puzzled then.

Perhaps I smiled. Only she did not like the look of it. I said, "Then, it was she that told you I found out on the roof."

She shifted then, afraid without reason to meet my eye.

"Is this not so?" Perhaps I shouted.

She drew a breath, then let it wither. "There was a time you came to me," she said, "and you would tell me all you thought." But she saw the cold impatience in my look. "Yes," she answered flatly, "she told me then."

By the bedside she had left a platter with a few scraps of meat. Each had been cut in strips as one might do to feed a child. Greedily I crammed them in my mouth. The meat was barely warm. She watched me, her head resting on her bent knee. "You were ever kind to me," I told her quietly. "More than I deserved." But she was used to me. Her eyes by now were dry.

"Tell me what you wish," she said.

I smiled outright. "It is unseemly that you should see my nakedness," I answered. "If you will, bring up my clothes."

She retrieved the wine cup without a word, dropped her thin legs to the floor, and stood. "I will send a servant." A silence grew between us.

"But should you come yourself," I said at last and saw her lips pull back tightly from her teeth, "bring me your father's book."

Her mouth fell open. "You went to her!"

I nodded. "Such as it is, I have a name."

Behind the curtain of her yellow hair, flying through the door, for one last time I saw her smile.

I had come to myself slowly. In truth I had awakened before Grieve came, and slept again. But I remember how bright the day had seemed when I first woke. I had

watched the dust motes dancing in the air. They floated
in the glowing light, which slid in at the edges of the
window skins. Gaping and bemused, half knowing what
I did, I watched them as fish risen from deep water look
on air. Perhaps I took them for shining flies. I wonder I
did not snap at them. For I remember hunger then, a
pain in my belly that twisted like a knife. Truly hunger
was always with me in that house. The women ate stin-
gily. One small dove was hearty fare to them. It took
six portions to remind me I had eaten, to which I added
onions, cheese and bread in larger measures. Still I often
went away unsatisfied. The thin aunts, their dinners done,
would look up from their dry plates. Perhaps they thought
I meant to eat them too. I closed my eyes.

For hours it seemed the wind outside was still. From
the house below I heard in snatches the servants talking,
a low and intermittent drone too distant to make out the
words. It was with that, I think, that I remembered who
I was. From the yard there had come the crunch of boots
on snow. One of the servants had gone to brush the
horses or do some other work. Doubtless in the kitchen
the cook had been putting out the loaves. Life is as it
was, I had thought, so little note they take of me. But I
realized that Yllvere had hid everything from them. Even
her own women she kept ignorant.

But for Vydd, I thought. Surely she knew or guessed.
Had she not sent Ninmir soaring from the mountain to
rap on the window, to wake me from my sleep? But then
I thought, perhaps it was a dream. I sat up once more to
see the window clearly. The straps that bound the skins
had been retied. A few loose pieces lingered on the floor.
It proved no more than that I had torn them in my haste.
I groaned.

What had I gained from any one of them, I thought,
but children's tales and lies? Each answer only left me
more to ask. The memory of the fire ached in my head.
What Yllvere might have given she did not give. What
hope I had had was burned up in the flames. I will have
nothing from the Kell, I thought, and turned my mind
from them. It was no woman nor any man I waited for,
but only the dry pages of a book.

By the third hour, the light already gone upon Géar
Finn, Grieve had not come. I paced the cold room. In
time I grew bored with my nakedness and wrapped myself once more within a blanket. I sat before the grate

and stirred the coals. There were faces in the flames and shadows in the burning wood. Frail and beautiful, they flickered with passing life. Each regarded me with frightened eyes. Almost I thought I knew them. But the fire had changed them before I found the names.

At my back the door squeaked on its hinges.

I did not turn. "Let me see the book," I said.

"Give me your name." The voice was old and edged with care.

I whirled around and saw him. His feet were planted in the doorway. In one hand he held his book, in the other the long sword by which twelve men were dead. I did not mean to be the next.

"I am not armed," I snarled. "But even the small hands of a child should be enough for your old throat."

Silently he stood and watched me. His face was lean, age-lined. But it showed no hint of feeling now, only the marks of other sorrow pressed into his mouth. His long thin fingers curled upon the sword hilt. "You have been too long among the women," he answered evenly. "Had I wished you ill, I would have done it when you were still a boy and killing you was no great task." He was still a moment, his old eyes moving on my face. He lifted the sword. Even then I saw it strained his arm. "You stole this once when you climbed into the women's wood. Now I mean to give it to you."

My lips twitched bitterly. I remember his cold words to me, the millwright watching, the day he did not make me his heir. "What use is a sword to a one-eyed man?" I said. The blood flared in his face. His own lips parted.

"No better did I expect from you," he answered angrily. "Always you were the crooked stick among the straight. Nonetheless, I will keep to what I said." He went to the bed, then laid the great sword flat across it. "It saw good service in days that are now gone. And it has kept its fame if I have not."

I did not know what to make of him. I drew back. But though I hid it, he saw or guessed the question in my look.

"It was my father's sword," he said, his voice soft as the murmur of the fire. "And my grandfather's before it came to him. In better days when Meroc ruled, the king's own smith had made it for my kin. My father gave it to me when he died." He paused as if in thought. "I have had it since I was a child."

And still my heart was hard. The struggle between us was only part in words. The firelight brushed his face but brought him no relief. I saw how his mouth had tightened.

He stared, his deep eyes narrowed, cold once more. "Would you have me hand it now to Sanngion or Ryth?" He gave a bitter laugh. "A fit thing, do you think, to stir a pot or skewer a chicken?"

I turned to the window so as not to look at him. He could but wonder why I had pulled the strings away and tore the scraped skins down. The night was black and fierce with stars. Beyond the mountain I saw the faint paired lights which mark the north, the travelers' stars. I knew then I would go. And since I did not mean to stay, it mattered little what I said to him.

"There was a time," I said, "when I would have taken the smallest gift you gave me. And thanked you for it. There was a time, the night they held the rite for me, when Jjared and the men came up from the towns, I thought that I might even be your heir."

His old face set hard and cold. "Heir to what?" he asked, his voice grown soft as though his breath had gone with it. "To two dead wives and my dead son?"

I started. Perhaps I pitied him. "It is said," I answered haltingly, "that once you were the king's own man, the first of all his soldiers."

"I killed what he bade me, even among those that followed him." His eyes clung to my face. At length he said, "Take the sword. It is better given late than rusting here for want of use."

I went to the bed and lifted the weapon, hefting the cold metal in my hand. Though I had carried it once before, until that moment I had not felt how deadly a thing it was. I held it up before him. He saw how readily I turned it to my will. I did not forget.

I said, "I have heard it said you meant to kill me once."

"Once," he said. His voice stayed quiet but his eyes had slipped away from mine. I saw them shrink into his head as though he found some memory. "I loved her once as well," he answered, his small voice hushed in the stillness of the room. "You are too young to know how that can drive a man. She was lithe as an eel when I first saw her. I remember how lightly she would spring into my arms. When she came back, fat with you, riding another

59

man's mare two winters after she had gone, I would have killed. There was a dead child in this house before. I knew the look of it. I would not have turned from it, but first I wanted your father's name."

"So you beat her for it."

He nodded frankly. "I have done worse things than strike a whore."

I was silent. "She would not tell you," I said finally, getting past the word.

"I taught myself to wait," he said. "You would not be a child forever. I knew one day you would make her tell you."

I glared at him. "And I would say what she would not?"

He shook his head and frowned at me. "I have children of my own within the house."

A sound came out of me. I had been a fool not to think of it. "Where is Grieve?" I shouted.

His lips pulled into a smile that blazed across his eyes.

"She did not tell me," he answered evenly. "There was no need of it. I found her rummaging among my books. I knew she would not pick through them idly. More, I knew the thought to take from it."

He kept perfectly still, his deep eyes laughing, even when I grabbed his neck and held the great sword ready to plunge into his throat. "Where is she now?" I cried.

"I sent her to Yllvere," he answered, pleased.

"To what place?"

He smiled. "Where your mother always goes when it grows dark." He watched me. "You know that in the kitchen, at the back of it, there is a door."

I felt the flames shoot up in my head. Before he finished, I was gone.

I took the steps in a dozen leaps, pushed into the hall and passed it. There were still some women squirreling about with lamps and bedding. They screamed to see a naked man run by them with a sword. In the kitchen I faced the cook, who, hearing the noise coming at her from the inner rooms, had a cleaver ready in her hand.

"Keep back," I warned between my teeth.

She stared at me as one would watch the mad.

I made my way past her to the door. Before I touched it, I saw the latch draw up, heard something move behind the wood. The door came open with a groan. They stood together looking at me, the darkness at their backs, their faces flushed with heat. Grieve had her thin arm about my mother's waist. She leaned on her. The edges of her yellow hair were singed. A patch of blisters had already risen on her cheek.

"Grieve," I cried to her.

I heard her speak, her voice dry and distant so at first I could not make out the words.

Something moved in my mother's face. She lifted her pale hand. Touching a strand of my sister's hair, she drew it out between her fingers. The ghosts of the fire burned brightly in Grieve's eyes. She whispered but then I heard the words.

"You have gone where no man goes," she said. "What you have looked on, no man must see." She paused, regarding me as I had seen the women look at Urien.

I turned my back on her.

"Finn," she called out after me.

I let the small voice fade, unanswered. It echoed softly between the walls.

6.

I HAD THOUGHT MYSELF IMMUNE, SECURE AND safe against the worst outrages of my fate. In that, I had been no more than a child. True, I had lived with sorrow and knew that more must come. Yet when I looked ahead at troubles, I expected what I knew. It was gentleness that disarmed me and took me off my guard. I had trusted in that, in Grieve's kind ways. Urien's vengeance was the fruit of old betrayal and his pride. In my anger there was room enough for him and even space for Yllvere's indifference. I knew them both for what they were. Grieve alone escaped from me, she who I had thought was mine—possessed, as one might enfold a dove in the hand, wrapping fingers over its warm body, feeling its small heart flutter against the palm. But when I had gone to look for her—to save her, I had thought— even as she stood before me, I found her gone. I knew then I had held but empty air.

The Kell are what they say, the spawn of nevermen and harsh old dreams. The women of the world are one. All their lives are memory. There is no new thing in them. When it came to the test, the Kell blood raged as wild in Grieve as in any of my sisters. In time, the sea longing would surely beat against her brains and she, like the rest of the winter brood, would creep down the mountain wall to the western ocean to wait upon the shore for their impossible lords to come cold and gleaming from the waves. But I was done with that. Before morning I would be gone. Eastward, a direction for which the Kell care nothing.

I had no horse of my own. In the stable I saddled Yllvere's, not a war-horse but nimble-footed and tireless, a gift, the women said, from my father, grown old since its giving yet strangely far from dying.

If I went like a thief, I felt no shame. What was a horse in the balance? My father left me no legacy. Naked I had been born into the house. If I left with little added, it would be enough. What, after all, was a bastard heir to but himself? I took a longshirt, bundled three loaves of travelers' bread and Urien's sword. There was no one to see my going. The women had retired at last to their chambers. My sisters, I imagined, their hair night-snarled and their wide mouths slack and damp, were long in their beds. Grieve, for all I knew, had gone down once more with Yllvere to work at the fire.

Just beyond the gate I turned and gave the house one last salute. In the darkness with all the doors closed and the windows empty, Morrigan had a cold, stupid look like the severed head of an aurochs. It was a house, I was certain, that Death kept—bought with murder, enthralled by a dead boy I could not replace. And were not the Kell dead themselves, I thought, their deep hearts cold as dreams?

Caught up in my thoughts, I did not notice the horseman until he was already close upon me. I had not looked to be followed. Yet he came not from Morrigan but seemingly out of darkness itself, as though a boulder had been given the shape and form of horse and rider. Without appearing to hurry, he gained on me. The iron shoes of his mount struck blue sparks from the stone. A heavy war helm hid his face and a great cloak covered his shoulders. Yet by his size I knew him well enough.

"Hold, my lord Finn," he cried as he drew beside me.

The flanks of our horses touched lightly. The mare gave a cold shiver.

"Go back to Yllvere," I ordered.

Tabak shook his dark head. Stolidly he rode beside me. I saw the slits of his eyes through the cleft of his helm but could read nothing in them. He looked straight ahead, surveying the road. If he meant to stop me, he gave no sign of it.

"I am leaving the house," I said. "Never shall I return to it."

"I have heard you," he replied and rode on as before.

I stared aside awhile to master my anger. Though we were matched in height, I was not his equal.

"What business do you have with me?" I asked at last.

"To follow."

"I seek no company."

A brightness had come into his eyes, like the cunning in the eyes of a dog who in all its life has learned one trick and waits to perform it. In the darkness he smiled. In the cleft of the helm, I saw the lips had parted.

"I waited for my lord's birth," he said. "Fifteen winters have come and gone since first I heard you cry within the house. Fifteen winters I waited outside your mother's door, my ax at my side, that Urien would not come to her. She is a young women even now, and you were to be the last of her children. So it was decreed. I did what I was bidden, though it was clear to anyone who watched that Urien had spent his seed. Yet I was faithful to my trust. I waited. Lord, I saw your first steps in the house. I watched you, when you were grown, go off into the fields and saw when they carried you broken, near death, from Gwen Gildrun. Fifteen winters I stood my post. Now my young lord goes forth and the waiting is over."

It was the longest speech I had heard from him. There was a solemnity about his words and much that made me wonder. But I could not get past the mistake and laughed. "You have the years wrong," I said, for I knew my age.

He shook his head. "Why do you listen to the women?" he asked. "Surely my lord knows the Kell could never count."

"I do not know it," I threw back at him then added, "but should it be so, what does it matter?"

"You have been too long on this mountain," Tabak

answered gravely. I meant to question him more on it, but a wind sprang up and blew away our voices. I wrapped my cloak across my face and, glad only to be done with it, rode on. For the moment let him come, I thought. The important thing was only to be gone.

Toward morning it rained, a gray cloying drizzle that clung to our eyes and made the stones slick and the footing precarious. We were forced to dismount and lead the horses to keep them from stumbling. By dawn there was no brightening. We went slowly, feeling our way as much as seeing it. There were places where the road, because of its steepness, became rough stairs cut into the track. This the horses found difficult. They fought us and we feared for their legs as much as our own. We cursed them, breathing in the dampness till it hurt our lungs. Beyond the wheeze of our breaths we were as mutes, moving in a world of wet wool. Our sodden boots on the rock made little sound. Except for the occasional whinny of the horses, there was no other, not even the bark of the wild dogs that hunted these mountains. They at least were safe in their dens, tails curled, their muzzles sunk deep in their fur. Not for the first time I thought of my dry bed beneath the eaves. By now the servants were bustling about, the smoking fires brought once more back to flame.

Tabak's absence would be noticed by the servants before mine. More would be made of it. They were used to my wanderings. But the loss of the horses would trouble them. The stableman would be taken before Yllvere and flogged. She would likely do it herself, not trusting the others to beat him soundly. She would not flinch when the skin tore and the welts oozed blood. To her they were lesser creatures. For their part, they expected no more. The idea of cruelty would have surprised both servant and lady.

I put that behind me. Morrigan has lost us both, I thought, and turned my mind instead to Ormkill. Soon I would see for myself if the books were true. I thought of Tinkern, where it was written the presence of the oak god still lingered, where the leaves whispered prophecy, and a man, if he knew how to listen, might hear his destiny. So the hours passed.

A mist held the land in a shroud that stretched from the ground up to heaven. But the track had broadened and we rode again. In the darkness we had come down from the peaks and into the lonely waste of hills the maps call Menhirs. It was a place well named. For here there were no trees or huts but only huge upright stones, man-high but sunken to their knees in the soft earth. It was an ancient place, already old when the road makers were at work in our mountains. The stones themselves were blank, the dark mountain granite worn smooth of runes. If they were god-shrines, time had forgotten them and eaten away their memory like old flesh. Only the acrid smell was left. Indeed, something yet hung in the air and burned my eye. I squinted into the mist, seeking to keep the road. The mare snorted. I had to nudge her belly to drive her on.

Tabak's swollen eyes moved cautiously across the ground. He looked weary, yet he kept to the task. We dared not rest until we had passed the stones. No wind stirred. The horses plodded on. Grown impatient, they sniffed the air. They wanted meadow grass and our weight from off their backs. But throughout the murk-bound world there was only the smell of godstones and the damp. I too had grown restless. I had not slept since dawn of the day past and in all that time only tasted a bit of travelers' bread. Beyond all, the darkness wearied me.

At length the horses grew too exhausted to carry us. We dismounted and went on foot. We led them through the weary end of the afternoon. About an hour after sunset the cold deepened and a biting wind sprang up. I began to fear we would not escape this land. The great stones did not diminish. They had become, if anything, more numerous, surrounding us like an army through whose silent ranks we passed as captives.

Once I heard a stream. Lured by its faint slavering, we abandoned the track, thinking the water would lead us downward and away from the hills. But the sound was deceptive. Caught among the stones, it echoed queerly. It was some hours more before the land gave way to the east. We had reached, I judged, the outer buttress of the mountain. Below us was a valley, locked in night. Without forlorn hope I started down, Tabak beside me, his mount's bridle jingling in the stillness.

Partway down the slope a rough figure jutted out of the earth. Its features were gray like the rock and stern as the images carved upon the holy rock at Tinkern. It did not move. At first it seemed no more than a stone itself. But the horses knew it for a man and whinnied.

He was old. A stringy, earth-colored beard lay matted on his chest. His garments were in the olden style, now mostly rags and covered with filth. A feeling of foreboding leapt in me. There was no horse near him. What sort of man, I wondered, would walk these hills in such ill weather? For his part, he studied me from behind his large black eyes. His flesh glinted like slate; the ridges of his features were sharp as broken stone. Slowly, like the action of a man who had not moved in a long time, he raised his hand to us, the gray palm outward in a sign of peace.

"What house are you?" I shouted across to him. Being uneasy, I had kept a distance of some yards between us.

"You are late, Finn," he called to me, his deep voice hollow.

I glanced back sharply at Tabak. "You know this man?" I asked. "For I do not."

The old man raised his eyebrows. An odd light momentarily softened his hard gaze. "Do not think, my lord," he said, "that your name lies only in your servant's keeping."

Fearing wizardry, I answered. "I have a name, it seems, from each that knows me. But the name you give me I had not until I left the one who gave it. At that I tore it from her. Now it seems that it was hidden only from myself, and every beggar on the road has it ready to greet me with."

"It is known far, my lord, if not as wide as that," he answered back.

"I do not know you, sir," I said. The place was strange and the meeting unexpected. Though I bore animosity to no man's kindred, I kept my guard. For there were those who hated Morrigan for the blood that Urien spilled. Others, the threads of whose lives Yllvere had twisted with her sorcery, bore us ill. What power this one had I could not guess. It was enough, I saw, to master my own name even before I myself had grown accustomed to the taste of it.

"Your house, sir," I demanded.

A flicker of amusement crossed his face. "These stones," he said.

"That is no fit answer."

Once more an icy smile had turned his lips. "Indeed you are his son," he answered mildly. "But you are late in coming. I had looked for you last spring. From what is spoken you were fair-sized then, had climbed Gwen Gildrun and brought down the children of the air. It was then that you were needed. Now you have wasted a full year's turning. Be warned, Finn, the way is long and at the end your father waits."

The mention of my father, more unlooked-for than my name, took all my breath and wrenched my heart.

I gasped. "What do you know of him?"

His cold eyes gleamed. "All that may be known by one who only stands in this one place and listens."

I had no patience with his riddling. The blood beat at my temples and I no longer thought. "Answer what I ask!" I cried and pulled my sword. Poor weapon that it was, so long unused, it was weapon enough, I judged, to frighten one old man. I brandished it before him. At my back Tabak had been shouting. In my anger I made no sense of it. Quickly I advanced upon the man. He did not draw back.

I would have struck him. But Tabak was at my side and stayed my hand. Then, before I knew, I saw him kneel, his thick neck bent, and yet he kept his eyes on the man.

The old man smiled. "Your faithfulness, Tabak, has not escaped me." The voice, though full of echoes, nonetheless was kind.

"He is a child," said Tabak, "and raised by women on the mountain. Sadly, he knows nothing of the world." I stared at him.

"Teach him quickly, then," said the man. "For the world he enters now grows perilous. Since Dagda first set me here to guard the riverlands, to set both Anu and her wood apart and keep the Kell, I have marked the days and watched the seasons turn. Since that first time which no man knows I have seen the darkness creep above the ground and the greater darkness falling from the sky. But I have seen it beaten back. Eight times the oak kings, masters of the lightning, the sun on their shoulders, have ruled it. So much was promised. Now once more I ache from darkness and the dread of it. I feel it cold and biting, gathering before me. But of my company only I remember man-speech. Like the very stone they sleep. And who shall waken them? Who is there who will speak the word? The High King has hidden himself and will not be found. Eight victories were promised. That only. The last was left in doubt. Tabak, you must teach him well. Already it grows late and much is surely lost beyond recall."

As he spoke I felt, like a vast shadowy river, the huge expanse of years roll over me. Along its current marched the shapes of men and kings. Above their heads fire flashed from the sky. The broad land grumbled. But the swords in their hands were rusted and their eyes were empty. The river took them.

When I saw again, his words had broken off. I heard his grunting breath and came close to him to listen. It hissed away. The cold eyes were no longer on me but on some chaos I could not see. Even in the bad light and the mist I saw the cracked and pitted surface of his face, almost looking like a man. For an instant the hairs on my neck rose up with gooseflesh. Then the blood rushed to my face. I turned my back and would not look at it.

Ignoring me, Tabak went up to the stone and made a sign of reverence before it. There was a hush then.

"What is he?" I whispered, hoarse, amazed, afraid to keep the silence.

Tabak's eyes had narrowed like a lynx's.

"Tabak," I said, my voice a cry.

The muscles rose on his clenched jaw.

"I command you."

He bared his teeth, white like stones, the lips pulled back like those of a dog that guards his master's house. "I am your father's servant," he said.

"It is his son that bids you speak."

Tabak paused. "Do you claim him, then?" he asked. "Above Yllvere? Denying all the Kell, forsaking them, the house and women?"

I pleaded then. "I have left the house," I said. "Why do you test me?"

"A child may run away and still not leave."

"No," I said, for in that moment I understood, "you shall not bait me. More than I know myself, you know what I am. The women only speak in riddles. You are no better. Answer it yourself, for I cannot."

When he heard me out, he smiled. It angered me.

"Hear me," I said. "Whatever it is I am, I am no farmer's boy that the night wind frightens me. The stone spoke. How, I do not know. Yet I will not close my ears to it. I see only that it touches on my father. Either you will explain it to me or you will not."

His dark lips twisted into speech. "Indeed," he said, "you are his son."

I felt my hand close on the pommel of my sword. It gained me nothing. I let it go and swung out my arm and pointed, first east, then north, then west. "Where do I seek for him?" I asked.

He shook his great sad head. "I am to follow you," he said. That only.

I faced the stone again. But the life that flickered about its scornful face had gone. Whether god in fact or druid-stone, whatever mystery had made it move and speak had vanished. The chance, such as it had been, was squandered. I frowned to myself, knowing the loss and took the fault, for it was mine.

"It may be that I am yet no more than a child," I said aloud. But then I remembered my honor, so kept the rest to myself. Without another word to Tabak, I found the mare and mounted her. When I was about to leave, he came.

7.

WE WENT EAST.

In time the land had softened into undulating hills. The grass, at first no more than stubble sticking out between the stones, by slow progression turned thick and fragrant. We went slowly. The horses grazed. By daylight there was life again. Badgers and hoarpigs rooted in the meadows. As we rode, foxes, barking and flattening their tails, scurried from our path. A host of early flowers sprang up on every side; a light breeze lifted their heads. They were a good sight after the rain. Still I took no joy in them. The dead that are everywhere lay here in shallow graves. I saw their markers in the grass. The fairest lands are boneyards, say the *filidh;* but they make songs of what is sorrow. I did not know these dead nor what battle felled them. Still I grieved for them. The aunts say I had not the stomach for a warrior. Perhaps they were right. The dead have always saddened me, while the hearts of warriors, they say, are glad.

We went on for several miles and by midmorning had found the road again. With good footing we made better progress. The road turned slowly, edging the larger hills and leaving the mountain over my left shoulder. There were no signs of other travelers. Since Urien returned to this mountain, the men of the North rarely came this way. What little trade there was went north by sea along the Bay of Cassiterides and inland from Tywy to Haman and then no farther. Still, the world was a broad place and there were other folk than Urien's kin. Yet from the higher ridges I could mark the road as it ran like a ribbon through dells with grassy sides and stands of birch and hazel. Over the miles I looked, nothing moved on it. The sun shone fitfully. There were still rags of clouds.

"High up, there is a great wind," said Tabak. "It drives the last of the storm beyond us."

"I am glad of it," I said. "I have had too much rain. The cold has yet to leave my bones."

"Be grateful we are down from Géar Finn," said Tabak. He turned on his mount and looked back the way we came. I followed with my eye. "This rain is snow there yet. Winter lingers on your mountain."

I shivered. "It is its only season," I answered softly and let the matter be.

We clambered uphill and down. Yet overall the road went lower, running more between the hills than on them. The day wore on. I remembered there was bread within my satchel. Taking some, I passed the rest to Tabak. We ate in silence. Wide grasslands stretched before us.

"Is this not Rasoden?" I asked.

Tabak nodded. "It is often called that, the plain of horsemen."

I looked around. "Are there not towns then where the Undain flows onto this plain?" For from the house I had seen them, a few brave specks of light, their fires at Teimhne. Once when I was small, men came from one of them to speak with Urien, grave men on some errand for their lord. Their stay was brief. For I doubt they found in Urien the man that they remembered or they sought. "Surely there are such towns," I said. "Yet all we see is grass, not even the river."

"We are south, my lord, of where we should have been."

I thought aloud, "I would see the river and the men of towns."

"The river goes south with us," he said. "In three days we shall cross it near the ford at Stephen's Well. There the Steward holds a company of his soldiers, four hundred men, I think, enough at least to satisfy your curiosity. Still, we must be careful if we go among them."

"Surely a man may pass unnoticed among so many."

Tabak gazed at me with fine sad eyes. He scratched the back of his broad neck and said, "Many men might, though they are wary of strangers. Many, but never you or I."

"Am I so different, then?" I said.

Tabak threw back his head and grinned. "They are small, these men. Far easier for a wolf to hide among rabbits than for you or me to walk unregarded in their company."

"They will fear us, then," I answered quickly. "So much the better. And I shall go then wherever I please unbothered."

I saw him laugh, but quietly and to himself. I made no more of it.

The sun sank low behind the mountain's rim. Smooth, bare and endless, with the sky on every side but back of us, the grass, when the wind had touched it, rolled in waves and swells. It seemed, I thought, like what the sea must be. It was strange to me. For I knew only the mountain pastures. There nothing was straight or long, but all things broken by the rock and walls, the very earth heaved up and torn. For the first time in my life, heedless of how great Tabak had said we were, I felt myself small.

The sky was slowly filling with stars. The night breeze blew light and cool. On such nights as a child I had looked out over the mountain wall and to the land that sloped away downward to Rasoden. There was such savor in the sight, it is difficult to describe—to see the world laid out like a silver tapestry, the distant river like a thread of ice.

There was yet no moon.

"I am weary, Tabak," I said. "Since I left my bed at Morrigan, I have not slept."

"Patience, my lord," he answered almost tenderly.

"One more hill. Beyond it there is a hollow and in the hollow a pool of clear water."

He was not mistaken. As I leaned against the saddle, I felt the mare come to a halt. I blinked. The road, which had dropped suddenly through a cleft of leering, jagged stones, passed beyond the ridge and entered a small valley. Stands of birch circled the pool, though there were places where the shore was clear. The water stretched before us, black and still. At its soft margins reeds with feathered crowns reached up into the dark like a host of useless spears. I dismounted and let the mare, unfettered, drink. I went down after her, to wash the dust from my face.

Behind me Tabak pushed into the trees and pulled at a branch of twisted wood to be broken for a fire. I wanted only to sleep but would not leave the work for him. At the border of the pool I saw the green spikes of arrowkin. I went into the mud to dig them with my hands. The roots were thick and pulpy, tangled in runners, and almost not worth the effort. But, baked in the coals, they would help us endure the night without discouragement. When I had collected enough to fill my arms, I bundled them in my longshirt and climbed the bank.

The fire crackled warmly. I huddled close to it, my cloak across my shoulders. Tabak came from the horses. He had unstrapped his leather satchel and laid it down between his knees. His helm was off. The lines of his face were drawn. He was, I saw, as weary as I. Yet I knew he would not speak of it. I had spoken once already of my weariness and would not do so again. He said, "From this place to Stephen's Well the road will be more traveled. I will watch while you sleep. Now always one of us must stay awake."

I poked at a root with a stick to keep it from burning. "Then I shall watch first," I said.

He gave a slight nod. "As you will," he said and made a show of yawning.

After he had eaten, he laid his head across his bag, his arms drawn down to either side. I watched over him, keeping the fire. Perhaps he slept, but his face was turned from me where he could see the road. When, as much as the fare permitted, my hunger was appeased, I lay back against a rock. In time the moon rose, a bright crescent clasping a gray rock. A few small clouds scudded by it. The rest of the sky, between the stars, was black. I lay

72

beneath the enormous vault of heaven. It seemed only a moment.

The birds in the thicket announced the morning before it came. The air was still dark. I pulled myself up on my elbows. Tabak squatted on his heels before the fire. In his hands he held the bare carcass of a hoarpig which he had skinned and split along its belly, making one deep cut from its throat down to its balls. He was intent on his butchering. The best meat he tore away in strips, some of which he impaled on wood skewers. The rest was hung to smoke on a rack of green branches laid above the fire. He had been some time at the task before he decided to notice me. His gaze brought the blood into my cheeks and I was of half a mind to offer some excuse. He saw it.

"Finish this," he said curtly. "Someone must see to your mare."

"I slept," I admitted.

He seemed not to have heard and walked off leaving me with the fire. I stretched the last of the meat above the smoke. The smell was good and took away some of the weariness. Yet I was angry with myself and glad to be alone. The sun came all at once, flooding the horizon from one end to the other. It was not like sunrise on the mountain. It made me uneasy to be so much in the open. But it was a thing past remedy and I would know the world.

In time Tabak came up from the pool leading the horses. He had taken off his longshirt despite the chill. His face and thick shoulders were still wet where he had washed. His flesh shone bright in the sunlight. The sight of him caught in my mind. So the sealmen must have looked to the Kell, I thought, huge and raven-haired, rising out of the foam. But then his fine sad eyes smiled at me and when he spoke it was the voice of a man, like any man.

"I am hungry," he said.

I turned back to the fire.

Along the way I gathered what I could, the small fruit of tinviel, green, astringent and filled with seeds, and the harsh bulbs of allium, hastily dug. But the meat was good. I carried it wrapped in a cloth on my saddle. We paused at midday under the open sky. The land ahead was empty as the land behind. We ate in silence. Then went on.

73

The road was now broad and well planned. Nothing put me in mind of dwarves or magicians. It was men's work, solid, earnest and well tended. Grieve had said the riverlands had fallen into ruin, that small lords warred with one another and the farmers starved. If that were so, the ruin lay further on within the Steward's realm; Rasoden was ordered yet. We saw no one. But clearly someone kept the road. Everything seemed quiet, peaceful. It was hard to believe that the High King had fled. A sure hand ruled this place, albeit invisibly.

We passed in time along the edge of the fields. In places there were stout gates and hedges. Once in the distance I saw the thatched roof of an outer farm. No smoke came from its chimney. But there was a dog. Yellow-haired, suspicious, it ran from the horses. It was not like our mountain dogs, that took delight in their courage, in bristling and challenging strangers. I thought it odd but soon forgot it.

Toward evening we found shelter by a prodigious wooden gate. It was set alongside the road, its wide posts carved with the figures of men and birds. A path led away from it into an empty field. It served no purpose I could see, but then I did not know the ways of men. Still, in part, it hid us from the road and this seemed to please Tabak. I undid the girths of the mare and tethered her to the gate. Beside it, for the horses, was a wooden trough, which still held some dampness from the rain. I unloaded blankets and took from my sack the tangle of roots and bulbs which I had gathered. I looked forward to the leaping flames in which I meant to roast them. Fire, if it is also the destroyer, still gladdens the heart of the traveler. In those days I thought it walls and a roof against the dark. When I had it crackling, Tabak came in from the field where I had seen him walking by himself.

"See that you do not build it too high," he said.

Ready for him, I grinned. "From the road you cannot see it," I said.

Without blinking Tabak watched the fire. On its fluttering edge, in the play of light and shadow, huge as he was, he seemed no more than an apparition. He said, "What keeps to the road I have no fear of."

"This is a tamed land," I answered. "In all of Rasoden I have seen nothing more frightening than the sun rising and the sun going down."

"When you have looked, you have not seen," said

Tabak quietly. I saw the tenseness in his brow. Then all at once he reached into the fire. Taking up a burning brand, he held it so the light fell brightly on the wide posts of the gate. "What do you see, my lord?" he asked.

I saw a post entwined with the figures of birds and men. The wings were outspread, the great arms straining. Such was the craft that looking, as on my own flesh, I felt the thrashing of those terrible dark wings. The arms, unsubmitting yet weaponless but for one poor stone raised against the onslaught of the air, were like my own. "I see a gate carved with great skill," I said.

Tabak did not lower the brand. "You have not seen," he said.

I pressed closer. The hosts of figures I saw were in fact one man, one bird, their images repeated and repeated in a coiled battle about the post. Awestruck, I stared into the face of the man. The face, unflinching yet edged with pain, with those deep eyes, that face was mine or one so nearly like it that I cried out.

Tabak watched me. "It is not you," he said.

"I thought—"

"In this place," said Tabak, "your father fought the crow of Anu. He saw her as she passed overhead, a shadow between the earth and the highest stars. He knew her, and though he was alone and weaponless, he spoke her true name so she could not flee from him. Like an arrow she fell at him. But he took up a stone and pierced her eye. It was a great thing. Until that time no man had marked her. You alone know the cost." With these last words a sudden gentleness had come into his voice. He saw how it struck me.

"Whatever is bought is paid for, lord," he added softly. "It was her due and settled before your birth."

But I did not like to hear it, for Gwen Gildrun had been my glory. I spat into the dark. The silence was deep and painful. I felt a chill deep as the marrow of my bones.

"Do you swear," I asked bitterly, "that it was my father who stood upon this place?"

"He was here if you will see it. He had this gate put up to mark the deed."

I looked once more upon the gate. Was this indeed my father's face? There was no grandeur in it. The lips came together in pain, a bloodless line, haggard, almost broken. What victory was there in this? It was not, I decided, a fitting memorial. I wondered if the artist mocked him knowingly. He who had known the hidden name and called it, contended with the anger out of the sky and beaten it, in the midst of his glory, did he see only ruin? I could not believe that it was so.

"I trust," I said arrogantly, "he had the woodcarver beaten for his work."

Tabak looked at me as one might look upon a dog boy who had failed a task. "No, my lord," he answered. "Your father praised it as was just. Indeed, the work so pleased him he gave the man the swiftest of his horses and a saddle, such as are made by the men of Bede, a wonder in itself, a king's gift, of carved leather and studded with good silver."

But I mused. "There is only pain in my father's face."

"So there was that day," said Tabak. "He was not a fool. The law is one. He knew it. If you cast a stone at heaven, will it not fall to earth? If you steal the eye of the first of Anu's children, will not another of equal prize be taken in return?" His dark eyes fixed on mine.

Through stiffened lips I answered him. "I am lessened by this. The one thing that was mine, Gwen Gildrun and the crows, is mine no longer. I am made but his reflection. He acted and it befell me. Nothing more."

Tabak threw the brand back roughly in the fire. I watched the figures on the gate dissolve into the dark. "He knew what he did," he said scornfully. "But what can be said of you? Is it from Yllvere, the winter queen with her pale looks, you get that raven hair or your stature over other men? Did the runty earth of Urien's holding give you those bold legs? When you look, what do you see?" His eyes were cold, his features dark with scorn. "You are your father's son," he said. "His seed it was that gave you life, both fair and foul. The great oak makes an oak. Can it be otherwise? Or did you dream that when you found him you might keep your precious bastardy?" In his anger he seized me roughly by the shoulders. Too late he saw what he had done. He had a warrior's pride but he was my father's liegeman first. His oaths held him. Not a nerve, not a muscle of his stirred. His breathing seemed to stop.

Later we lay down to sleep. There were branches near, but I let the fire fade down to coals. In the darkness I saw my father's face. It floated before me. There, within a hand's reach. A doubtful substance, yet I might have touched it. Great dark wings beat about his forehead. It will pass, I thought. Yet inwardly I cursed myself because I feared that it would not. I pressed my palm into my eye. In the rush of pain, the face melted. But in my mind I knew the shape of it; without hearing, I knew it groaned.

"It cannot be," I said and, although it was barely cold, I trembled. A feeling of loneliness rose in me. I had seen him whom I had never seen. In the wood of the gate I met him face to face. As though I had looked into polished brass—eye, hair and bone, looking back at me, sharing my own flesh. It filled me with horror. I had seen him and yet learned nothing. After all, what comfort is there in a mirror?

Tabak stirred. "Did I hurt you?" He moved a little. Yet he was like a corpse twitching after an execution— huge upon the ground, his movement thoughtless and unconnected. The poor light of the fire showed none of his features. When he grew still, he might have been a stone. In all things there is both life and death. I thought of the Menhir. Perhaps, I thought, even the great earth grieves.

I looked into the hollow of the fire, into the place where the flame had raged hottest, that was now but scales of ash.

"Did I hurt you?" he said again.

Even in the ashes there is the memory of the fire.

"No," I said. And then again more gently, "No."

Tabak let himself lean back. Once more he became a man. I cast a branch on the fire so we could look at one another. The wood was slow to catch, and we waited for it.

"How old was he then?" I asked after a while.

"As you are, fifteen in the spring."

But I was not listening. Something came back to me. I said, "She told me she would not know his face. Men change. I remember it exactly. She would not know the look of him. But when she spoke she looked me in the face."

Tabak smiled. "Men change," he said, repeating her words as though he tested them. For a moment he closed his eyes. If he started to say something, he changed his mind but then went on. "You must remember she did not know him then, not yet. When she did, he was different. And when she had gone away, back to Urien, he was not the same."

The fire grew. His features, disheveled from the journey, cinder-red in the firelight, seemed suddenly old.

There were hollows under his eyes. "A man begets himself in a child," he started, "but time works on them both. It was not always so. The first men, when at the world's beginning they came upon the land, did not change. Their backs never bent. They loved and fought, but when at last they slipped back to their sea kingdoms they were as they had been. But their magic we have not. Perhaps they no longer have it themselves. Who is to say? Myself, I am not what I was when, at my lord's bidding, I followed Yllvere to her house by Anu's wood."

I sat with my chin in my hand and looked into the fire. "But once," I said, "he was as I am now."

"You have your father's youth in you," he said. "But his old age you have not." Something lingered in his face when the words left him. I saw the years on him, like the dust of the road that goes on and on and finds no peace. I said, "How old would he be now?"

Tabak let his eyes rest on the fire. "The time that binds him is as your own," he said. "He was twice nineteen when he met Yllvere and lay with her. It was the height of summer then. The oaks were full-leaved, the acorns green. I heard his laughter through the grove. It was light on the air, easy at heart, despite his cares. I was his man in that as in other things. That day I held the horses on the far side of the island and watched both the road and the sea. He was hunted then, fearing discovery on all quarters. From the spring which followed when you were born until this time are fifteen more. Together it is three-and-fifty years."

But I did the sums myself. "No," I answered. "It is fourteen, which makes fifty-two."

Tabak lifted his black head. "I will tell you once more and then be done with it," he answered gravely. "The Kell cannot count, as I have told you. All Anu's folk mark out their time by the tides. They care nothing how the water lags behind the moon. They are shore folk who never went to sea. They do not track the stars. When winter comes too soon, they say the snow is early. The spring surprises them. Yllvere, inland on Anu's mountain, counted the tides in memory, not what she saw. So did her women. In that a year was lost and more besides."

He stopped. His rough face drew close to mine. With one hand he had gathered up loose stones from the ground. As though counting, one by one he dropped them to the earth. As they knocked one against the other, the sound of their falling echoed against the darkness. Presently, he said, "If you would be free of the Kell, you must measure your life as it is."

I felt the fire on me. I remembered Vydd in her hut marking her stick with her thumb. I did not attempt to reply and turned from him. In time I slept.

During the night I tossed and dreamed, I thought, of the god Duinn who had filled the great belly of the goddess Night with stones. Long into the night I heard the clang of boulders dropped one by one into the dark's wide craw. In my dreams I beheld the darkness, cold, implacable, immune to the cries of men, and yet I knew the god had tricked her. I stood alone at the saw-edged rim, the abyss below me. Death was there. It was our first acquaintance. He did not beckon. I slept. The late moon rose.

Toward morning the breeze had freshened. A whisper rose from the grass. In the lingering dark the breeze carried the smell of horses. I stirred, sleep still on me. Without waking I lifted my head. Swords glittered under the moon. I heard the riders call to one another, watched them from a great distance, pointing, trying to decide, brave men but cautious. Slow as dreams they rode down upon us, not knowing what we were. I saw them as through a gauze, like creatures under water, five men and a string of ponies. The ponies had thick haunches; great dark packs were buckled to their backs. I lay as though asleep, scarcely breathing, awaiting them, the first men I would meet abroad in the world.

I did not move. The horses circled.

"Are they men?" asked one gruff voice.

"In form," said another. The voice was hard but there was reason in it. He brought his mount nearer. "But see the size of them. They are larger still than the folk we saw two winters past at Tarn. Mark me, they are giant kind or nothing else, such as the *filidh* say live undersea. Though how they came to this place, I know not."

I saw then they thought us corpses, for Tabak slept like a dead man and I lay still. I rose to meet them.

The four fell back; their little mouths dropped open. But the one, his hair in flaxen braids and a grim sword in his hand, pressed forward. He advanced until he brought his sword within a yard of my chest.

"What manner of thing are you?" he demanded.

"A man."

79

The rider looked at me with stern but puzzled eyes. Though I had spoken no more than the truth, the horsemen looked at each other in wonder. Their confusion gave me a moment. Stooping, I shook Tabak till he blinked and yawned.

"Wake," I said. "The day has brought us company."

Laboriously, like a bear just roused from winter sleep, he stirred, turning his sleep-slackened face at first to me and then instantly alert back to the horsemen. Then, without bothering to hurry, in one unbroken motion dwarfing them he stood. Though they rode and we but stood upon the ground, our eyes came level against theirs. The riders watched us with dismay in their faces. At length the one spoke up again.

"Give me your name and tell me whom you serve," he said. Though the four wavered, I saw that his sword had not once faltered. Spurred by his boldness, the others closed beside him. Strangely, I was disappointed. The men of the outer world, like the men of the villages I knew, were as children. The greatest of their company, he with his ring shirt, battle gear and crested helm together, was scarce four elhws and lean as any of my sisters. The others ranged down to a span shorter, about the size of the servants and the women of our house.

"Your name and liege, sir," the one repeated.

"Lately it is Finn," I answered. "But I am no liegeman."

The horseman frowned. Behind him one of the others sniggered. They were small men. But armed and mounted they outnumbered us. The one who laughed had a thin nose and hollow cheeks. Tufts of spare yellow hair grew from his chin. A new sword rested in his lap. Boldness, I saw, may set its root in the poorest soil. He laughed again to make a point of it.

"Finn," he sniggered. "You were right at the start, Ceorl, we have caught us fishmen."

But the one hushed him. "We are men of Bede," he said. His voice had darkened. It stiffened the men beside him. "We are smiths and tinkers, but we are soldiers too. We have ridden this land from one sea to the other, wheresoever a fair price may be had for a bright sword or a shirt of twisted rings. But though the High King's gone and the Steward sits in his place, from the one water to the other the law's the same: a man must give his kin and name the lord he serves. Think again, sir. You do us discourtesy at your peril."

I might have pulled him down with my bare hands. Perhaps he saw that. It did not chasten him. Yet I kept my hands off him and answered mildly, "I am called Finn, as I have told you. I serve no lord. These last days I came down from the twin-peaked mountain. You see it at my back. If you are strangers to this place, I will tell you it is called Géar Finn, though the women of the mountain call it Anu's paps. There I grew to what I am. But now I go toward Ormkill, where I have never been."

The horsemen eyed one another. It was a fair answer, but I saw they doubted it. Tabak came forward, keeping the sun at his back so that they squinted at him. His eyes had sparks dancing in them.

"Would you not know me also?" he asked. "Or is your honor so small a thing it takes offense but one thought at a time?"

The horsemen muttered. But the one looked steadily at Tabak. Unmoved, he answered, "I know good metal from dross," he said. "Nor does it take much wisdom to tell the servant from his master."

A wolf's grin tore at the hard edges of Tabak's lips. Both anger and irony darted in his deep-set eyes. "The men of Bede travel back and forth in this country to little purpose," he said. "Or else so much journeying has joggled their small brains. Surely, even in these days, memories have not grown so short." He broke off, laughing coldly. I did not understand his meaning. The horsemen found no words to say but gazed at him.

The one was troubled. I saw him grip his sword more tightly than before. "Give us your name then, man," he said. "I ask it honestly."

"You know it, Ceorl," said Tabak. "As did your father and all the wandering men of Bede from one shore to the other." He paused. "I am Tabak ap Ewyn," he said. He looked around at them and then at last at me.

A stillness fell upon the horsemen. It fell on me also, creeping on my heart. Yet it was their stillness that had taken hold of me. For myself, I drew nothing from the name. From the time I was a child within the house I had heard it. I looked back on my life as far as memory took me. In gentleness and anger Yllvere had used it, calling to him from the locked door of her chamber. Vydd knew it, smiling to herself. But Vydd would smile as secretly at a thrush in a thicket and find grave portents in the colors of the moon. My sisters spoke it, slyly, for they feared him. I waited to understand. But nothing came of it. The horsemen had not shaken off their silence. I turned to Tabak, facing him.

"Your name has taken their speech away," I said. "Is it only foolishness in me that I am left unmoved?"

"It is not foolishness," he answered gently. "You were mountain born, cut out of a woman in the sight of Anu's wood and reared apart by her own folk. The names men speak you have not heard. So it was kept from you. Even in the book of names you would not have read it. The book holds the majesty of the land. There is no page there for its servants."

But, thinking I had wounded him, I said, "It was never hid from me that you were a serving man. Truly, I never thought you less for it."

"There is nothing to dispute," he answered. "You showed as much courtesy as you had learned. No more was looked for."

"Yes," I said, "these men take the name of a servant as a great wonder."

Tabak smiled then. Looking back I see it was because he knew such words were fated. Something like this must have crossed my mind. For seeing no reason, yet my heart pounded.

"It is not the servant they hold in awe." Though the men heard him, he spoke only to me. His voice was clear but something gathered at the back of it. He looked pleased and perhaps a little sad. Afterward he added, "In knowing the servant, they know his lord."

Around us I felt the horsemen pressing near. The air smelled of horses, of the leather satchels tied to the backs of the ponies, of swords and armor, the acrid smell of iron. To this day I remember it.

"Who is it, then, you serve?" I asked him.

"Ar Elon, Lord of Hren and all the lands between the seas," he answered.

Though backward and mountain born, I knew the name of the High King.

II.
Undain

8.

A MAN'S LIFE IS NOT STRAIGHT. LIKE A SERPENT, it turns back upon itself. It sucks the wounded places. In my heart's core I knew it. Nothing is ever forgotten. Under my breath, like a thing still secret, I tasted my father's name. Ar Elon. I thought, there is not a gift given that is not also a curse.

Nothing is forgotten. The name Urien sought, both waking and dreaming, first from the lips of his servants, then last and longest in the chronicles of Gedd, folding back pages till he nearly went blind: that was the only name he knew without looking. Nothing can be cast away. Slowly I went through it all. I thought of the tower room where I had crept in good and bad weather, close behind Grieve, to hear the old tales. Those bold men and faithless ones, all out of the wide Eastlands, those who were but names in my memory, were now my kin. So the serpent turns back upon itself.

With the sword I had stolen to climb Gwen Gildrun, that which I now carried, Urien killed Lot, the High King's man. With that sword he won Morrigan. Little he dreamed when he plunged the blade into the guts of the man, when he saw the man squirm, coughing up blood before the feet of my father, that all the blood would buy him was his ruin. So the serpent turns back upon itself. For a death my father gave Urien Morrigan and the lands upon the mountain, a murderer's fee. But, taking Yllvere, my father cursed the gift.

I thought of Yllvere. Against the wall of flame I saw her face, crimson with the heat of the great fires under the house. Over the long leagues in my mind I sought her. There was blood on my own face, she said, that night when Vydd cut me from her womb. Then it came to me out of the tangle of my thoughts. I heard her words within the roar of burning wood: "There was another born that night. I clove the name."

It is written in the Book of Gedd that I wept when I heard the name of my father. So to this day the wise *filidh* tell it. But nowhere it is set down what was in my heart.

"They go toward Stephen's Well, to the Steward's holding," Tabak said again, for at first I had not been listening. "If we should go with them, by midday you will drink from the river."

The horsemen muddled behind Ceorl but were mostly silent, not knowing where to put their eyes. I looked over them. Tabak was still talking. I shook my head at him. I meant to take the place he had raised for me. I said, "The days we rode together you gave me no answers, only riddles and sawed-off words. Now, before men I have never seen, you unfold my father like a banner."

But Tabak would not be rebuked. His look fell hard on me. I saw he meant me to keep still. To Ceorl he said, "You have heard what was said here and you know the claim."

Ceorl did not look away. "I have heard it, Tabak ap Ewyn," he answered. "You do well to speak openly. Though I am not eager to be part of this, it would be folly to bring a king's heir to the Steward's holding without swordsmen at his back."

"It is many years since I was elsewhere but the mountain," Tabak said. "How is it with Thigg?"

"There is fighting still," said Ceorl. "The Steward was never easy with his might. The barons bite at his heels. There are holdings, not many leagues distant, where the inconstant vassals would take up the name of the King's heir whether they believe it or not. Should they master Thigg with him, there would be time enough to judge the claim."

Tabak looked across at him and smiled. He stood in the fresh sunlight. The mist was all but gone from off the ground. "And how, Ceorl of Bede, do you judge the claim?"

"I do not judge it."

"You have but to think on it."

Ceorl's pale face was solemn. He stared at Tabak a long time from under his helm. "The lad heard me if you did not," he answered. "I took you both for giants."

"You know the High King stood well above all other men."

"I have crossed mountains and many rivers," said the

horseman. "In one place it is spoken that the High King came out of the East, where smoke hangs always before the sun, that at his summoning the crows of battle flock down from the crags of Morg. In another, it is said that he was seaborn, risen on the foam, and that the great whales there did him service. Though here on Rasoden and along the river they say that he was only a red-haired farmer like themselves but that one day Dagda spoke to him and in that moment raised him over other men."

"And what say the men of Bede?" Tabak asked him.

Ceorl laughed and let his bright sword fall back into his lap. "In Bede," he answered, "if a cat claims he is king, it is thought best to kneel, at least until we have had a chance to see his teeth."

I glanced quickly at Tabak but discovered nothing in his face. He was looking east, his dark head lifted. The breeze twisted his hair.

"Tell me your name again," said the horseman.

"Finn ap Ar Elon," I answered.

The horseman studied me with careful eyes. "I will ride with you, Lord Finn," he said. "At least as far as Stephen's Well. I for one would see the faces of the men of towns when first they looked at you."

I saw the horsemen mutter. But his word was given.

In the early afternoon we came down near the river. On the uplands there was heather on the sides of the hills, the grass in flower. But the borders of the river were thick pinewood. We went into the wood along a narrow path. Here, even at midday, there were shadows and in the dampness, flies. The horses went single file. Because of this there was not much said among us and I had my thoughts to myself. Yet even before I saw it, my thoughts were filled with the river.

The Undain flows out of the mountain north of Morrigan. There I imagined it was like the streams I knew, nightmare torrents echoing among the rocks. But on the plain, they say, the river was both broad and still, smooth as a mirror. Here deep-keeled boats came well into the midlands, stopping at towns to trade, the oarsmen sitting at their ease at dockside after a stiff day's work. I longed to see such boats and the masters of water.

The path ran from one turning to another, twisting among boulders and great trees. As we went there were times when I was cut off altogether from the company though I heard the sound of hoofbeats close at hand. It must be that the horsemen lost track of where I was. for in time I heard them speaking openly. The long boughs of the pines drooped over me. In the breeze the needles whispered.

"I had not thought Ceorl so empty-headed," said a voice. It belonged to the one with the yellow beard. who had called me fishman. I remembered well the sound of it. "Yet he will pledge his sword to any upstart that comes down from the mountains."

"Tabak ap Ewyn rides with the lad," another answered.

The man sniggered. "If the tales are true, Tabak has ridden with the green mares of Tir-na-n-Og. By that you would have a horse at Ormkill in the King's chair."

The other laughed. "Better a green mare than Thigg."

"Be careful," said a voice, "or you will find the doors of this land shut to you."

"Look to yourself, Wend. If the lad's the King's heir, as they say, there is not a door between this place and hell where they will let you in."

The yellow beard muttered. "King's heir or not, he has no allies. When the High King fled, his liegemen scattered. Of those who served him all that are not dead are men too old to lift a sword. Look to yourself. If the barons take him up, they will cast him down soon enough when it pleases them. Think on it. In faith, who is there who will come to him?"

"It may be there are some of Bede who would not fear to serve him," the other said.

The yellow beard answered. But a fly buzzed in my ear and I missed the words. Later, when we had come into a clearing, I looked to see the man who rode beside him. Our eyes touched for a moment. His corn-colored hair hung from his temples in long plaits like the others', but he sat a head taller and was coarsely made. Strapped to his back was a great broadax. I set it in my mind to remember him. The sun was overhead.

Once more the clearing passed into a shaded wood. But now the ground was steeper, the mare uneasy. I leaned forward and patted her thick neck. She thrashed her tail. Shortly we came down a high ridge. The trees parted. Then nothing hid it from me.

From one stony bank to the other the Undain spread before me like a silver meadow. I was not prepared for its quiet. Its peace sank into the marrow of my bones. Yet beneath its voiceless surface I knew it moved. I felt it, invisible and deep, shifting under the sky, a kingdom of water, black, dark green and silver, all colors and none at once, sliding with none to stop it toward the sea. It enchanted me. At the edge of my mind I was thinking of Grieve. With her tales of the great ocean she had set my heart on traveling. Then I remembered her face as she came up from the fires beneath the house. A chill ran down my neck. I drove the thought from me.

The mare checked at the water's edge and nickered. Sliding from her back, I gave her to herself. She was a gift to Yllvere from my father. Perhaps she knew this bank, or it may be only that she thirsted. Yet she did not drink, but lifted her old head and whinnied. Her cry sounded thin and shrill along the bank. The horsemen, where they knelt on the flat stones, looked up with stupid faces, their small mouths dripping.

High above us a rider broke from the cover of the wood. He stopped on the promontory and held there. He was a stern man with the mark of service on him. On his thick chest he wore a bright ring shirt and yet his head was bare. He did not look at us but spoke over his shoulder, calmly as though scarcely interested in the sight that had greeted him. At his word a mounted column came out of the trees. They took their stations along the ridge. All were clothed in the same fashion, red cloaks on their shoulders and helms with nosepieces jutting down. These were Thigg's men, I judged, or at the least men of his vassals. They knew their number and had not bothered to draw their arms. When their chief saw they were ordered, he pointed down to us.

"Drink deep, men of Bede, then gather your ponies," he said in a booming voice to carry the distance. "My captain at Stephen's Well has need of axes and spearheads."

But Ceorl called up to him, "In Bede we are free men and come and go as we choose."

The man spat. "My captain is not poor," he cried out sourly. "He will pay a fair price if the work is good."

"We will come or not as it pleases us," Ceorl shouted back. But I saw it was but talk to keep up his spirits. He was quite still.

Tabak stood next to me. "Rather a poorer price than an honest one, I should guess," I said lightly. "Else his captain would not send so many swordsmen to harvest so few smiths."

"They are a patrol only," Tabak answered. "I doubt they rode out seeking either one thing or another but come by chance to shark up whatever they can find."

Then, for the first time, their chief seemed to notice us. He leaned forward. His red hair was cut close to his head; his mouth was twisted. "You are not of Bede," he announced loudly. He made it sound like a great discovery but at the same time one of doubtful interest. "You had best come with us as well," he shouted. "If you are as strong as you are big and can handle a sword without cutting off your knees, my captain may have a place for you."

When I heard this, I saw he took us for farmers. I thought less of him for that. But the truth was that he was looking down at us from a height and so could not take our full measure. By then several of his company had descended to the bank and come even with us. One pointed me out. I saw they had already begun to mutter among themselves. Exchanging a final word with his companions, the one that had stretched his finger at me set his mount to climb the ridge again. Regaining the promontory, he spoke at his chief's ear. When the man had done, I saw their chief twist his thick neck to sweep his glance along the shore. When he was satisfied as to our number, he spoke.

"I am Eoghan," he said in a measured voice. "Behind me are thirty men with swords and lances. My captain at Stephen's Well has four hundred. He is a fair man but quick to take offense. This river and the lands both east and west he holds in Thigg's service." He made a wide gesture with his hand by which he meant to show the extent of the holding. Then he added, "It is Thigg's law between the two seas. In this province I am Thigg's eyes and my captain his right arm."

I glanced aside at Tabak. "Why does he waste words on this?" I asked, for the speech had puzzled me.

"You have made him unsure of himself," he answered. "He knows the folk of Rasoden, and you are not one of them. His man has no doubt told him you and I are twice the size that men should be. He fears now you may be someone of consequence. But not having seen it at the first, he dares not ask you who you are. So he tells you his name, counts his own and his captain's men, and drags in Thigg and the whole countryside to puff himself up. By this he thinks you will respond in kind."

"And if I do not."

"They are still thirty and we are seven."

"We are six at best," I said darkly, but there was no time to explain it to him.

I walked to the mare and mounted her. With my hand I bade the men of Bede do likewise. I saw Ceorl smile to himself. He threw his leg up over his pony. When his men saw it, they followed him.

Eoghan scratched the beard on his cheek and stared down at us. The few that had come down the bank stood now some distance off. They kept looking up at him yet he would not signal them. At last he roused himself, calling out to me in his great voice.

"What do you do in this place?" he shouted.

"When I have a mare that thirsts, I let her drink," I called back to him.

He did not know what to make of that.

"I am Thigg's eyes," he said again. "I keep watch at this place and at others. What I see I tell my captain. When I tell him of you, he will be curious. And what is the name of the man whose mare thirsts, he will ask me."

"Then you must tell him that you met a one-eyed man with half a name," I answered. The men of Bede looked at one another with troubled faces. For their sake I added, "If you wish you may also say that I have lived my life in Morrigan, which Urien holds, he who was friend to the High King."

If it surprised him, it seemed as well to suit him better. Eoghan nodded. "The name is not unknown to me," he said. "You are his son, then?"

"I have lived in the house," I answered. "If I were his son I would have said it." Even his own men saw I had answered well. Yet I could see Eoghan was displeased. I doubted he was accustomed to being answered so. His gaze wandered impatiently around our small group of horsemen.

"My captain will have many questions about the North," he shouted. "Seldom is it that men come down from the mountain kingdoms." Into his face there came a kind of smile. "It would honor my captain," he continued, "should one who has lived in the house of the High King's friend stop at his holding."

Neither Ceorl nor his men nor any of Eoghan's company spoke. It was between us only. But it was a thing I was not used to. For I only had my sisters to match wits with. Yet I knew clearly enough his courtesy was hollow.

What was odd was how surely Eoghan, with his twisted smile and pompous bellowing, expected me to see the lie. Seeing no better return, with lies I answered him.

"Your courtesy indeed is welcome," I called out. I saw that Tabak winked at me. It made me bolder. "You must tell your captain that when I come to Stephen's Well I shall seek his company. Pleased I will be to tell him that in Eoghan he is well served." I saw now that among his men some eyed one another, their faces on the edge of laughter. I would have continued in this vein, but Tabak, who had brought his horse near to mine, kicked my knee lightly to hush me. Chastened, I picked up the reins and turned the mare's head to the left along the shore. Over my shoulder I called up to Eoghan. "I bid you a fair journey," I shouted. Then slowly I rode from the place, Tabak and the men of Bede beside me.

We rode a little way, just beyond the rocks where the river turned. When we had passed the rocks, I said, "He let us go. I had not thought he would."

Tabak shrugged. "The bank is steep between this place and Stephen's Well. If you will watch the rise, you will see in the spaces between the trees that we are followed."

But I was angry then and would not consider what he said. "At last," I said, "we will ride into Stephen's Well as men and not as captives."

"It comes to much the same," he answered.

Still I would not think of it. I spurred the mare and let her gallop.

That night, camped along the shore of the river, with Ceorl and his men on watch by turns, I did not sleep. But when Tabak found a place beside me, I had nothing more to say to him. We had no fire, seeing little need to make it any easier than it was for those who followed us. Now and then we heard their horses. My ears strained, listening for them. I was uneasy. Just before morning it rained —a soft spring rain, the sort that farmers love. I rolled myself in my blanket.

When I woke there was a boat out on the river. My clothes were soaked through, but it was warm and I was in no discomfort. I stood, peering out into the river. In the mist I could see little but the long shadow of its bow. I heard the oars splash, and ran to the river's edge. The water was gray. Already birds were fishing. I looked carefully. For a moment I saw the mast, a naked tree, the sail furled. I wished it closer. But it stayed well into the current and soon had disappeared in the rain. Ceorl saw me staring out at the mist. He came beside me.

"It is a river like any other, lord," he said grinning.

I said, "I have seen no other."

"I see then that I was wrong."

"In what?"

"When first I saw you, I took you for a sea mage."

The rain had lessened. A fresh breeze was clearing the mist. I looked down at myself. Steam rose from my arms and my damp clothing. "My mother is a witch of Anu," I told him. "In my blood is mixed the salt blood of the Kell."

He was thinking but I could not see into it. After a silence he said, "Whatever else the Kell are, they are as mortal as any that live upon the land."

"It may be so," I said but I thought of Vydd and then of Grieve. "Or it may be they go mad in place of death."

"I have heard that also," said Ceorl absently. He held my eye, his thought already gone ahead to something else. "What runs in your blood from Ar Elon, I wonder?"

I looked out at the river, across the flat sheen of the water, thinking of the tales I had read within the Book of Gedd. "He was king of the land between the two seas," I said. "But whether he drew his strength from the water or the earth it is not written. In my life I have known only the rocks of the mountain. Though I have sought him in the stonefields, he was not there." I met Ceorl's stare again.

"Then you must seek him here," he said.

"I do not swim. There was no place to learn." But already I knew that I would do it. I sat on the bank and drew off my boots and then my longshirt. But as I did this, the yellow beard came down on us.

"So it is wash day for the mountain king?" he asked of Ceorl, the smirk still lingering after the question was done. We were still a moment, looking at one another. At Ormkill, I supposed, a king's son would have struck him. But at Ormkill a king's son would have had a troop of housethralls at his heels. Yet how easy, I thought, to kill a man. Nonetheless, I let the anger drain from me. In the fields above Morrigan I had sometimes seen a small blue snake coiled on a certain stone. Its bite, the women said, would kill. Yet I had gone by it a dozen times and left it whole. Wisely or not, so it was then. Small evils, I judged, were best left to themselves. Otherwise a man would fill his life with nothing else but taking heads. I waded into the river.

The water was cold against my thighs. But since the two watched me I moved quickly out beyond the shallows. Free of the shore, the current tugged at me. The icy ripples rose against my chest and circled my neck like a collar, so that for a moment I felt myself like one of the bodiless heads the great *filidh* sing of, such as guard the gate that leads to Duinn's realm. I lifted my feet from the stones below. For an instant, closing my eye, I felt as though I flew. Still I knew it was not the earth that moved beneath.

It was quiet in the river. I went down and opened my eye. The water was black. I could see nothing. I turned to see the river's roof shining above my head. Its brilliance startled me. I turned from it. The river carried me. I heard it then, whispering among the stones, the water song, the river longing for the sea. An icy lassitude came over me. I passed into dreaming. I thought, there are gods in the river and long-armed demons with bodies like sunken logs and fingers like wet branches. The thought chilled me. I shot out my legs to stand. My feet did not touch the stones.

"Finn," moaned the river.

I will not drown, I thought.

The voice of the water laughed. "Stay with me," it murmured, "for I will bear you in such state as fits the king's true son, past the little maggot towns and out past rancid Tinkern, out beyond the man-trodden islands at my mouth. Beyond the faint and crawling life on land in the Great Sea, you and I will dive to the oldest of halls, crystal-roofed, limitless and cold. There is a place for you among sea stones where you may hear talk of the first things and the last, such as none before you ever heard."

"You are a ringing in my ears," I said. "No more."

"I am your blood," the river sang.

"My blood is not so cold nor yet so pale," I cried. But my head rang with echoes. The river's laughter drummed against my ears. It mocked me.

"I am the blood of Yllvere and of Grieve," it sang. "In you I am the same."

"No," I cried out. "I will be king upon the land." I knew it, then for the first time. It was a sign to me, like a hot coal found in ashes. I warmed myself before it. The river squealed among the stones. I would not listen.

"Finn," it sighed but I would not heed the whisper as it fled.

I came up into daylight. I drank the air.

9.

FISH WEIRS JUTTED UP A HUNDRED YARDS FROM shore. Here the shore flattened and the trees were cut away. On the banks old men sat with nets draped across their withered knees, mending the torn places with wooden shuttles. A few naked children of either sex swam among the rushes. Ceorl rode at our head and was the first seen. The children ran out to him, swarming around his ponies, fingering the packs to see what might be found. The yellow beard, who was called Wend, followed and after him in a knot the others of Bede, their new swords scabbarded. Tabak and I, for we had been talking together, came last, riding out of the trees. The sight of us daunted the children and killed their laughter. Backing away, they hid themselves among the scrub. One red-haired girl I remember, her eyes wide with fear, hugged a bawling infant in her arms. An old women hobbled out of a hut. Giving me a nasty leer, she claimed them under her apron. A thick-set man in a leather jacket and bearing a broadax stepped out into the light. At his back, ducking under the door frame, came two stout boys with hoisted spears.

Ceorl and his horsemen halted. Tabak and I did likewise. Men continued to emerge from the huts. There were perhaps twenty of fighting age, each armed with a long spear. Still they stayed back from our horses. Ceorl studied them critically, picking out their leader.

"You know us, Cram," he said. "Two summers past I traded ax blades with you and hooks of good metal. If it was honest work, you have no cause to turn on me an ax of my own fashioning."

The man, his eyes narrowed, shook his head. "I have my worries, smith, as other men. Along the Undain there is little peace. There is no breach of courtesy if my people are vigilant." Having said that, he advanced toward Ceorl. Ceorl slipped from his mount and met him on the ground. Cram let his anxious eyes rest sharply on Tabak and myself.

"The men of Bede bring more than metal," he said to him.

Ceorl gave our names. He had met us, he said, on the road that come out of the north. Cram nodded slowly, without conviction. I could see this did not satisfy him. Behind him an old woman stamped her feet, muttering to all that would listen that we were water trolls. The young men laughed at her. Still, they did not send her away.

Cram called for chairs and a table. "I would hear of where you have been in two years' roving and of your meeting with such bold men as these," he said. Then he placed his hand on Ceorl's shoulder and abruptly smiled. "Such talk, no doubt, will make us thirsty." He gave another command. The young men dragged a table from his hut. But seeing it was too small for so many, they took down a door and set it upon barrels. Chairs were placed around for us and one for Cram and two old men at his side. The young men stood around. They did not put down their arms.

"What is the danger," Ceorl asked, "that your young men bear their weapons and do not sit with us?"

In the meantime a woman had brought forth a pitcher and cups on a platter. Cram poured the beer into the cups himself.

"Young men are not as you and I," he answered with a sigh. "They do not always know when they should be afraid and when they should not."

"Then let them learn," I said, speaking for the first time.

Ceorl agreed. "I am not so young," he said, "that I would sit with a beer cup between my fingers when boys like these sharpen spear points at my back."

"Drink, then, and be at ease," said Cram uncomfortably. Without waiting for us, he lifted his cup to his lips and drank deeply, wiping his mouth with his arm when he had done. Then he called one of the elders of the village and bade him take the spears and pile them in the middle of the clearing. It was done as he commanded, though the young men grumbled. Cram filled his cup once more. "Now, what news?" he said.

Ceorl looked at the faces of the men and at the children clinging to the women in the doorways. He answered, "I have never heard there was fear in the eyes of children if men were strong."

Cram drained the cup.

"Things go ill, friend," he whispered. He would not meet Ceorl's eyes.

"Has it ever been otherwise?" said Ceorl. But then he added, "Perhaps Thigg's service lies too hard upon the land."

"No!" Cram exploded. Then he was excited all at once, shaking his big head and looking up and down the table at us. "As I am a man who hates evil and villainy, I swear it is not so. Thigg is a fair lord. Let them sink my body in the marshes if it is not so."

A murmur of astonishment ran through us. There is madness in this man's blood, I thought, and perhaps in his drink as well. Ceorl put down the cup which he had raised. Even the yellow beard, who was seldom without a word, sat quietly, his cup untasted. His squinty eyes, watching Cram, grew harder. There was no sound to be heard save the aspen leaves rustling gently in the wood beyond the village yard. On either side of Cram, the old men trembled. Cram's eyes started stiffly out of his head.

"If you will not drink, then we will trade," he said. From off his hip he drew a small bag of coins, which he flung clumsily upon the table. They scattered and rolled from one side to the other. Though of no great worth, it was more than I had thought would have been held in the whole of such a village. I took that in and did not miss the warning in it. The trumpets rang.

The horsemen rushed out of the wood. I knew the red cloaks and the helms. I seized my sword. The men of the village rushed toward their spears. Yet I saw well enough that even armed they would stay back. We alone were Eoghan's prey. They knew it. Perhaps Cram had been paid to have his young men take us and, seeing he could not have us addle-headed with his beer, had lost his nerve. Who is to say? Tabak, who had his wits about him still, cast away the chairs to give him room to fight.

The men massed forward, waving spears and swords from upon their mounts. The first of the company drove at me. I hewed the neck of the first horse that reached me. With a scream, it reared its great forelegs, toppling its rider. Before he could crawl away, his arms still in confusion, I caught him in the face. The skull split open under the metal. He was the first man I had killed, but I had no time to think of it. By then the rest were plunging down at us. Ceorl struck one in the side. Tabak drove two back, cutting the knees of the horses and pulling down the startled men with his bare hands. After that they did not press as close but mustered among the huts and before us, cutting off the way to the river. They held their broad shields before them. By ones and twos Cram's men joined the mounted soldiers. It was not long before they had us in a ring.

I saw Cram move among them; his mouth was slack and his gestures uncertain. Eoghan came at last, his mount trotting easily out of the trees. A shout went up from the horsemen. Eoghan surveyed the work of his company, the men in order, the corpses on the ground.

"Better you had come with us at our first meeting," he called out gravely.

Cram was at his side. "There was to be no murder," he whimpered.

Eoghan laughed at him. "They are my own dead."

Cram shook his great head and wailed. "It is in the eyes of the children."

Eoghan did not answer him. When he rode on, his men gathered quickly at his back.

None of the soldiers' horses would carry me. So they gave me back my own but kept her fettered to two others. The ropes they bound me with cut my wrists. They had needed six men to take me. Yet not one came close enough for sword or ax. Rather they ringed me about and threw stones until I fell, my face bloody and my shoulders bruised with wounds. In this same way they had taken Tabak, even as the men of the mountain towns cripple a stag in its pen. At the feast of the new year I had seen it. The memory came to me as the stones fell. To them we were as monsters. As such, no warrior's honor bound them. Ceorl's men they took in a more manly fashion. Their wounds were deep. Still none of our own were dead.

In that way I stood my first battle and kept my life. We rode the rest of the morning. The soldiers were still, thinking of their comrades. Myself, I thought of the man I killed. In the quiet, with only the footfalls of Eoghan's soldiers, the wind hushed, I remembered the look in his glazed eyes, disbelief more than anguish, before the small face fell apart. There was no glory in it, some farmer's son, no doubt pressed into service by his lord, no quarrel between us but Eoghan's word to him. It was not as the *filidh* tell it. He was a clumsy man. He carried his leather shield too low. His own men left him for the flies.

They had Tabak ride in front of me. Because of his wounds, he kept falling. Later they tied him to the horn of the saddle. He shivered though there was no wind. My heart was in my throat to watch him, once my father's servant, half-slave to Yllvere and waiting fifteen winters, now bidden to be my guardian in the eastern lands. How still he was, grim but strangely without anger. He would take his fate, both good and ill, just as it came. I met his eyes. What must a man bear in service to his lord? I mourned for him more than for myself. My trouble was at least of my own doing.

We rode through meadow lands, close to the river but below the road. I guessed by this that Eoghan meant to take us in secret into Stephen's Well. Twice, when in the distance I saw a string of farm wagons climbing the road along the hill, Eoghan ordered our column halted. He sent two men to pull me roughly from the mare. They pushed my face into the grass. When they let me raise my head, the wagons had gone. The second time I would not mount. The soldiers glared at me.

"I will dress the wounds of my friend," I said.

"A soldier takes his chances," mocked the man. "What is it to me if this one dies?" Then, to prod me, he drew his sword. Still I would not do what he wanted. Eoghan, looking back, saw his man armed and came riding down the line to us. The soldiers drew aside.

"I have ordered that we ride," Eoghan said harshly.

"He will not," said the soldier.

Eoghan regarded me distastefully. "Mount," he said.

"When I have done," I answered. "First, I must wipe the blood from my friend's eyes and close his wounds."

Eoghan's small eyes turned full to me. "That he lives at all you owe me. By right the men who took him should have scattered his head and limbs from one end of the village to the other. It would be only just to lay him dead among the death he made."

I only stared at him.

"Take his arms," he ordered, "and lift him."

Putting up his sword, the one came forward and three more from the ranks of the soldiers.

"If he struggles," said Eoghan coldly, "you may beat him. Only leave him enough life's breath that tomorrow he may answer what our captain asks."

It was not the threat of pain but simply the humiliation that tormented me. It made me reckless. "By Anu," I hissed, "the first that touches me is dead." The soldiers grinned.

They were men as any other and laughed at the name of the goddess. I do not know what made me invoke her. For I was my father's then and had reasons enough of my own to hate the mysteries of the wood. Yet, once it was spoken, I saw the use of it. With my boot, since I had not the use of my hands, I drew a figure in the twisted grass. The pattern burned in the air as I made it. Poor thing it was, a hearth spell such as any of my sisters used each night to start the kindling. Even the serving-women knew it. Yet, it frightened the soldiers. They were plainsmen. Among such folk the old religion had been dead a thousand years.

"He is a man witch," a soldier whispered. The others muttered and made quick signs against the eye.

"Fools," Eoghan scoffed. "You wounded him. You bound his hands and made him ride with us." He turned his horse about. "Set him on the mare," he said. He looked at each man when he had finished. A vein beat in his temple. He was accustomed to being obeyed.

The soldiers were silent a moment, uneasy, waiting for one of them to speak. It was a gray-haired man who came forth, a slight man even by their measure. He had a scar across one cheek from the left nostril to his ear. Yet he had a bold voice and made certain that the others heard him. "Who is to know what a man witch chooses and what he does not?" And then to me, "Lord, mage, I would have peace with you."

Eoghan spat. "If he had power, think you not he would have used it?"

Still the soldiers grumbled. Eoghan stared in anger, without a word.

the mysteries are greater. A man, if a priest tells him, will plant a rind and throw away the seed. It was not my

I saw then that the authority of men is one thing, but

cunning taught me this. In the faces of the soldiers, still as celebrants, afraid, I saw it. It ordered my mind.

"Take down my friend," I said. Several soldiers came out of the column, uncertain, unbound the ropes and slid Tabak to the earth. They knew what they risked from Eoghan by that. It was to him I spoke. "I will go to Stephen's Well," I said. "I am eager to see how your captain marshals his four hundred and by that how Thigg is served in this place. For as Thigg is served, so he serves in turn. It marks the stewardship which is his until the true heir comes."

Then men of Bede looked one to another. Eoghan was watchful of it.

"Untie my hands," I said.

Out of their number, even in front of Eoghan, a man came forth.

The sun declined toward the horizon. Ocher and huge, it bathed the farthest clouds in copper light. In the east, some leagues before us, rose the walls of Stephen's Well, bright on the one side with the sun's death and on the other, by the river, deep in shadow. Fresh with the spring flood, the water came up to the wall, sucking at the old foundations. Although far off, already I felt small before it. On the landward side the holding jutted a hundred elhws above the trees. Until that time it was the greatest work I had ever seen of man's fashioning, though surely among the most plain. Its steep walls were laid unmortared. Without spires or carvings, bald as a skull, it was a soldier's keep, made to a soldier's rude imagining. Immense it was. Yet it was said that Stephen's Well, for all its height, would huddle in Ormkill's shadow.

From the road broad steps went down to the harbor. Even at a distance I saw it. On either side, backing away from the steps, huge storied buildings loomed above the rock. Each was several times the size of Morrigan. I felt a mountain boy again. But it was the ships that took my thoughts. There were four in the harbor, each of good size. One, whose double sails were bellied full, was setting out downstream to take advantage of the night wind. On the deck as we drew nearer, I saw a man in a blue cloak, hooded, shouting orders to the crew. I could not hear the words. It was still too far and the wind was from the north.

"It is the same ship that passed us in the fog," said Ceorl.

"Perhaps," I said, wondering how in the darkness of morning past he had seen anything that marked it. Yet I judged it was not the ship he wished to speak of, though it may have been that it reminded him of something. For he had seen the look on my face when I had come from the river, my hair shining, the steam rolling back from my shoulders. He had heard the claim that Tabak made for me and bound, on the strength of it, his men and honor to my service. Yet I knew well enough it was Tabak that bound him, the fame of Tabak ap Ewyn that gave him certainty. Now Tabak lay limp against his saddle. With the soldier's leave I had bathed his wounds and worked a salve into the cuts. Still I had not Yllvere's or Vydd's skill. Whether he would live I did not know. I saw Ceorl feared that he would not.

"My lord Finn," Ceorl began unevenly. "You know that we are few."

"I know it. And fewer still when we ride inside those walls." Then watching him, I said, "You are free, Ceorl, you and those of Bede."

He flinched and I saw that, without meaning, I had shamed him. "I have not taken away my word," he said. "I meant only to speak plainly."

"Then speak," I told him.

Ceorl looked up at me. It strained his neck to do so. The leather of his face was cracked; there were creases about his mouth. Like Tabak, he was older than I had first realized. "You have humiliated Eoghan, my lord. You knew that. Even now he rides at the back of us, his command broken, as much a captive as if you chained him. Yet if he enters Stephen's Well, he will have his captain's ear."

"I cannot help that."

"You might," he whispered.

I thought of Urien.

"Would you have me slip a knife in him?" I asked. So this is the way it comes to kings, I thought. It angered me. "Do you think that would gain me better entry or shelter for Tabak or time to heal his wounds?"

He shook his head. "I would not have you enter here at all."

"Is your word one thing, then, and mine another?"

He looked perplexed. "I do not see," he said.

I answered sharply. "Twice I have said I meant to come down to this place. Before these men I said it."

"You are not bound to them."

"They called me mage and begged my peace."

Despite his fealty Ceorl laughed. "For that small fire you scratched in the grass? Forgive me, lord, but in the hills I have seen a farm wife suck a better blaze out of the air to start her supper."

I knew the truth of that. Perhaps I smiled. "Fortunately for you and me, these folk are not as widely traveled."

But Ceorl had dropped his eyes. "Here they can kill a man as readily as anywhere."

"I do not doubt it."

Ceorl made a deep obeisance. "My lord, I pray you. Only ride past Stephen's Well and I shall go with you wheresoever you require."

I set my eye on him. "Do not bind yourself to me more than you must. I do not know myself what drives me or what, in time, I may require of those that follow me."

We were then within the outer perimeter of the town. Small outbuildings grew up about us. In the lampless doorways I saw the shadows of men—guards, I judged—spears resting in the crooks of their arms. In the poor light it may be that they saw no more, nor maybe wished to see, than a company of their own men passing.

Ceorl rode at my right, on my blind side. "Truly, I am already bound, Ar Elon's son," he said. "I will follow as I can." I turned to look at him, to fix his face forever in my mind. He was the first man who swore his life to me. Though he thought me wrong, pigheaded, yet he followed me. If I had been able to think then or had foresight, I would have thought, this also is the way of kings. In the years that followed, into the hall that was mine, with the barons like my hounds fighting over the scraps of my table, Ceorl would come in the spring out of the north from the lands I had ceded him. Yearly, the most trusted of my counselors, he would sit at my hearth at Ormkill in the place I kept for him, to drink and remember what we did. Then, before he fell asleep in his beard, he would recall how I disregarded the first advice he gave me. Even now, the god only knows who was right and wrong.

We rode in the middle of the line. At the front, before the tower, I heard a watchman call out.

"Eoghan's company," said a soldier.

"I do not see him." said the watchman cautiously.

"He comes," the man answered.

By then we were abreast of the tower and the light of the torches poured over us. When they had a look at me, the guards came to life. Someone lifted a horn to his lips. Its shrill sound called forth other horns within the holding. There was a clank of metal, footfalls and the squeal of hinges. The wall itself was a warren of tunnels, alcoves and small doors. Within I heard men running and orders being passed. Soldiers ducked out of creviced shadows I had thought were stone. In several black lines they wormed out of the rock. I saw little of their faces, small dwarfish men like the rest I had seen in the East, helmeted, clothed in leather studded up and down with iron. Silently they formed in columns about us, pressing in. Out of their number someone bade us dismount.

"Be careful with this man," I said, gesturing toward Tabak. Without further comment a litter was brought for him. When they had settled him, an immense wooden door, pulled by four men, opened in the holding.

Eoghan, who had come up from behind, now entered at the front. He ran a distrustful eye along his company and, taking the watchman aside, spoke to him privately. The man, staring at me all the while, ran off when Eoghan had finished.

After a moment a burly man without helm or weapon came down the stair along the inner wall. His eyes passed over the line of soldiers, lingering on me in astonishment, then stopped on Eoghan.

"Why would you have your own men put in irons?" he asked sternly.

Eoghan, who had come before him, answered. "The prisoner," he said, "has witched them."

"What prisoner?"

Eoghan pointed.

The man pulled his beard, stared a time and shook his head. "It is an odd sort of prisoner who rides into my holding bearing his own sword."

Shouts rose among Eoghan's company. Eoghan himself cried out above them, his nostrils quivering. No sense could be made from the howling.

"Silence!" the man cried roughly, grasping his beard between his fingers. His eyes gleamed beneath their heavy brows. He extended his hand toward me, pointing. "Bring this one to my chamber. And the giant on the litter." Eoghan was about to protest.

"And you, Eoghan," he grumbled. "I did not mean to

forget you." Then, turning, "And you of Bede. Yes, I know you. I mean to have this settled." He gave a swift glance toward the watchman. "Now bolt the door," he ordered, his voice grown heavy. "I'll have no more marvels at my door this night. If any but Thigg's own messenger come banging, you have my leave to turn them back."

The watchman nodded. As they had come, the soldiers vanished. Like worms into wood, they were reclaimed by the walls. Then, even before we had left the yard, the torches were put out.

10.

I WAITED ON THE BENCH. EOGHAN HAD ALREADY begun to speak, his loud voice choked with anger. The captain, whose name was ffraw, had dismissed the guards though I guessed he had them stationed outside the door where he could get them quickly enough if he had need of them. He sat on a low stool before the hearthstones. It was his own chamber, and not some prisoners' hall, which I thought odd. There was a bed in one corner and a plain table in another. With his own hands he had pulled the drapery over the window. It was the one luxury in the room, a wide cloth woven with gold and silver threads. Among the folds of the fabric I could pick out the images of an aurochs and a team of horses. The aurochs was crimson, the horses green.

ffraw took no part in the questioning but let Eoghan go on for some time. Once he rose to add another log to the fire. He had a great black kettle boiling on a tripod. He stirred the contents with a stick. With his back to Eoghan he listened, staring into the flames. His brows hung over his eyes; a harsh frown puckered his forehead. When Eoghan had finished, he restrained a sigh and smoothed his matted beard.

"A fire, you say?" he half-asked, half-demanded. "No more than that?"

Eoghan was adamant. "Out of the air alone," he said, his cheeks flushed.

ffraw stared inquisitively at Tabak, laid like a corpse on the litter, before at last he turned to me, his eyebrows raised.

"And did you?" he asked.

I took my finger and tore a livid fragment from the air. The flame, pulled out of emptiness, fell smoldering on the floor, where it expired.

ffraw nodded without surprise. "You asked his name?" he said to Eoghan, waving his stick at him.

Eoghan bit his upper lip with his yellow teeth. It was not the sort of inquiry he had expected.

"You did ask him?" ffraw repeated.

"He is from the North," said Eoghan. His voice was bitter. "From the house which he calls Morrigan, of Urien's line. So he told me. But from the sound of it, my guess is that he means what we call Sléibhte-na-Ban, the mountains of women. In truth he called out the name of the goddess."

"His *name*, man," ffraw shouted. There was a commotion at the door. Two guards, hearing the shouting though perhaps missing the words, came in. ffraw did not wave them off but held them at the entrance with a stare.

"His name," he said again.

"He did not give it."

"Or to any there?"

"Not that I know."

ffraw drew himself up, wiping his hands on his long-shirt as though to fuss with something. No other reason. The muscles had changed minutely in his jaw. Yet if he were weighing some action, it took only a moment.

"Guards, take this man," he said.

For an instant the spearmen did not understand. They moved toward me. ffraw's eyebrows arched still higher and he thrust out his stick to make it clear. But Eoghan knew it from the first. A brief spasm twisted his lips. He flung at me a look of feverish hatred. The spearmen grabbed his arms. There was a blade at his back, in the hollow right above his buttocks. When he felt it, his small eyes turned their astonished gaze at ffraw. His shoulders quivered.

The captain watched him quietly. "Take him to the deepest part of the wall and chain him there," he said in a low voice. "Let no one speak to him. If he so much as whispers, you may kill him."

105

Eoghan raged and shouted but did not look back when they pushed him through the door.

As though he had forgotten him, ffraw turned once more to poke the fire. Pulling a strip of meat from a rack on the wall, he added it to the kettle. "Ceorl, you know a soldier's life," he said, giving him a wink. "No maid or wife or even an ugly widow to do a man's cooking." A smile compressed his lips, but his face grew no softer. He found his place on the stool again. I did not know what to think of him. Ceorl, I saw, was uncomfortable. ffraw looked sidelong at Tabak. A secret lay behind his eyes.

"Will he live?" he said to me.

"He is not dead."

"Not a few of mine are," he observed. "And by his hand." Slowly his expression took on a certain thoughtfulness. "You have done, I suspect, all you can for him."

"What could be done," I said.

In a moment he was up again. "Come," he said, "sit at my table." Then he pounded the floor with his stick. A new man appeared at the door. He was squat and gray; a dullness sat in his staring eyes. He had not the look of a soldier.

"Beer?" he asked.

ffraw smiled, rubbing his hairy hands. "A man must drink," he said. "And my guests, I judge, have come a long way without much comfort."

The man hunched his shoulders when ffraw spoke to him. ffraw said no more, and the man went out again. In the next few minutes he went back and forth, bringing knives for the meat and refilling our cups. Lastly he brought a platter piled with soldiers' bread. When he was not needed, the servant stood before the fire. Ceorl kept his eyes on him. We were both uneasy but made the best of it. For some time now I had felt my ignorance. I had not eaten at a table since I left Morrigan. In truth, I little knew what was expected at a man's table. For I was accustomed to my sisters whispering to each other and my aunts holding counsel while the servingwomen hovered. I spilled my beer. I had been thinking of Eoghan.

"Ah," ffraw sighed and put down his heavy cup. His wide bare forehead glistened. He pushed the meat away, having had his fill. "And are there still barons in the North?" he asked. "We hear so little news from there."

"Such barons," I said, "as the High King left. We have kept the holdings much the same."

ffraw bared his great blunt teeth. "But we are Thigg's now," he declared. His eyebrows quivered. "You don't deny it?" I caught the sober glitter of Ceorl's eyes.

"He is Steward," I acknowledged. Somewhere within the walls I heard muted oaths and men laughing. The soldiers' quarters are to the left, I thought, and set that fact in my memory.

ffraw stirred. "To be candid," he said, "we never did know much about the North. Yours were never friendly folk and held aloof since I remember. It has been a dozen years, I think, since we took a harvest from the hill farms. The *filidh*, I hear, no longer go there." He looked up. "Yet now and then," he said, "a word comes down to us." I noticed that his lips were parted slyly. "It is said, for instance, that now the men are weak and women rule there." The sneer was not hidden from his voice.

"I am born of such a one," I said.

"Cu, fill his cup," ffraw ordered blandly. The servant came from the hearth. "A witch woman, is she?" ffraw added as though it pricked him just to think of it.

"Of the Kell," I answered.

"Well, I don't suppose a man would lie about a thing like that," he said. "Though it does seem, lad, a queer sort of lineage." His deliberate black-haired fingers took up his stick again. "Still, of all that's said of them, I never heard the Kell suckled giants."

I made no answer.

Ceorl coughed, wanting my notice.

"Damn queer, I think," said ffraw, the muscles knitting in his jaw.

There was a heaviness in the air, a thickness that the fire could not dispel. ffraw scowled, and I caught in his twisting gestures a piece of the mystery that held his thoughts.

"Like any man," I said, "I have a father."

All at once the room seemed very small. I stood, feeling the floorboards sway beneath my feet and the nearness of the ceiling to my head.

ffraw held himself erect. Without joy, he smiled.

"I know you, Finn, Lord Ar Elonson," said the captain of Stephen's Well, spreading his black hands on the table. Having spoken, he blew out a great quantity of breath, like a sprinter who has run a race. Then, his duplicity done, he found his voice again. "Since the last winter storm closed in on your mountain, from that time to this, I knew your coming. All these months in the northwest I sent out my patrols. I did not tell them what they sought. I knew that they would find you. A man eight elhws high cannot pass unseen along the roads. Yet I have thought and taken care. Eoghan, my own right arm, I have cast in irons for you. He is no fool. If he were, I would not have made him what he was. Shortly he would have guessed just what you are. Even half a word is sufficient to a thoughtful man."

All the while he spoke his eyes were fixed on me. His eyelids were blue and weary. "My lord," he said with dignity, "I have tried my best to think what must be done. I knew that you would come, that, before others, I would receive you in this land. Yet I had no guidance. I could not tell whether you would make your way openly or if you were better served in secret. If anything, I have erred on the side of caution, assuming you meant to keep this to yourself and to me who was given warning. Yet you alone can tell me if I failed."

I shook my head, for I had yet no words for him. His speech surprised me. I thought of it in silence. Much as well remained unsaid. I knew that too. Beyond the window the night had deepened. There was stillness at last within the walls. The guards, if they yet kept their stations outside the door, could not be heard.

"How came the warning?" I said at last.

ffraw beckoned to his servant. "It is time, I think," he said. The man went out.

When he had settled himself once more, ffraw spoke. "It was after that last storm, as I have said. I was walking in the practice yard. The day was bright and as I had been long within these walls, looking up, the sun near blinded me. It was, I believe, because I was almost blinded, and so not looking at the world, that first I saw it, a vague hard thing, iron-black and falling from the sky. I knew later that I was meant to see it. Yet perhaps I saw it before its time. High it was and treacherous, I thought. It bolted from the north. I did not take it for a servant. I was about to tell my bowman to shoot it down, when it called my name."

Cu came through the door. He had his arm outstretched, wrapped all in leather. His face was apprehensive. Before him, its huge claws crooked about his wrist, he bore the crow.

The cruel mouth snapped open. "Hail, Finn, lord to

be of the lands between the seas," she croaked, her voice a grating whisper.

She tilted her dark head at me. Her eyes shone redgold in the firelight, distant, beyond all pain, like Grieve's when last I saw her.

"Ninmir!" I exclaimed in wonder.

"So you have named me," hissed the crow. "And so I am."

In that way I began my life at Stephen's Well. For if I were of any mind to hurry on to Ormkill, Tabak's wounds had put an end to it. Morning and evening I climbed the winding stair into the tower in the eastern wall. There they had carried him so that high above the holding, out of its shadow, he might lie day long in the sun for healing. From one day to the next he slept. As he had watched once at my bedside, now I kept the watch at his. Who was the servant now? I wondered. But it was just. Yet, in honesty, I desired as much to stand in that high place. For there above the backs of men I could look out far along the river and the plains.

There, though I told myself my thoughts were all on Ormkill, I often watched the north. I half expected to be followed. Yet I saw nothing but the distant hills and beyond them, gray and hooded, the mountain along whose hard ridges and furrowed glens I had come down. Nightfall often found me there, watching the clouds float southward across the peaks. By midnight the wind would tear them away. Then I would see the belt of stars which men called Undain after the river. A thing of dusty light, it girdled the sky from west to east, as though it alone kept the heavens from falling asunder. I would stare tensely into the velvet dark. Sometimes, despite my cares, I slept. Once in a dream the Menhir, his craggy shoulders thrust into my thoughts like a great gray hill, spoke to me. But on waking I had not the words.

In the mornings white mists shimmered on the water meads. The sun would rise watery from the eastern sea. The green of earth returned. It was spring then. Men called out to one another along the river, their clear strong voices ringing in the morning air. The boats knocked at their moorings. I would look out. Above the fields, descending slowly in wide circles, Ninmir hunted. She would come if I called. Yet I knew I had not tamed her. My eye ached dully. I thought of the tangled lives of both our kindred, the crow's and mine, twisted one about the other like the maze of ivy spiraling about Gwen Gildrun, fastened on each other like the figures on the gate.

Ceorl and those of Bede had taken up their craft again. When I wanted him, I would find Ceorl in the forge, his face flushed with the heat, his chest and arms mired with soot. Hammers rang on anvils. Two men kept the furnace, one to feed the wood, the other at the goatskin bellows. It was hot, brutal work. Yet Ceorl would stay at it both early and late.

"How is Tabak?" he would ask me, shouting above the hammering.

"He grows stronger," I shouted back at him. "Soon we shall be on our way." Yet I felt keenly how the days came and went, how each new morning found us as we were.

In the afternoons I walked into the yard. I had grown accustomed to the slow stares the soldiers gave me. Word of the spellfire had passed quickly among them. A lame horse was brought to me to cure and a ewe from one of the farms with some complaint. I built a mound of green wood and darkened the yard with great quantities of smoke. Not knowing anything beyond that, I mumbled a Kell song I had heard as a child. To my surprise the chestnut mare recovered in a day or two. I never heard what happened to the ewe. But after that I could have filled my days with doctoring. Knowing I woudn't be twice lucky, I put a stop to it. Nonetheless, it was widely held I was a mage of exceeding power.

Word of my claim, however, seemed to have stopped with ffraw. As things stood, that suited me. For himself ffraw acknowledged the claim but hadn't, I thought, quite made up his mind what he should do. Though I watched, I saw no messenger dispatched to Thigg at Ormkill. Of course, patrols went out each day and the ships pulled away from their moorings to float downstream. It would have been no great matter to have the word sent secretly. Yet it did not seem he did. It was Ninmir, I thought, that restrained him. Like a rope around his neck, she tugged at him. His old thoughts failed. When I went to his table, when the meat was eaten, he would bid me bring her forth. Deep was his silence when he gazed at her.

It was late. The cups were drained. ffraw twisted his

fingers in his beard. "Is there another," he asked, "the like of her?"

"He I called Ninguh," I answered. "Both in the old tongue. I took them from the tree. It was at the time I came to manhood."

He was silent, his eyes vague as though he looked into himself. "Who taught them speech?" he said.

"One of my mother's women, her sister, who lived apart on our mountain."

"It marks you, lad," he said. "Though I am but a soldier and have not walked the way of the mysteries, I have not heard that the children of the air spoke to men since the days of the beginning. Though men forever speak of such things, in my life I have never seen a sign. Yet this is one."

He laid his hand on mine and leaned forward, as if to tell a secret. "You know the land is troubled. Thigg sits heavy upon the barons and they grumble. Yet if a new king comes he must master each of them. When you ride to Ormkill, you must send Ninmir before you, as she came to me. She must perch on the High King's chair where Thigg now sits. And when the barons are with him, she must make your claim. In that they will know you are your father's son."

I nodded, thinking, she is my inheritance. It took me by surprise, for since I was a boy I had thought my father left me no gift but life. Then I told ffraw how I had climbed to the nest, the marvel of Gwen Gildrun, and how, bartered by my father, I had lost my eye. It was a fair tale, he decided. Though he was sorry there was no murder in it and advised me, should the *filidh* make a song of it, to invent three trollish warriors. Then he took pains to tell me the strokes that I must say I gave them and how, though ill matched and a boy, I took their severed heads and set them on the tree.

"I have lived longer and will tell you this," he said. "A king must have blood on him if he would make his own men brave. For what man would follow a milky ewe among its enemies? Your father was not squeamish. At the four corners of Ormkill, beneath the posts, he placed the hearts of the barons who betrayed him."

I was slow to speak, for I had not heard this. "You saw it?" I asked when I had mastered my feeling.

"I was a lad myself then," he answered. "When Ar Elon first came up from Hren, where it is said he walked fullgrown out of the sea. Rumor spread from Tywy and Cassiterides and on again to Haman that a giant, as of old, had come once more among men. The people rose to meet him. He gathered them as he rode inland. It was the barons who named him last, when they had no choice, when already he had an army at his back. Even then, some diehards would not swear to him. Those he slew with the people watching. I stood among the many, cheering when he did it. I had left my father's farm to follow him. I was then not yet seventeen."

He drew a breath. I looked at him. His hair was gray to the root. He had a barrel chest and the thick arms of a warrior, but the strength was old.

"And would you be young again?" I asked him.

He was not a stupid man. He knew what I meant.

"Since Ar Elon fell I have held this place in Thigg's service," he answered softly. "Yet I remember that day at Ormkill, the people cheering, your father standing over us. A great figure of a man he was, his black hair shining." He drew his brows together and laid his fingers flat on his closed eyes. "I will swear to you," he said after a little while. "But what good are my four hundred against all that Thigg can muster?"

He knew I could not answer him. Yet I laughed and made some boast. Lord, Dagda, it was long ago.

In the evening I sat by Tabak's bedside. The sky above the tower and to the north was dark with storm. Curtains of wind-blown rain pummeled the roof stones. The gale sang through the holding. Tabak drew the blanket high upon his chest and coughed.

"Your mind is set on it?" he asked.

I nodded, looking into the storm then southeast along the river. Nothing moved on it. The smaller boats had been dragged onto the bank. "When you are able," I told him. "When the storm is done with us and the river calm."

Tabak drew himself up, slowly like a man from some great labor. His eyes were bright but his face was pale. He coughed again.

"The light is poor," he said. "Let me see your face."

I turned to him, straightening, trying to look a king.

"I will send Ninmir before me," I said, "to perch on the Steward's chair. She will proclaim my coming before the council of the barons. So ffraw advised and it seems good to me."

Tabak threw back his head, sharply, though it pained him. "So Thigg shall hear of it and will have his horsemen lie in wait for you." He laughed. I had not known him so cold.

"ffraw has sworn to me," I protested. "I shall ride at the head of his company."

He answered bitterly. Almost I did not know him. "It takes but one man to kill a king," he said. "Thigg with his armies should safely manage a boy."

His hard words cut me. "I *was* a boy in a house of women," I shouted at him. "For all I knew my father was a maker of fish weirs. You put it in my head that he was king. What would you have me do? Am I not his heir?" I glared at him.

He made an awkward gesture in the air with his thick hands. Perhaps he tried to grab hold of something that was not there. The pain ate at him. He murmured. But the storm was in my ears and anger filled me.

"It was your word to me," I cried. "His blood, you said, came down to me."

He moved his hand again and I saw then that he was trying to lift himself.

"To you and to the child I took away," he whispered, his voice haggard, his lips on fire. His hand raked out in front of him. I might have taken hold of it. But a chill ran through me and I cried out.

Even in his pain he watched me. From somewhere behind his eyes where the fever had not reached, a silence waited.

"Where?" I pleaded.

Once more the coughing racked him. There was fresh blood upon the mat. He fell back against the bed, his staring, wild eyes rolling. It was only then I touched him. But he did not know me. That night I stayed close at his bedside till the fit was free of him and he slept.

11.

THE SEED IS IN THE FLOWER. THE RIDDLE'S AN-
swer dances about the words that spoke it. Things fall
back upon themselves. The prophecy no man could
fathom is always plain when the tale is done. So a man
carries his death with him all his life, unaware. Had I but
listened to the *filidh,* I would have known it. It is the one
true song of kings. But I had other things to think of.

All night by his bed I pondered it. When he groaned I
turned to him. But when the tendons in his neck would
loosen and his forehead cleared, my eye wandered east
beyond the tower to the place where rain and river met in
one gray line. The Undain, swollen with the storm, swept
on before me, toiling toward Ormkill and the sea.

Unlike Urien I did not need to seek the name. I had it
before it was given me. "Géar," I said to the darkness,
tasting it. "Indeed we two are mountain born." I thought
bitterly of Yllvere, knowing all the while it was not simply
a woman's capriciousness but Kell work to the heart. For
among the shore folk each well and hill has its own name
and the name and its history are one. So it is among their
children.

The smell of rain and the wet smell of the stone came
to my nostrils. In one tower I thought of another. I remembered Morrigan, its sheer walls cut from the mountain fastness, the blueness of its stone, old beyond
imagining. It is the place I know, even to this day, best
among the places of the earth. There I came to manhood.
Storm-filled, its sky crawled in my dreams; its stony pastures were in the shape of my heels. Yet Géar knew it not,
except in the red hour of birth and that is beyond recall.
What place, I wondered, was in Géar's memory? What
house haunts Géar's dreams? I knew such places, wheresoever they had been, would count for nothing. The name
was given. We two were wedded to the mountain, even as
the nestlings, though early I had stolen them, were Gwen
Gildrun's still.

All night I crouched below the storm, in the wind that racked the tower, muttering the name. The sound was wonder and it was terror. I felt it wash into me like blood. In the shaping darkness I touched it. In the hiss of the rain upon the roof tiles, it beat against my ears. Géar, my father's child and Yllvere's, Géar. It was a god's name but it was a goddess's as well. I do not know which name was older. It was not, I knew, the name of a king. What then need I fear of my father's child?

But Tabak slept and the answer with him. The rain drew away to the south. The morning reddened. I did not wake him. When he stirs, I will have everything from him, I thought. But for the moment I went down the winding stairs and came out by the outer wall and the broad steps that led down to the harbor. The pacing sentries were used to me and let me pass.

I went into the morning. The early light was brilliant as it is after rain. Now I began to hear the din of the docks ahead of me—the sailors' voices, the grunt of men lifting thick barrels, the inland gulls, the rushing river. I walked forward among the ranks of rivermen. In the evening, ahead of the storm, a great ship had sailed into the harbor. It was an odd sight among the lesser craft and I went to have a closer look at it.

It lay at the far end of the wharf, rolling at anchor, the mud-gorged river slapping at its massive sides. Bright oak it was and fitted with iron. Its high bow arched above the deck, even then looking seaward. Its golden wood was cut in the likeness of a salamander, its eyes painted. Someone had hoisted a shield into the rigging. It was meant, I judged, as a sign of peace. I saw the reason. For they were strangers on the river, sea folk by their dress, their yellow hair loose below seal caps, and here by ffraw's leave.

The sound of the sea folk's voices grew less when I came among them. Those who had put their weapons down looked to see they were in reach. So I have always made uneasy those who do not know me. It may be their silence passed to those below the deck. Soon a man came up from below the planking. Seeing him, the sailors touched their brows in deference. He had a great corn-yellow beard and eyes as blue and piercing as the sky on that spring morning. Something stirred in me but I could not place it. By his carriage I took him for the shipmaster. Why are sea folk so far inland? I wondered. Curious, I stepped forward.

"It is a stout ship you have, master," I called to him.

"Aye, man, it is that," he answered.

"Nor have I seen the like of it," I added, "for it shines like a cup of gold."

There was pride in the shipmaster's face. "I saw to the cutting of the boards myself," he said. "The trees were of my own choosing. On rocky Hren I took them, from the high grove that watches on the sea."

He saw how my breath stopped. "It is a holy isle," I said.

He nodded and laughed. "So I was told by the folk who live along the shore that faces it. We camped the summer there when a storm had left us ruined upon the place, my own ship broken on the rocks. When they saw what I meant, the women came out on the beach to shriek and tear their hair. But when I went over the narrow water and took the trees, their men, though armed against us, would not cross. So I took the trees in peace."

As I listened, something prompted me. "I would stand upon those planks," I said. It was my own doing. In after-years in the hall I wrested from Thigg, my own wine loosening their tongues, I have heard the *filidh* tell it, their honey words seeking to flatter me. It was a great ax, they said, that the shipmaster had which tempted me, that seeing it I desired it for myself and so went up to take it. In my own hall I never foreswore it. This was a thing men could understand. But, in truth, I wished to walk upon godwood.

"I will come up," I said.

The seamen heard me. They saw my size and, thinking I would swamp them, they murmured, their small eyes darting back and forth like flies. But the shipmaster, as though he had a purpose of his own, did not forbid it.

"Only step lightly, man," he said.

Gladly, I went up and stood upon the deck, in the center, keeping my balance. The planking held. The men who watched me looked relieved. Though I doubted there was much chance of my bursting through, still, men will gawk and I think I must handle all I touch like eggshells.

"Now indeed," cried the shipmaster, "I have a ship of wonders." But for an instant he would not look at me, his blue eyes vacant, as though he took counsel with himself. Then it passed. He laughed again, though grimly, and gave his hand.

"I am Pendyved, Gwynedd's son," he said.

It was an ancient name but fairly given. It may be he is named after those of old, I thought. So I sought among the names I owned for one to give him in return. Yet a silence held me. Perhaps the god made me cautious. But the day was bright and I threw off the warning, giving him my own. "I am Finn," I said and the seamen heard me. Yet in my own ears it sounded clipped, a broken thing, but half a name.

When the names were given, the seamen crept closer to see me, and Pendyved called for wine. His boy brought it in an earthen jar. It was red as currants when he poured it out. As he looked at it, Pendyved shivered and bit his lip. "So the sap ran when I cut the trees," he said. "Red as berries, redder still like blood. The men complained loudly when they saw it, but I held them to the task." With his own hands he passed me the cup.

I held the cup, small in my fingers, before my face. "What wine is this?" I asked. "I do not know the look of it."

"Rare as druid's breath it is," said Penlyved surely. "I found it in a cave on that same island, wrapped in a mantle and behind a wall. Who is to say how old it is? It has the bloom of some ancient summer in it, though. Drink and you will see."

Truly I thirsted, for I had spent the long night at Tabak's bedside without relief. Its fragrance sprang rich to my nostrils. Full of the scent of the vine it was, of the broad ripened earth at harvest, old but without sourness. Blessed it seemed like a remembered summer.

I took it greedily, pressing the cup against my lips.

"It pleases me," I said.

Pendyved stared. He had not touched his cup. "Drink deep," he urged. But all at once the cup was far too heavy for my arm. An anvil weighed upon my eyelid. I fought it. My heart leapt in me but my veins were thick as stone. Then I saw the sea folk were not men at all but only shadows. The sun shone through their flesh and I knew it was not human flesh but only rags on bones. Pendyved laughed, his parched lips twisting into snakes that fell and hissed on the deck. His yellow hair burned down to ash. The wind swept it smoldering from the naked skull. He had no eyes but dark holes out of which he laughed.

With what strength I had I tore my gaze from him. I felt the great ship shudder. Fleshless arms cast off the mooring ropes. Bony hands ran up the sails. Like webs they were, made of threads and holes, but the wind filled them. Voices that had no sound cried out. The dead crew cheered. Into the white-toothed current the ship turned. On the broad black of the Undain it glided, but not on the sunlit river, rather some dark memory of the river, flowing out from underneath or out of time, I knew not which. Despite my fear and the wine's burning, I made myself still. This is Death's ship, I thought, but Death shall not have me. I did not climb Gwen Gildrun or stare into the fire that burns its root or tear from Yllvere the name she hid that I might perish unsung, before my time. So I boasted to myself. But I felt myself shaking. Still I listened to my thoughts. What harm, I told myself, can the dead hold, being dead? Has not life eaten all their strength and gnawed what force they had, both blood and muscle, down to these pale bones? Else how are they dead? And then I knew it. It was the wine and not the dead that kept me, that drugged my limbs. I will sleep, I thought, and when I wake I shall be free of it.

Then seeing me composed, the eyeless dead nuzzled up to me and huddled near my warmth. Like hounds they were, pawing at my knees, whimpering without breath or sound. It is said that in my sleep I grinned at them, though who among the living saw it I know not.

The stones of Morrigan, spidered with lichen, swung back into my sight. The wave bore me up along the wall and then fell back. Above me the tall elms ringed the yard and the grass was the grass of summer, green as emerald. The cold wave lifted me almost to that high bank before, gently, it drew me back again. It did not seem odd that the sea came high before the walls. The foam danced about my head, stringing out my hair. I floated. In my nakedness the water lifted me, high to the brink of stones where watched the women of the house, their eyes unmoved. Grieve stood among the others, my sisters—Sanngion in white and Ryth in purple. Vydd stood back of them, bent upon her staff. Her head was lifted. Like the very stone of the house she was, gray-eyed as the sea. I lay strengthless before her gaze. The sea wave rose and fell.

A door opened from the oven room. Yllvere came out to walk beneath the trees. She moved in their green shadows, her women at her back—the cook in her apron, the other aunts in robes. She came to rest at the sea edge to watch my bare legs splayed and carried in the heaving tide. From the nameless place that, secret, she kept within her she watched me, her deep eyes distant and chill as stars. But I was used to her. The brine washed in my mouth.

"Tabak I have left at Stephen's Well," I told her.

Even as she smiled, her long white fingers tightened on her arms. "Is it only him you think of, Finn?" she asked.

The women raised their faces. There was a dark-haired girl among the rest. The canopy of leaves moved over her. Her face was smooth. It let no feeling out. Her black hair drifted behind her like a cloak. The west wind blew at it. She shivered, her deep eyes moving over the waters where, watching her, I rose and fell.

"Give me your name," I said.

Motionless, as he waited, Pendyved watched me with no eyes. The night itself was voiceless; the bank, hushed and hidden in the darkness, passed far to either side. The ship, finding wind where there was no wind, sailed on. My breath caught as I woke.

"The wine has passed?" he asked me.

If I do not dream, I thought. But even in my mind he heard me.

"You dream the dream," he said, "the living take for life."

I was silent, watching him. The river was black and solemn, but the ship, disdaining darkness, glittered red as gold.

"What is it the dead wish of me?" I asked.

"To hasten you." His voice was like a wind from underground. It smelled in the air, the breath of caves. His skullbone gleamed beneath the stars. "So Ninguh came first to you at Morrigan," he said, "and the Menhir after, the very stone, ancient and asleep, awakened to bid you hurry. And when still you lingered, these spare bones from my cold grave, brought back from dust to stand and call you forth again."

I heard him but thought, what if I am mad? I raised my arm and found the strength of it. I unfolded my fingers and closed them. The nails scratched at my palm. I thought, it is the body of a man I have.

"Such as men are, so you are also," he sighed.

But I seemed to myself only a burning shell. I blinked and rocked my head to clear it.

"You are a plague of dreams," I cried, the faces of the women still in my eye. "I know when I wake and when I sleep. I know the sea does not rise to Morrigan except in dreams."

"We ride the river," said Pendyved simply. In the shadows I saw the memory of his yellow hair against the sky. As though I had opened a door to a place that was but was no more, so I found him. The flesh where there was no flesh was lined; the lipless mouth was stern, for care had turned it. I made myself stare at him.

"What are truth and lies in this?" I asked.

"The ship is as I said," he answered quietly. "I hewed the wood on Hren, taking back a suit of flesh to do it. Yet even as I was, I stood in wonder of the wood. Dark and old it is, brooding on headlands which face the sea. The trees are tall and terrible to behold—trees that draw breath and listen. Before them the ages of men pass as an hour. It is no wonder the Kell cursed me; but they could not stop the work. Still they screamed their oaths and blistered me with spells. Till he that holds the place, the stony ground and even the trees themselves, took pity on the Kell and veiled the island, piling the darkness up to heaven so the sight was hid from them." Then he was quiet again. A mist rose from the river and mingled with his flesh.

I shook my head, thinking, what cause is there for such a ship? What purpose worth the price of felling godwood?

"To take you out of Stephen's Well where you had lingered," Pendyved answered, though I had not asked. "The ship was fashioned to tempt you upon its decks. So he who rules the island placed in my hands such wine as even the dead may not drink, so that having walked here you would stay."

Despairing, I looked into those vacant eyes beyond whose emptiness a greater darkness moved. His features twisted. I saw the pain it cost him to keep his man-shape and pitied him.

"What lord would wake the dead?" I wondered.

The skull that had been a man looked grim. "He has dared greater and done worse. He is not patient, yet he has learned to wait. The strength he has, though it has waned, surpasses the strength of any who still walk upon the land. That which he is able to do he does. You must know it. In you the king's blood drips as well."

I groaned. "Am I then his toy?" I asked in anger. "The mirror of his will? So, if he pushes, I must fall? Say plainly, man, who calls me. Is it his voice in the stone, in the crow's mouth, that seeks my going?"

The skull laughed upon its bony neck. "Each man is himself," he said, a thing, no more a man.

I raked the face that was no more.

"Yet I am called," I cried but found no words to make him answer.

"Speak!" I shouted. But the voice had ceased or else became one with the wind that blew down from another heaven than the one I knew.

The Undain turns east above Ormkill into the face of the sun. I watched its simple round orb rise out of the river. It was the sun I knew. I bathed in its clear light, shedding the darkness like an old skin. Before dawn I had awakened, in the gray hour, cramped and shivering. But now the early mists were gone, the dead with them. Their bones, like ice, had melted in the air. They only serve, I thought. My argument's not with Pendyved but his lord. But the memory left me in a sullen mood. I am called, I thought, but given no counsel. Yet even as I thought it, I knew it lacked for truth. Such words as could perhaps be given Tabak gave me, though often I had received them bitterly.

The ship bore me on, its sails of cloth firm against an earthly wind.

Villages grew out of the soil on the banks. Green walls of sticks now poked above the earth, fresh planting, the defenses of one man against another, the new hatred of the spring. The yellow smoke of cooking fires coiled up from the compounds. I cupped my chin in my hands and gazed at them. There were gardens and cattle here. Hogs snorted at the boles of trees. And there were men, doll-like, distant figures on the bank. They called out in words that could not reach me, pointing to see what seemed a bear, or might have been to them, in man's clothes, larger at least than living men. Alone upon the deck beneath the unmanned sails I watched them. The ship was shining. The air shook with the smell of gold.

So I passed the towns which later I would rule—Arbereth and Elderwyn, Gest and old red Hwawl, upon whose rocks once in the years that came, I dragged the body of the river mage, his hair a nest of moss and snakes, my ax sunk deep in the slime of his oily chest. How the people cheered me then, for the troll had harried them, overturning boats and ripping the hands and feet from the bodies of the men who fished there for as long as anyone of them remembered. Yet then I did not know the names and the towns might have been no more than piles of sticks and fenced-in places for men and beasts, mere scratches in the earth. Yet even then I was not unmindful of my purpose. The name of king was sweet to me, else I would have been more cautious or, alone on Death's ship, more in fear. It was not guile I had but great imagining. I saw my life bent toward kingship as a sapling is bent over in a gale. For surely it sought me first, seeking me out before I turned to look for it. Like the river it bore me—spilling me unthinking as a cataract over the mountain wall to wander across my father's lands toward Ormkill. Long had I dreamed of that great hall before I knew it was my father's court. So I looked with interest on these towns and tried to read the faces of the men who were too far away to see. It did not matter what was hidden or seen. Already they had shaped themselves within my mind. Here is a proper world, I thought. It was a song in my blood. This is the true place of kings. For this I came away from Morrigan. Still, doubts rose in me. Cries went up from the bank. I wondered.

Will they come to me, I thought, as once men came to Ar Elon? For I was yet unschooled in the ways of state. Nor had I the mastery of words to heat the souls of men or hammer them as Ceorl would hammer iron, finding each flaw and hardening the edge. Yet at the last I did not fear the lack. Things came to me. Had I not killed a man? Had not men sworn to me? And if they who had sworn were but a handful, was not the swearing alone the test of it? In this way I talked to myself, puffing myself up, eager for fame. It cannot be called the way of wisdom, yet, I know, it is the way of young men when pride burns fiercely and discretion seems but the infirmity of advancing years. So, it was with me then. And still I sailed.

The wooden towns gave way to towns of stone, the fenced-in yards to broad acres of cultivated land. Now and then there were heralds posted on the shore, holding their stations on walls that snaked along the water's edge. Stairs led up to terraces, roofs piled one upon another. I had not seen the like of it before. My eye was filled with it. People stood thick as bee swarms at the gates. I had not thought the wide earth held so many.

So it was that the baying of the hounds surprised me. The ship had drifted in toward the shore, along the great walls. The town was hidden back of them and only sounds came to me. The hounds yelped wildly. They have scented something, I thought. A horn sounded. I heard it echoing among the houses. What beast, I wondered, is hunted through streets and lanes? Yet I could see nothing, only the high stonework and the roofs above. I heard the clatter of horses racing down stone streets; men called out. I began to wish that I could see the hunt. So I pushed the anchor from the deck.

The howling rang out fiercely. I thought, the hounds are near their quarry. Their baying rose up to heaven, eager, joyous, imagining the kill. I listened. They had turned, I thought, toward the river.

All at once a dark head thrust itself above the wall. The eyes were dazed with fear, the mouth gasping. The shoulders followed, the hands madly seeking hold among the stones. I felt my heart leap. For I knew then what thing was hunted.

By an act more of will than strength the man pulled himself to the top of the wall. He could not have been a man of this place or he would have foreseen the futility of his climb: the hounds behind him but the river too far below, the jump too treacherous. I caught his eye as he saw this. He had his head thrown back. His thin chest heaved for breath. The eyes, empty at first of all but terror, fastened beseechingly on mine.

When first I had seen the shape of the man, I thought, it is a runaway servant or a thief more likely, some grasping beggar surprised with another man's gold. But this man, I saw, was richly dressed. He wore a fur collar, his waist wrapped with two heavy belts of silver. He stood, his eyes opening wide at the sight of my crewless ship, golden in the blue water.

"Hear me, lord," he cried. "If the High King's law is still held by any in this land, I claim it." —

"I hear you," I answered back.

What seemed wildness passed suddenly from his face, surprised, I thought, by courtesy. He lifted his hand, saluting me. He looked grave now and proud, despite his labored breathing. He was a man of middle height, no longer young, and, I saw, weaponless.

"Why do the men here hunt you?" I asked.

He smiled grimly. "They mean to take the one thing I would not gladly give them."

"Which is?"

"My life."

I said nothing. But I had begun to think. Surely this was more than a thief and more than a townsman too.

"For what cause?" I asked. Behind him, out of sight, I could hear men calling out for ladders and the hounds yapping.

"For a song, lord," he answered, having found his breath again. He looked about himself, carelessly, as though all at once the hunt had become a sport, some lesser matter. It did not seem fool's courage now but somehow cleverness. His eyes were gray; his hair blackened, sleek as a cat's.

"I will tell you, lord, since you have asked me," he said evenly. "Last evening I sat at Thigg's table. When the meat was eaten, Thigg asked me for a song. Since that is an art I know, I gave him one, such as had not been heard in that dim hall since Ar Elon ruled, a song of the world's beginning.

"I see no offense in that."

"Oh, but there was, lord," he answered.

I had grown uneasy with his web of words. "What was the song?" I asked.

"Of Tân," he said. "My lord must know it. He was the first man, Tân, whom the gods made out of fire and Rhiain, with him, the first maid, whom they had fashioned out of mist and ice. I sang of the agony of that first love and how Dagda at the last did pity them and gave them shapes of blood and flesh that they might lie down with one another."

I frowned at him. "What is the offense?" I asked again.

"None," he said, "for any that is a man. But Thigg is a withered tree. His women laugh behind his back. Believe me, lord, my song cut deep."

"It was a rude song then."

"Thigg is a rude man. It found him as he was." The small man straightened, some faint amusement in his eyes. "But rude or not," he said, "it breaches the king's law sorely to kill his bard."

I thought about this for a moment, recalling the great names that moved through the book of wars, for the king's *filidh* was not unmentioned there, a man so skilled in song that it was as a sword to him.

"Are you Fyris then?" I asked. "Ar Elon's man?"

We stood facing one another. I felt the ship pitch beneath me. The tide had turned and now was running toward the sea. "Answer, if it is so," I cried, "and if you seek my aid in this."

But before he spoke I saw a ladder top the wall and then another. A band of men came quickly upon the rampart, no more than a hundred elhws from where the small man stood. There was a chief among them. I knew him by the standard-bearer who went ahead of him and by his linden shield painted with an aurochs. He cried to his men to lift their spears and then, looking across to the man they sought, he shouted, "Hear me, whoreson, I come to give with point and blade the gift you earned at Thigg's table."

The *filidh* grinned at them. "May Thigg's generosity be rewarded in fair kind," he answered. He threw back his head then and laughed. There was music in it.

The chief cast the first spear. A swarm of spears flew after it. With a yell the men raced to the place where Fyris stood. Yet before the first spear fell, the *filidh*, sinking a moment to his knees, leapt from the high wall, hurling himself out into the river far below. It was a powerful leap, belying the man's slight stature and his age. It carried him beyond the rock just short of the ship's bow, where the water was deep almost to blackness. The soldiers knotted together on the wall. The bubbles broke in the air.

That same instant I jumped. The water lashed my face and shoulders, my belly heaving at the sudden cold. Yet I kept my wits and swam beneath the broad keel of the ship, looking for the place where his body had entered. He was my father's man. If there was nothing else between Thigg and me, now there was this.

The current was swift but I held myself to a rock. The river floor was patched with weed and strewn with cracked stone from the building of the walls. The mud should have been stirred up where he had fallen. But the water, though dark, was clear. I pulled myself deeper. The pressure hardened against my ears. I had taken a good breath before I dove, but I felt my chest grow tight. Dead or living, I thought, I will find him. But there was only rock and riverweed and, after a moment, a pain against my heart. I looked around me one last time and then shot up through the cold emptiness of the water, three body lengths before I broke the air.

Under the river I had turned myself about and so came up in open water facing the other shore. The shouts of men directed me to the bank. I swung my head around, pushing the straight hair from my eye. The men had pulled the ladders up, then dropped them on the river side of the wall. I saw them, man after man, descending. Some had already made the bank, their spears retrieved and lifted with their voices. Yet when I rose, head then shoulders, wading toward the bank, their howls came instead as murmurs, as though they had seen some wonder. Indeed I was not the man they looked for.

It was only then I saw the ship was gone. I swept the river with my eye, twice, astonished, before, I truly knew it gone. Not drifted. It was too huge a ship: its bright sides massive, golden in the sunlight, its paired masts tall as forest trees. It had not washed behind the great wharf wall that jutted into the Undain there, but vanished, without whirlpool or ripple, on the calm face of the river, put out like an extinguished star.

So the men of Ormkill found me, staring and open-mouthed as a babe, soaked to the skin, my black hair steaming, a river giant in the place of the man they lost.

As I walked ashore a golden acorn knocked against my thigh. I hid it, shining like a piece of fire, in the darkness beneath my shirt. Then it was that I stepped upon the land.

12.

"YOU ARE NOT FYRIS," SAID THE SOLDIER CHIEF. I saw his anger and his puzzlement. He was tall for a man, coming nearly to my shoulder. He stood poised on the balls of his feet, like a mountain cat about to spring and yet held back by uncertainty. His light brown matted hair stuck out beneath his helmet like a ledge. But his beard was a tangle of dark curls. A scar grew out of it, red and new, branching across his cheek from the jaw to one gray eye. Though the bright sun made him wince, he was no less fierce for it.

His soldiers walked around me, staring at my size. One or two half-held out their hands as though, if they had dared, they would have touched me to see if I were real. But when I shook myself to drive the water off, the soldiers drew away lest the water fall on them. I saw they feared it held some magic to change the shape of things. Only the scarred man stood his ground.

By then, hearing no death cry and grown curious, a crowd of townsfolk, mostly men and boys, had found a way to mount the wall and stood looking down from its height. I heard the buzz of their voices. Further back from windows under the eaves of the near houses, I saw old men and scattered here and there a few women, sleek and groomed, their bare arms hanging on the sills and looking out to see what happened to the hunt. With each moment new faces appeared above the wall. I should have been uneasy among so many, but I thought, these are my father's people. How then can I be stranger among them?

The scarred man blinked and cocked his head. "I chased a man," he said, his voice cautious but with an edge to it. "My hounds were at his heels until he climbed that wall. With my own eyes I watched him jump and saw the river swallow him, even as it spat you forth." He stopped to watch me. "Were you not so unlike him, you would be dead."

It seemed too proud a boast. I said, "I had not heard they hunted men with dogs in Ar Elon's kingdom, running after them as boys chase hares. I thought the best of men contended here, one with another, as men are made for, one strong arm against another."

The scarred man frowned. Anger warmed his cheeks. "This is Thigg's land, not the wizard king's who fled," he answered. "Thigg's law was broken. It will be Thigg's price that must be paid."

I looked down at him. All saw I was not armed. The sword I had I left at Stephen's Well. "There is but one law for all the land between the seas," I said. "The king's *filidh* is sacred. He may not be harmed." I spoke loudly. Even on the wall the people heard me.

The man's lips whitened. For a while all there were still. I gazed at them with my one eye. Perhaps I did not look wholly human then. The river mud was smeared about my knees. My chest was wreathed with riverweed.

"It is the god Duinn," someone cried out from the wall. At this the rest stared for none knew whether to believe or not. Yet others took it up and I heard it whispered back and forth.

If he had meant to lunge at me, the scarred man thought better of it then. I watched his eyes. Fear had crept in them, if not belief. I saw he had no mind to quarrel with me more, with the crowd uncertain. For indeed a strangeness hung on me. Like the mists of the water from which I came, I seemed to have risen out of emptiness, cold and veiled. A chill wind blew across their faces.

The scarred man shivered. Yet he could not let the matter go. "Where is Fyris then?" he said.

I could not answer him. As he fell, the *filidh* had not the look of a man who leaps to death. Still, the best guess was that he was drowned and pulled into the deep channel at the river's heart where it runs most quickly seaward. I saw it would serve me poorly to say as much. Better to let them wonder whether I was some underwater thing or god or Fyris himself transmuted into giant kind.

I said, "What answer can the hunted give the huntsman?" No more than that and, turning, made my way along the shore.

A great silence full of eyes was all about me. I went a good distance, the soldiers lagging afterward. Farther up the shore, beside the wharf wall, I found the stairs. The steps were crowded with the folk who had come down from the streets above. They were better dressed than the folk I knew. The men wore fur and silver, the women rings and necklaces of blue stones, carved gold and crystal. Beneath their astonishment their eyes were cool. They gave me room as I walked up but did not avert their eyes. Had I been less than I was, I have no doubt I would have amused them, dressed as they found me in a ragged longshirt, the water, if I stopped a moment, making a pool at my feet.

I had little time for such musing. I took a pace forward and then another. I had come to the top of the stair and walked into the streets of Ormkill, my father's city. It filled my sight, for I had been only in towns. From the river it had not looked so huge. Now I saw the books were true. The streets were not the crooked lanes that I was used to but broad avenues, paved with washed stone. Nor did the houses lean, rotting and uneven, over streets, crowded in like starved dogs about a bone. Rather they were set back, poised and stately, behind fine mortared walls and gardens, not meant for herbs and cabbages but planted with hedges and flowering trees. Some rose three stories upon the backs of the hills. Above them, on the highest ground, the proud hall of my father shone as though its stones were fire. Its polished ridgebeams seemed the fairest of metals, glittering in vivid sunlight, not the rough oak of which in truth they had been hewn. It took my breath. I longed to stand beneath its arching roof, in the longroom where my father once heard all who came to him, in whose chambers he judged and made the law. But not yet. I knew it. The strangeness that held these folk and gave me space to move as I willed would wear thin. There would be treachery. I was not ready. Tabak lay sick in Stephen's Well. Ceorl and those of Bede, ffraw and his four hundred, when they had found me gone, might guess where I had gone. But they would not ride so openly up these paved streets, unknowing if I walked freely here or rotted in Thigg's prison.

There was a stir behind me. The soldiers, their dogs whimpering and uncertain on their heels, trooped up the street, the scarred man at their head. I saw his eyes, dark and disquieted as those of his hounds. His brow furrowed like that of a man bested in a game whose rules he only half perceived.

"Hold, sir," he called out after me.

I stopped and waited for him by the gate where two streets met. The pillars of the gate were fashioned of forged iron and hung with heavy rings. A piebald mare and two gray geldings, their muzzles deep in bags of feed, were hitched there. Upon the lintel in broad letters of the Western script was spelled Y Gasgen, or The Cask, which I took for the name of the inn whose wide doors opened into the great guest house beyond the yard. "Well, what is it?" I asked when he came even with me.

The scarred man rubbed his chin. He leaned forward, his soldiers close behind, clutching their spears. "Tell me your name and the chief you serve," he said.

I let the silence drink up his words.

"Are you Thigg's herald?" I asked when I had waited long enough.

"I am a sergeant of his company," he said as though it were some great thing.

I shook my head.

"Tell Thigg to send his herald," I answered. "When I have eaten and rested I will speak to him."

Once more the silence fell. In the streets the men stood silently and stared. For a moment I did not know whether I had dared too much. A handful I might have killed, but not so many. Had I known the spells that blunt men's wills, I would have murmured them. Instead I made a hard smile play about my lips. Nothing else moved. But I could see in the eyes of the people how they measured me, how the quiet filled their ears.

The scarred man hesitated. He was a year or two older than I and bore himself bravely. Alone, or before his own men only, he would have held. But the hush of the people was too much for him. He himself had watched me walking from the river and heard the voice cry out I was a god. After a long moment, he turned on his heels and was gone. For myself, I turned into the yard, thinking it best to leave the people to themselves, lest some man among them find his voice again.

I met the landlord at the door. He eyed me warily. But if he had seen the commotion in the street, he gave no sign of it. He was a strong-built man with thick brown arms, accustomed I judged to keeping the peace among his guests. The whole of his face, apart from his ears, which were covered with coarse hair, was scarlet. When I told him what I wanted, he shook his red face sadly. He had, he said, no bed to fit me. All the while he kept his gray eyes fixed on my ragged shirt and my wet boots. I found a large coin and dropped it in his hand. The grudging shadow passed slowly from his face.

"Perhaps," he said, "perhaps." And led me down the hall, past the dim common room where three hooded men sat at their cups. It was a large, nearly circular room with a great hearth on either side. Doors ran in and out of it, the largest to the kitchens, the others, I later found, down narrow ill-lit corridors to the guest rooms on the first level. The doors were all of carved oak, dark with age. I heard one creak open. Two of his women peeked in at us. He sent them scurrying for fresh bedding, pillows and a water crock. We had not gone much farther when he knocked at another, calling for his boy. When he found him, a small spindly lad with a worried look, the landlord bid him drag a second bed into a certain room and gave instructions how it was he wished them lashed. The boy, who could not keep his eyes from me, had to be told twice.

"His name is Rapp," the landlord offered when the boy had gone. "He's not a bad sort like some his age. But overcurious, if you catch my meaning. Curiosity's no virtue for any that work in a public house. Still," he added with a wink, "should you need anything, just bang on the wall and he'll come around."

He led me, my head and shoulders stooped, along several passages and down a few steps toward the back of the inn. At last he stopped before a door and opened it. "This should do," he said. Indeed it was a good-sized room with a high ceiling, but the walls were piled with shelves. It had been, he said, a pantry once that he had made into a spare room for travelers who were none too fussy, some years back when trade was better. "There's not much need for it nowadays," he said, "but, as you see, it might have been made with you in mind."

I thanked him and waited for him to go.

The landlord's eyes looked at me thoughtfully. "You've no horse, have you, to be looked after?"

"No."

"Or," he asked, "a pack to be brought in from the street?"

"No."

The landlord scratched behind his ear. His lips moved, puzzling over some new question. But at that moment there was a faint knock at the door. The women, loaded with bedding, crept in. They were small and dry, their thin faces pinched with nervousness, their dark eyes darting back and forth. Annoyed, the landlord ordered everything dropped in a corner and told them to come back when the second bed had come. The women blushed and turned hastily away. "After sundown I bring the supper out," he said. "But beer is poured both early and late."

I stood before the room's one window. My shadow fell over him. He stepped backward, then pointed out into the hall. "Beyond the arch is a door to the stable yard. The well is there, should you wish to wash the river from your hair." He glanced up as he said it, his small eyes fastened hard upon my face.

"I will sleep," I told him and put my hand to the door.

Later the boy came dragging the second bed, the women slipping in behind him. The women worked quickly and were shortly gone. But the boy lagged. I saw clearly he was taking longer than was needed.

"What did you see?" I said at last.

His troubled eyes grew round; they burned in his head. Still there was no need to press him. The words spilled out of him. "I was in a tree by the wall," he said, the words like a rush of air. "Truly, sir, I did not mean to look. I was only getting ospreys' eggs. No one was with me. It was by chance only I was there, before I heard the hounds, before the soldiers came chasing the running man who climbed the wall. But they were only looking at the man." He paused, shy all at once and gazing at his feet. When he spoke again, his voice was low. "So it must be," he said, "in all the city I was the only one who saw it."

He faltered. His voice trailed off, afraid. I wondered at him. It must have seemed, I knew, that I loomed over him, more like a cliff than a man, a huge crag that might, at a word, drop down to crush him. Yet he had brought it on himself.

"Saw what, lad?" I said.

He turned up his small thin face. "The ship, sir, the one that you made vanish when you dived."

I thought a moment. "Who have you told?"

He shook his head. "No one. I swear it." He wiped his nose on the edge of his sleeve. For the first time in many days I smiled.

"You are called Rapp?" I asked.

He nodded.

"And who is it, Rapp, you think I am?"

For all his sniveling he was a smart lad and answered cautiously. "The old people whisper you are Duinn himself, up from your kingdom undersea."

I looked at him squarely. "And do you believe them?"

Despite himself, at the corners of his mouth, he grinned. "I think, sir," he answered, bold and yet not daring quite to lift his eyes, "that the Lord of the Dead would not stink so much of riverweed nor would he come without a servant to clean his boots."

I laughed outright, the first time since I had left Morrigan. Then kicking off my ungodlike boots, I gave them to him and sent him off. I heard him whistling down the hall.

That day I slept. If Rapp came back, he found me already in my bed. No herald came. There was the sound of horses led along the lane, the whisper of the landlord's women in the hall. In the inn yard, wood was being split for fires. But, for the most part, during the day the house was quiet. I slept again. It was not the house sounds that intruded into my dreams.

When I woke the moon was rising. I saw it outside the window, above the houses mounting the steep path of heaven. Like the mouth of a boiling pot it looked, filled with the smoke of clouds. The wind was up. From time to time between my dozings I heard the sparse hard patter of rain. Once for a half hour a rough squall buffeted the house. Outside, on the sloping streets I imagined streamlets building, converging from back lanes and open avenues, falling riverward. It is the Kell blood that makes me think of it, I thought. From the time of my crossing into manhood my sleep had been filled with dreams of water. Since I had come down from Gwen Gildrun the night tides, older than memory, had beaten against my sleep. It was the women's blood. I was sure of it. I thought of Yllvere and Vydd, who counted by remembered tides and counted wrong. They lived in dreams, in the madness of dreams, it seemed to me. In Morrigan, high beneath the mountain wood, the sea forever hidden from them, they waited and did nothing. In the dry cold of mountain rooms they sat, my mother in her chamber, Vydd in her smoky hut along the hillside, spinning idly or working useless charms, excuses of inaction, doing nothing as if waiting was all that mattered. And Grieve, I knew, was like them now. I thought of her, listening to her heart beat, hearing the small sounds of her breath, till she had eaten up the day and nightfall flooded all her sleep with ocean dreams. I lay awake, my eye open, facing the dark window.

I thought, I have come to Ormkill to be king, not dream of it, idle as a woman.

I pulled myself up. Groping, I found my boots where Rapp had left them. Perhaps, I thought, they are still serving in the hall. For all at once I realized that I was hungry. Indeed, it felt as though my belly were an empty sack. I lit the lamp. The light bit into the darkness.

I threw a handful of water on my face and rubbed my fingers into the greasy sockets of my eyes. My flesh felt oddly thin beneath my hands. I thought, I must try to look more lordly, and searched about for a mirror. I meant at last to comb the weed and matter from my hair. After some moments I found a sheet of polished brass tucked upon a shelf and brought it down. Absently, I set it before the lamp. But when I saw myself, my flesh froze.

My beard that I remembered as little more than a swath of down beneath my chin had grown thick and full. Black it was and wild as the great tangle of my hair that fell newly to my shoulders. The skin about my eyes was dark and drawn. It was a man's face, not a boy's. I saw the old roundness of my flesh devoured as a flame melts fat. I stared. I dug my fingers into my face as though it were a mask that I might rip away. The new hard features held. I turned the mirror in the light.

About me I felt the quiet of the night. All things age, I thought. There is not a man who does not at the last shrink down to dust and bones. Yet for what had come upon me there was no accounting. I sat with myself for a long time and listened to the night.

At last I drew a sighing breath. No longer looking at my face, I brushed the weed from my hair and stood erect. My hand found the door and opened it. In the hallway, stooping beneath the low ceiling, I paused and listened. Voices, dulled by the twisting passageway, drifted down from the guest hall. I heard the easy laughter of men at their drink.

The gathering that night was large and mixed. There were perhaps thirty altogether. The loudest sprawled on benches near the smoking fires, telling stories with waving arms or singing half-remembered bursts of songs, the carnage of a *filidh,* just dismembered limbs and fingers of the tales, with nothing whole. The men of cities drank, I saw, like other men, hanging onto one another for dear life or out of friendship or merely to keep their dazed heads off the floor. It put me in mind of what Morrigan must have been, though on a smaller scale, when Urien still had his strength and his company of men in other years before the death of the gray-eyed boy. I hung in the doorway, unnoticed, alone as a ghost that looks down from the wind on the lights of living men. A stranger here, I watched them. Servingwomen and a troop of boys moved with studied care among the revelers. They bore large platters and in their hands were pitchers to refill the cups. The log fire blazed and reddened almost every face. Yet in the shadows a few vague figures, tucked into the deeper corners of the hall, hunched over their tables. Their tankards unlifted, they sucked privately at their pipes. I sought no company. So I made my way among them and found an unused corner far from the fire.

I sat across from three men, the same I thought that I had seen before when the room was nearly empty. Yet I could not be certain. Their faces were well hidden within their hoods and their shoulders obscured in the vague folds of their heavy cloaks. Perhaps they were full of drink. One may have been taller than the rest. But in the bad light I could not make it out. They sat slumped in upon themselves, mute and unmoving. The coals of their pipes glowed faintly in the darkness. The fumes that now and then escaped between their teeth were the only sign that they breathed. I nodded out of courtesy. They let me be.

Still I was thankful when Rapp came and set a platter and a full tankard before me. Perhaps the three watched me as I ate. But while I satisfied myself I took no more note of them. I had put the tankard down for the last time before one spoke.

"You eat, friend, like a man who has just discovered food," one said quietly around his pipe. He turned a little and saw the gleam of his dark eyes. But the mouth was hidden.

I did not answer.

"Sir," he said accusingly, "I spoke to you."

"Hold your noise,' said another. "He will not speak to the likes of us. He is the one we saw come up from the river, scaring Thigg's poor soldiers. Best let him be. He is too grand despite his rags."

The first looked at me suspiciously. "He is the size of that one, sure enough," he said. "He has but one eye, too." I saw in the shadow the thin lips twist into a smile. All at once he straightened, pushing his leg boots out against the floor. As he did he seemed to grow. I saw his bearded head, unexpectedly huge, now only half-concealed within his hood. The cheeks were swarthy; a wolf's grin tore at the edges of his lips. Yet it was not until he threw off his hood that I knew him.

"Tabak," I gasped.

"Be still," he whispered and put his great hand before my mouth.

Slowly the others pulled back their hoods. So I knew them, Ceorl with his yellow braids and ffraw, his mad bright old eyes shining. But it was to Tabak I spoke first, in disbelief and then in joy.

"I left you in your bed at Stephen's Well," I cried. "Two days ago you seemed near death."

He shook his great head. "It is a year, my lord," he said. "ffraw will tell you. For all that time he kept us, even against the grumbling of his men."

ffraw gazed at me and then over his wide shoulder like a child who cannot help himself, frightened and yet knowing he is too old to be afraid. "It is so, my lord," he muttered thickly. "We have lived. For the world does not stand still. But long, my lord, we searched the shore for you. Far along the river's rock we went to see what the flood would wash there." He hesitated. "Even now, though here I see you, that sight still freezes me when I looked out and saw you step upon the planks of that great ship that rested in my harbor. With these tired eyes I saw it fade." His mouth turned, awkward and confused, only then remembering the point that Tabak wished him to make. "From that day unto this," he said with sudden sureness, "it is one year."

By his eyes I saw how deep this went. For I knew what he must see, what Tabak saw and Ceorl as well, they who were the first to swear to me, though then it was a boy they swore to. Green I was then, new as mountain wood, no man that ruled. I saw how they studied the changes in my face. But already my mind had turned from them.

Instead Pendyved's face rose smoking in my thoughts, the peeled lips cracking backward to the skull. I heard once more his ice-cold breath and felt his pain. One year. The thought came at me like a knife.

I thought, truly Duinn must pity the dead he keeps, for he makes their time pass quickly. Else how could it be borne? Then only did I see the thing the god had placed on me. The night had worn upon the Undain but not as the earth's night wanes. On the earth the long spring had lingered, turned summer and waited until at last it tightened into seed. One season passed onto the next. The red sun rose and fell. But where I rode the river, morning and evening, it seemed one day. If Pendyved's lord had meant to hurry me, it was by his own strange measure. So ever the Kell had counted, my aunt upon her staff, my mother dreaming at her fire. I groaned.

Yllvere's shape rose out of my memory. I saw her as she looked that night I had taken my name though I had come seeking my father's. "How shall I know his face?" I said. Behind her the root of Gwen Gildrun hissed upon the hearth. Her small voice was deep when she answered, but it was sharper than the tongue of the flame. "He will have changed," she said. The words caught in her throat. "Men do." I set my teeth. This night at Ormkill, had she looked into the shadow of my face, she would have found a stranger there, like him she lost, no man she knew.

III.

The Girl in the Oak

13.

TIME CREEPS AS SLOW BLOOD DRIPS FROM SORES or spurts like heart's blood from new wounds. Either way, life goes with it. It is the way of things. Yet, looking back, it seems time laid hold of me more roughly than it did other men. For like a wolf, it watched me and where I went it followed at my heels. Three times before I ruled I felt its horned tongue lapping at my veins. The first was that spring I crossed to manhood, stumbling stupid with dizziness down from Gwen Gildrun with the crows. Then it took a month. And when I looked on Yllvere's fire, it drank a winter dry. I remember the sheet of flame and how my mind sank into emptiness like a stone thrown in the sea. But the Undain was a gaping wound. A year fled out of me. I felt the dryness at my heart. To fight it, I took the hand of each of them and pressed it. But to ffraw I said, "Where are your soldiers?"

We had gone from the hall and down to the high room the landlord had given me. Though I had pinned my eye on him for the space of several breaths, old ffraw was silent.

"Lord, they left me and I left them," he said at last, his gruff voice dark with anger. "At first I led them as I always had. We went along the river, seeking the ship that took you. We marched as far as Hwawl for news of you. But summer came. The flies got in their mouths and they were sick of tramping through wet bogs and mire. Though they would not speak to me, I heard them grumble. You were a river troll, they said, no true man, and so worth no more chasing than the mist. Their eyes grew hard. When I pushed them, I saw their necks stiffen. Then word came down to me that Eoghan was released, freed by the guard I put on him. The men I had left went over to him. The message that he sent was for the rest to join him. My soldiers heard it. They were like children. With little thought, they went, forswearing me." He snorted. "The wise look forward. All they knew was the weather and the flies."

Tabak shook his head. "They knew Eoghan was a man much like themselves."

But ffraw said, bitterly, "Finn walked among them. Though we kept among ourselves the secret of his claim, they knew him as a man set apart. They begged his peace and called him mage."

"You expect too much," said Tabak quietly. "They are only men. And men forget what they no longer see."

They were silent.

"And what of those of Bede?" I asked.

"Lord," said Ceorl sadly, "with them it was the same." His blue eyes opened and looked in mine. I saw the grief there.

But I forced my voice to steadiness. "Those whom I needed most held true." I made myself smile on them. Then in earnest we traded tales. Late into the night we talked. So I learned how those of Bede, whose spokesman came to be the yellow beard, had argued openly with Ceorl. For they were traveling smiths and hated any place that kept them long though there was work enough at Stephen's Well among so many soldiers. In that company, Ceorl said, were his own kin, his sister's sons. Yet they broke with him. As he related it, he nodded sorrowfully and passed his fire-blackened hand over his tired eyes.

"They have gone their own way now," he said, "west of the river, down to the great sea towns."

So I heard him out and more besides from ffraw. But Tabak said little, only that the year had healed his wounds. Yet he pressed me about the ship. I said what I thought prudent. I told them of Pendyved and how I drank the ancient wine and slept. ffraw pulled at his beard, his dark eyes wide. Yet for my part there was less to tell, for it had not seemed a year. But always Tabak came back to the ship and what I knew of it. I told him what Pendyved said, where the wood was cut and how the Kell women screamed at him. Tabak listened. The moon shone down on him through the room's high window. Its faint glow lay cold on the furrows of his face. His eyes were sad. I saw some thought was stirring up behind them.

He said aloud, "Where is that ship now?" His voice was stern. I remembered then how we had fought when last I saw him, the thunder booming about the tower room. In the hollow of my shirt, against my flesh, the acorn burned. Its fire ran through me. I set my teeth. Though I felt no mirth, I laughed. "We grow like two old women, you and I, hoarding our secrets as though we thought them gold."

His hard look did not soften. His teeth shone like a wolf's. He said, "Gold is as rust compared to that ship's worth." But I did not answer him. I thought, this one thing I hold of my own.

A stillness hung in the air. "The night wears away," said Ceorl. He of all of us preserved some gentleness. I owe it to his craft. He would rather fashion arms than bear them. "Let us sleep," he said. "We are a year delayed. We can surely wait till morning to decide what must be done."

All saw the sense of that. Once more we embraced and spoke our gladness. Slowly, one after another, they slipped out to their rooms.

I awoke to find a small figure bending over me. I turned upon the bed, half out of a dream. Still her face and those remote dark eyes, resigned, without hope or fear, looked back at me. It seemed a damp leaf brushed my arm. It faded. I was in the room again. Rapp shook my arm. The gray bad light was back of him. I yawned.

"Surely," I said, "it is not already morning."

Rapp shook his head. "I am sorry, sir, to rouse you. But even at this hour a man comes seeking you." I sat up sharply. "Do you know him?" I asked.

"He is dressed like Thigg's soldiers but grander."

I thought, it is the herald. "Where is he?" I asked.

"If you will follow, I will bring you where he is."

It did not suit me. I said, "Do you know the rooms of the three who sat with me last evening?"

He nodded loyally.

"Wake them," I said. "But see that they come quickly and come armed."

I got up when he had gone. Standing before the window I ran my fingers through my tangled hair, thinking once more to straighten it. In the dark street I could just make out a tethered horse searching for weeds in the cracks of the paving stones. The herald has come alone, I thought, and knew that Thigg was careless of who I was. Doubtless word had reached him quickly of how I had come into his city. It could not have been hidden. It was likely he would have heard it before his sergeant brought the news himself. Yet all that day had passed and the night besides before he sent his man. I made myself look at it.

Tabak came first with Ceorl after him, then ffraw, old and panting, still buckling his sword.

"Thigg has sent his herald to me," I said.

ffraw squinted and blurted out before he could stop himself. "It comes too soon," he said. "When your father came to this place, the countryside had risen up with him. He met the barons with a host."

But even Tabak, who disapproved, knew better. He lifted his ax to me. "We argued this when you left Stephen's Well. Yet I swore to serve you, even in foolishness. But have you thought what you would say to him?"

"I must look at him," I said. "When I have seen Thigg, I will best decide what follows."

Day came over the edge of the world. The new sun rising through the clouds seemed like a ghost. The herald rode slowly through the streets before us. Tabak bade me take his mare, but I would not. So I walked among the horses. The streets were nearly empty. I saw then that Thigg had given some thought to when he would call me, setting a time before men stirred from their houses. Still, it was the time that I had waited for. If I were unprepared for it, I had no one else to blame.

Not far along the road we came upon a mage, a spindly man, old, his hair uncut, clothed in a worn brown robe. Little he seemed to profit by his craft. But that he was a mage was clear enough. His face bore the look that such men have, still, drawn in upon himself, secretive as stars. He carried a bundle of branches on his back. Though not much to speak of, perhaps a dozen branches bound with cord, it seemed a cruel weight for one so old.

"Old man," I said, "I am climbing the hill to Ormkill. If you go there as well, I will take your load for you."

He shook his head, running his palm over one of the branches. "It is the last of winter wood," he said. "I saved it, setting it apart from the rest, for the first fire of summer. With great care I hoarded in, a holy thing. But for the High King himself, none but old men may carry it." His breath wheezed as he spoke.

I knew the custom. It made me think. "Indeed, a year has gone," I said, "with Beltane almost on us."

The old man rubbed his chin. "Not almost. As any

child knows, this is its eve. The very hills will seem to burn this night, that the summer may come without fault." Though there was fierceness in his voice, he coughed. I pitied him.

"That precious wood of yours will not burn at all," I said, "unless you get it to the hill."

"You see that I have started early."

"You are too proud, old man," I said. "And much too old to carry your burden far." With that I took the branches from his back and put them on my own. Yet at once the bundle weighed on me, not as a few dry sticks, but thick and huge as a great tree itself. I staggered.

The old man opened his narrow eyes a little wider. I saw, wondering, a swift softening spasm cross his withered face. "Dagda reward you, Lord Ar Elon's son," he said. "By this I know you. For surely in the world of living men there is no other who could lift that wood or bear it." He wiped his face and sighed. "Truly, lord, I am glad to be free of it myself."

The herald who rode ahead of us, not looking back, had yet to notice we had stopped. But my companions looked from one to another. At last their eyes had settled on the mage, amazed. The old man felt their gaze but passed it off. He stood very still, his head tilted. There was something unearthly about the hush that fell. He seemed to be listening to the quiet earth about him, to the folk still sleeping in their houses, to a far song of a bird, perhaps, from among the rest, to even the sun's hushed rising. He tightened the dirty rag that held his robe.

"You must bear these sticks to Thigg," he said, "and lay them at his feet in that great hall. It is a gift men will remember." He spoke in a half-whisper, grim and still, but on Tabak, just for a moment, he smiled.

I breathed again but my head was spinning. I meant, when I had caught my breath, to question him. But he turned and strode on up the hill, quick as a young man.

It was Tabak's eye I sought. "He knew you."

My leigeman nodded. "There are some yet, even in this place, who served your father."

I took a step and lurched under the burden of the wood. I spat. "He is no man at all," I grumbled. Sweat broke out on my brow. "There is no muscle and bone made that long would carry this."

Tabak eyed me. When he had thought some time, he answered. "Your father, when he left his land and people, forswearing rule of them, kept hold of his right. He yet rules and in his fashion keeps his court, though it has dwindled. Still, if no men will do his bidding, under earth and sea are things that will."

I glanced at him and then away. I might have pursued it. But it seemed, always, my thoughts halted at some edge. After that all were silent. The herald went on as before and we, at last, went after him.

How I made the hill I do not know. The wood tore at every muscle. The pains shot down my back and into my knees. But even then I was angered more because I could not understand all that Tabak said. I knew he tested me. It had been his way since the first words to me, hinting that I was more to be thought of than some mountain brat but always leaving more unanswered than I had started with. Always he had led me to some dark river in my thoughts. Again he had left me at its edge. But he would never show the way to cross it. I knew I would have to find the way myself. My thoughts were heavy and would not move.

When we made the hill, the city was already stirring. Children came out of doors and stood about, round-eyed, as I passed. Men of some importance pushed out of doorways. Gathered at the wells that ringed the outer perimeters of the royal yard, they drank the water and, rebuckling their arms, talked among themselves. By their bearing I took them for lords, the great barons of the land. Their sons attended them. The rest, passing the pitchers or bringing up swords for their masters to buckle, were servants, each dressed in the special livery of his house. These, when they had done their service, drew back, lest they seem to listen.

The servants saw us before their lords would look at us and yet their eyes were blank. It may have been, with my poor clothes and bundle of sticks, they thought me a man of their own station. If the barons looked up, it was to acknowledge the Steward's herald. But when at last they saw us, the barons stopped their talk and stared, not caring to hide their curiosity. A large man with a round face and rounder eyes spoke something to the rest. Though I did not hear the words, I saw them laugh. These were the men who would either fight or follow me when I came to rule. I meant to set their faces in my mind.

Their shrewd, impatient eyes stared back in turn, studying my size with interest as in a market men might judge the worth of an aurochs, but more thoughtful and abstracted. Doubtless they had had as boys, like any others, the run of stables and cattle barns. But now with me as much as cattle they left such day-to-day affairs to those of lesser rank. Their concerns, to look at them, had grown both wider and less exact. On their own lands, looking out they saw, I imagined, neither woods nor fields nor even the bent necks of their grazing herds but only the great curve of the earth. Perhaps they found it a more fitting sight. Their dress was heavy with silver and embroidered cloth. The ridges of their faces were hard, their small eyes without sympathy. Their word, in the land they held, was law.

The large man thrust himself out from the rest. With slow great strides he came up to me.

"Woodsman," he called out loudly, "do you not know the custom? It is old man's work to bear the last of winter wood to Thigg's fire."

Because of his height, his forehead was nearly level with my chest. He gave a short laugh. He was accustomed, I saw, to ordering men and thought nothing that I stood over him. His small round eyes were hard with mockery.

"Woodsman," he shouted, "are you deaf? I spoke to you."

I saw my chance.

"Lord," I answered humbly, bowing my head to his, "it is a fair thing to remind me of what is due. Indeed it is old man's work and, seeing you, it does me no honor I did not think of it. But as you have corrected me, I will not neglect what is right."

Without another word I drew a branch of the charmed wood from my back and with one motion placed it on his shoulders. At once, beneath its strange great weight, he fell.

The man groaned. His servant ran to him. But, struggle as he might, he could not pull the branch from him. Other servants followed. But though they pulled together, they could not lift it. From under his burden the man glared up at me.

I smiled at him. "You have nothing to complain of, lord," I said. "You reminded me that it was old man's work, and you, I swear it, were the first old man I saw."

Then still smiling, though it pained me, I bent down and, drawing off the branch, returned it to my back. I waited.

Before more came of it, the keeper of Thigg's door opened the thing he was charged with. The old wood whined on its hinges. The man peered out, squinting in the sunlight. In a glance he took in old ffraw, Tabak and Ceorl on their horses. If he saw me at all it was as one among the servants clustered about the man in rich dress lifting himself from the ground.

"Which is the man Thigg sent for?" he asked.

The herald pointed. "He with the wood," he said.

The keeper of the door screwed up his eyes. He seemed more goat than man. His fungus-colored cheeks were sunken and his beard a wisp of pale gray fur on his bony chin. He slid between a niggardly crack he had made between the door and its frame. He stared at me and scratched his head.

"That is the one, you say, that came out of the river and set foolish folk to whispering?" he asked, questioning the herald as though he were a child. "The one, you say, who wouldn't talk with soldiers but wanted Thigg's own herald sent to him?"

The herald shook his head. "I didn't say any of that," he said reproachfully. "But he is that same man or I would not have brought him."

"You are certain, then?"

"There are fools enough in the land between the seas," the herald growled. "Add not your piece to it."

"Be quiet," snapped the other. "It is with Thigg's own voice I speak in this."

The herald was still. The old man chuckled to have won. Then stroking his goat's whiskers, he motioned me nearer. With the load of wood still on my back, I came to him.

Arching his gray brows, he looked me up and down. "You say that you are mountain born?" he asked.

That sobered me. "I am that," I answered, uncertain, but thinking, it was no more than a guess.

"Of Urien's house?"

I stopped. I saw the quickness in his deep old eyes, his gray lips smiling, and knew it could not be blind luck that led him. "What need have you to question what, it seems, you know?" I asked.

He looked around. His sharp glances slid across the faces of the barons. "No need, I warrant, lad, as far as it matters to you and me. But not without interest to some men here."

I looked back at the barons, wondering what Urien's name might mean to them. Doubtless in the old days they had known him. But I could make nothing of the game the doorkeeper played with me.

"Their interest is none of my own," I said. "I have walked up a great hill this morning, early as it was that the herald came for me. Now that I am here, I will see Thigg."

"And so you shall," said the doorkeeper, nodding slyly. "This evening perhaps, or, if not then, tomorrow." And he closed the door abruptly and was gone.

There was a deep quiet. ffraw broke it.

"Lord, if you but ask, I will break down the door myself," he said hotly. "For I have never seen such lack of courtesy."

But I shook my head. I remembered what Fyris said was rumored and knew the use that I might make of it. "No," I said. "It is early and it must be that Thigg still lies abed with his women. Why else would a man act as he has done, a guest at his door? No," I said so that the others heard me. "It would be deeper discourtesy to interrupt a man at his pleasure."

I saw the barons grin. It was what I looked for.

"I will wait by his door," I said loudly. "Perhaps he will beget a son. I have heard he lacks one and it is said that morning on the Summer's Eve is the best time for making boys."

So I set down the wood—the barons laughing—and sat beside it on the ground.

14.

ALL MORNING MEN DRIFTED INTO THE YARD. Like wrecked lumber in a pond when the spillway's closed, they gathered, turning in slow eddies, barred, the hall doors shut even to those who thought they did the Steward's business. No little grumbling was heard among them—a pair of barons with matters of land rights to be settled, a merchant with a retinue of servants bearing sacks and scales, the sheriff with a dozen men-at-arms—proud men all, weighing the wrongs they thought were done them. And to each, word of my slander was passed. Each man, some behind their beards and others openly, grinned. But in time they wearied of it. The day wore on. All at once a stout red-faced man rose unsteadily from the chair his thralls had carried up for him. He had on a blue robe of rich new cloth. But he had been drinking to pass the time, and the robe was stained where he had spilled the cup. Around his neck he wore a greasy silver chain. His thick fingers were knotted with rings. With his left hand he knuckled loudly on the door. When no one answered, he lumbered across the yard to where I sat. The red of his face had deepened.

"Say if you are not the cause of this," he rasped. But his thralls came after him and, after some discussion, led him back. Yet I saw that when he had settled his flesh once more into his chair and had drawn another cup, he called to him the man that earlier I had shamed. Looking straight across at me, they talked.

ffraw winced.

"What are their names?" I asked.

"The drunkard is Hring," he said. "He is Lord of Reddmarch in the East. The other, Anhils, theid cousin some say to Thigg. At least he claims it. Together they hold great lands, though not the greatest here. Still, there is little to be gained in forcing such men to lie under one blanket." But I only nodded, knowing well enough what I had won and lost.

"They will fall of their own deeds," I said. But Tabak, who heard the boast, sat apart, keeping his eyes fixed on the ground.

"You are sullen, friend," I said to him.

"With reason, lord."

I shook my head. "I do not see it. Something guides me. Did you not hear how the people whisper of me? Something moves in this." Then I told them how I had met my father's *filidh,* or a being that took his shape, upon the river wall. "And then this morning that old man, if man he was, gave me such a gift of wood that giving it to Thigg would cause great wonder in the court." I was filled with a sense of the inevitable. "Nothing in this moves by chance," I said.

"It never did," said Tabak sadly and then he looked at me. "But there is more than one hand in the turning. From the first the only question was whose strength would prevail."

"I have put my own hand in at last," I said.

From under his old brows he stared. "Thigg knows you."

"That I am of Urien's house. That matters little."

"What matters," said Tabak, "is how he knew."

But then the great doors opened. The eyes of every man were turned to it and all were silenced. The keeper of the door appeared. "Thigg bids you come," he said. Then he leaned back against the door frame, scratching his chin bristles, watching the barons stir and rise, their servants, sobered, fumbling with their gear, gathering weapons and satchels, ready to move from one place to another. The butcher called his boy, who, because of some old fear between them, whimpered, his legs stiffening before the same fear drove him on. Then like one creature, the barons, loaded down with silver, wrapped in blue wool and prickly with knives, moved toward the door.

Inside, its shutters closed, the great room was dense with smoke. Worse, it smelled of sweat and old spilled beer, more the den of a wintering bear than some king's hall. A dozen pillars of thick trees held up the roof. But in the bad light I could not see if they were carved or painted. I saw only that the house was long and wide. Shadows filled it. Benches were scattered over the floor stone. The barons milled among them finding seats and, stopping the thralls that passed, demanding drink, already arguing whose rights took precedent. The sound of them beat against the walls. I was not the quiet of a court where one man ruled.

I looked for Thigg. But already there was a cluster of barons crowded before the platform at the far end of the house. Immense fires roared in the hearths at either side as though so near to summer the Steward still could find no warmth. I could not see him. I pushed my way in. The bundle of wood poked out from my shoulder. Because of it men stared angrily but cleared the way.

My three companions followed in my wake—Tabak with his cloak drawn back and dressed more bravely than a lord; ffraw in his soldier's garb and polished helm; and Ceorl, though a smith, clothed by his own craft in a wonderous shirt of rings, such as would have gladdened the heart of any who ruled the houses of the South. I only looked a begger in my ragged cloak, my beard and hair, defying all my efforts, still rank with the river. But it was the god, I thought, that shaped it thus. I was content to trust in that. And so I laughed.

All heard me. Thigg looked up; his barons startled, parting before his chair. He saw me then for the first time, standing in the middle of the hall like a thirteenth tree among the pillars that held the house, the wood on my shoulder. The sun was nearer setting then. The small light that entered through the louver in the roof reddened suddenly like a wound reopened. It fell crimson on my face and shoulders. Like a flame I burned before men's eyes. It is said that beside me all else seemed smoke and shadows, the barons shrunken and darkened, fumbling in their finery.

At last there was silence. Thigg did not move in his chair. Small and old he looked in it, a chair fashioned for my father, its feet carved with great claws, its massive back spread with aurochs hide. He seemed to sense how ill it suited him. For when the barons pulled back he raised his hand and held them close to him, comforted, it seemed, by their smallness, warmed by the vague warmth of creatures like himself. His gray eyes stared out at me. Yet though I felt that they would waver they did not. His hair was iron gray, pulled down into braids; his beard of the same color. On his forehead he wore a crown, new-made of beaten metal, too small to have fitted my father. We watched one another across the open space of floor. At length I spoke.

"I greet you, Thigg, Steward here, lord by grace of the High King till his heir comes. Morning and evening I have waited in the yard you keep, one day since your herald called for me. Yet I did not grow impatient. Pleasures, it is said, are few enough among men who bear the cares of the land. I would not cut yours short nor in them do I find a breach of courtesy."

Hearing me, all the court watched him with dark, wondering faces. Smiles pulled secretly at the lips of the barons who had waited with me in the yard. Remembering the jest, their eyes laughed. Thigg saw it, his eyes cold yet puzzled under the gray knit of his brows. The man nearest him leaned down and whispered in his ear. Thigg bent his head as he listened. When he lifted it again, his lips had whitened. The gray brows hardened. Still, it was not to me he spoke.

"By this deceit he only harms himself," he said. His voice was low, his anger well hidden at the back of it. Yet all heard him. It is said that in those years Thigg's rule was strained, that the barons grumbled and that he rode their backs as cautiously as if he rode on eggshells. If that were true yet, he had learned the trick of balance. It was not as I expected. I heard ffraw breathing at my back and knew he was uneasy.

"Well," Thigg said, fixing his stare on me at last, "what service have you come to offer?"

ffraw glanced at me and then away again. Ceorl muttered to himself. Only Tabak, now at my side, was still. They saw what now must come.

"Lord, it is the King's Wood I bear you," and saying it, I cast the great burden from my shoulders to the floor. It fell as a boulder might, with a crashing sound that shook the walls. So great a sound had not been heard within the house since first my father laid its corners. Even the men-at-arms fell back, gaping. Yet they were mindful of their swords. At the light's edge I marked the faces of the men who drew.

Still Thigg showed no alarm. He reached out with his thin hand, motioning the housethralls from their corners, bidding them come down and drag the wood up to the hearths. The servingmen crept forward. Several together, they tugged at the heavy limbs. All heard their groans. But when they could not move the wood, the thralls drew back with frightened eyes, none daring to look at his lord. It is now, I thought. Slowly, I turned from Thigg to face the hall.

"Hear me, men of this place," I cried, my voice light and high, soaring above the heads of men like a sword that is lifted on a hill, the harbinger of battle. "I am Finn, Lord Ar Elon's son." My bright words stung the air. I saw their brightness. Men stopped their breath. "This is the hall my father raised, the hall that I am heir to." I heard them murmur. Yet I felt how I stood over them. Their murmuring dissolved like sea waves on the shore. I felt it fade. In that quiet it was to Thigg I spoke, my voice grown full and booming. "Tabak ap Ewyn is my witness, my father's man. This wood my proof. Any who

would gainsay it, let him lift one branch to feed the fire."
So my words, grown huge, filled the room and the minds
of all men there. I waited.

Thigg did not move. Nothing altered in his face. At
last he spoke, his voice so small that almost I did not listen. "You have made you claim," he said, seemingly not
in anger but only weariness. "Have done it, as you must,
now go home to your mountain." His head was lifted
then, erect and cold. His eyes were iron right to their cen-
ters. "Take up goatherding or whatever Urien's folk have
come to now. But leave the rule of men to those more
fit for it."

I twisted. Tabak stirred beside me but I cried out,
"Have you not heard?"

"Heard!" Thigg shouted then. "You do not know how
many times. Not a summer comes but some green lad
stumbles down from a mountain or drags himself up
from the old sea towns, filled with his glory and sand-
fleas, too eager even to wash the salt from his hair. One
by one they come to stand before me, claiming kingship.
If all the tales were true, Ar Elon planted sons as readily
and in such numbers as any of my vassals sows his fields.
Every hillside grows an heir." He stopped. His thin lips
curled. "Go back to your mountain. It is enough to be
king of goats and stones."

I felt myself grow pale. He had made his moment
well. The barons muttered. Though I had stirred them,
now I saw a cold doubt touch them. Indeed for that one
moment I felt a stranger to myself. In truth, there was
one other born with me. Who knew where Ar Elon went
and what he did when he fled Ormkill? Though I had
not thought of it, it was not impossible that there were
other sons. My heart sank. My skin crawled cold upon
my flesh. I would have railed at him but I had no words.
Had I spoken, I knew I would have stammered. Sick-
ened, I sought out Tabak with my eye.

He that shared my height drew himself up, rising from
the hidden places in himself until he seemd nearly alone
in the hall and even I his lesser shadow. The features of
his face were stern.

"How lightly, my Lord Steward, you speak of getting
sons. Where are the round bellies of your women?" He
paused and looked around the hall, meeting the eyes of
all the barons, each in turn. "Where is the line of sons to
follow him? When breath goes out of him, who stands in

his place? Or does he mean to send his armies out to pluck heirs like apples from the wood?"

In the firelight his ax showed back the flame. For a time there were none who would answer him. It was a baron, the oldest there, who broke the quiet, one I had not seen, with thin bent knees. He kept two thralls close by his side to help him stand.

"It is little joy you bring to us, Tabak ap Ewyn," he said sadly. "Yes, I know you if these men do not. For most were boys then and the others here who should have welcomed you are either blind or fools, hatching their own designs. But what proof is there even if you name him? Thigg is just in this. We have had enough of bastards and their claims. And I will tell you, if it is too long you have been away, each claim, if any take to it, means war among us. Nor is there any certainty in marvels. You know yourself that there are women in my house who can throw a spell on wood."

For a breath's space there was silence. Then Tabak spoke again, his voice quiet. "There is one who knows," he said. I saw how his eyes caught Thigg's and pinned them. And it seemed to some that the Steward's flesh grew pale. In the glow before the fire Tabak laughed.

"Indeed, Thigg, you have grown overproud since we both served our lord," he said, "or else more careless than is fitting for a man who rules." Something passed between them that no man knew. Tabak's smile was grim. He took a step closer to the fire. "This long day you have heard her counsel, but having heard it you should have driven her out where none would see or question her." He turned then, gazing toward the hearth. He stretched forth his long arm to her.

"Lady," he called aloud, "what welcome is this for your son?"

Her figure bent above the flames, I had thought her but a crone, old in Thigg's service, slumped behind her cloak and scratching stupidly in the coals. Since I had entered, she had walked up and down before the hearth, her back to us. So I had watched her without seeing. But at Tabak's word she turned. I saw too plainly then.

The eyes that looked into mine were cold. No warmth they took from the fire she watched nor any joy, it seemed, in seeing me. Cold they were and kept their secrets. The chill in them froze my heart. After a long moment she looked away.

"He is the size of him I bore," she said.

Tabak frowned. "No more than this?"

"The hair's as black but he had not a man's whiskers." She seemed to think. "It is a year and more since last I saw him." The barons muttered. But again Tabak spoke, his deep voice thick with scorn. "And are there so many men, my lady, who have had an eye torn from their heads?"

She seemed not to have heard but came down to where Thigg sat, resting her light arm upon my father's chair. What brought her here I could not guess. Yet I knew well that, whatever for the moment bound her, she served herself, not Thigg. Her face was calm, white-masked like the moon's. She let her cloak fall to her feet; the gown beneath took light like alabaster. Boldly she threw back her head, shaking her hair from the coif that kept it. She was young yet and tall for a woman. Very like a queen she looked. The barons knew it. I saw it in their eyes.

"Long ago" she said, her soft voice pitched for all to hear, "I bore your king a son. Though Ar Elon was outlawed then, he was king enough and I only a woman. He knew whose wife I was and what we did. So with great oaths he bound me, that if ever a child should come of it the king's shame would not pass to him, nor his glory either. By all that is holy I took the oaths." She sighed, keeping her eyes down as though afraid. Then in a small voice that kept them still she said, "Now these oaths I break."

But then I could not bear it. My face, it is said, was wild. Fury twisted it. I lifted my arms. Men told me afterward they feared I would strangle her. The old pain boiled in my veins.

"Break now?" I cried. For bitterly I remembered how long those oaths had held, year upon year unbroken, when it was only a private thing between us. Her face before the fire held in my mind.

Yet even then I knew I spoke against myself. It was a king's secret, not a man's. I let the child's hurt die. "Speak, then," I said. "By Anu, lady, say as you never would my father's name and mine together in one breath."

I watched her, the mountain witch who bore me and ever after hid her heart. "He is changed," she said softly, quietly to all assembled, not to me. Her voice was so like

155

a maid's I only saw the complexities piled up behind it. She had gathered her gown in both her hands and knotted it between her fingers till the blood ran out of them. All who saw it pitied her. The men pressed close, their faces clouded. She allowed them to see how much she trembled. "I do not know," she said and shook her pretty head. "Men are like the sea that rings the earth, the same but every day they wear a different face."

Then Thigg spoke, his voice grown smooth. "Lady, that is no answer."

Between them I caught the half-curves of their smiles.

"There is a test," she said. She paused, waiting for understanding to come to them. Thigg nodded, his sly thin smile no longer hidden.

The old baron stood out from his brothers, free even of his servants. "It is his death if he is false," he said. "No kings while I have lived have done it, nor any in my father's time." Then he paused, the wrinkles of his face for one small moment smooth as though for that one moment he were young again. "But once," he said, "when men were not so far removed from gods, it was the one true mark of kingship to wrestle Life from Death upon the Mound."

Thigg smiled broadly, his gray eyes fixed on mine. "If indeed it is your right, you are free to claim it."

I flashed a look at Tabak, seeking an explanation for the trial they set, for I knew not what was wanted. Something stirred behind his eyes but I could not read it.

"What is the deed?" I asked aloud.

"Tinkern is the godshrine your father built," said Tabak slowly. "It shares its name with the island upon which he set it and with the oak grove, though both are older than the thing he made. At the grove's heart there is a great earth mound." He waited. I saw how he picked each word with care. "It is not your father's work," he said. "No man raised it and none but kings have stood upon its height. But few, having climbed there, walked down again. Most left their flesh for birds. There the god still lingers. Even the greatest warriors dared not go to bring the royal corpses back for burial."

"But what is found there?" I said, my voice too loud.

He looked at Yllvere. A servant, he had followed her fifteen winters, abandoned to the western mountains, far from his lord. In silence she returned his stare. Whatever their separate thoughts, they wove this one thread between them. She did not fear him now. Before the two of them I felt a child.

"Will you not tell me, then?" I said.

"What was broken will be mended," she answered calmly. Something hovered about her eyes and on her lips. "The old promise will be kept." She looked up. Her eyes under her white lashes were fixed on the servant she had lost, alone among the rest, a man the like of me but not myself.

"Lady," he said gently, "in this no oath is broken. What was taken now comes back. You know it or you would not send him to the isle."

She faced him, her forehead, set off against her hair, like a stone wrapped in wool. "Who is it that you serve?" she said.

"The son," he answered simply. "And you, my lady?"

Her face did not change. But she looked away.

No one spoke.

The old baron broke the quiet as he had before. "And will you claim it, lad?" he said.

"Claim what?" I cried. "No man will tell me."

"A fool's death," he answered gently, "or else the praise of all the folk between the seas, the king's lands whole again."

It burned in me, the quiet and the smiles, Tabak and my mother, the riddle of my life inevitably came round to. "What is the deed?" I said once more, despairing, expecting no answer.

He shook his old tired head. "Why, what we spoke of. Will you meet, like kings of old, the witch that waits upon the Mound?"

It was a child's answer I gave him, being unschooled in the craft that I was heir to. Only looking back did I come to know it was the only answer I might have given.

I thought of the Kell, the women of the mountain. They hung in my memory, thin and sour, pale as flowers drying in rafters—Vydd, a pipe between her mouse teeth, spelling words from crows; Yllvere, as much smoke as blood and bones, invoking ashes, whispering to flames; my sisters Ryth and Sanngion, their lips wrinkled and red with wine, whose laughter was like a curse to me. I thought of Grieve.

"I have," I said, "some familiarity with witches."

If he heard my bitterness, he did not remark on it.

"You will do it, then?" he asked.

I nodded.

Out of the darkness Tabak grinned and Yllvere with him. Thigg rose from my father's chair and laughed. Had that moment been cut loose from all that was before and what came after, they would have seemed, as in that instant they appeared to me, creatures of one mind, not what they were, travelers met at a crossroad and bound the next moment on their separate ways. But, looking, I saw only together how they smiled.

15.

So ONCE MORE SHE HAD LEFT HIM. THIS TIME, I thought, Urien will not have torn his hair nor climbed the battlements seeking her shape upon the roads. He was long past love of her. Yet, with what he hated gone, I wondered where he turned his mind. Perhaps, for a time, he would try to master his own house again. The village men would come to him. It was summer, after all, and time to set the service. With Yllvere gone, they would no longer smile behind their hands. Yet I doubted that the women would obey him. My sisters were accustomed to their own ways. The aunts had never done his will. Perhaps, his books and anger useless, he would come down to take his chair within the hall or walk his own broad lands again, barking to the thralls what should be set out and planted, which aurochs butchered and which let fatten for another year.

Grieve would not minister to him. The firelight leaping in her eyes, she would mind the burning beneath the house. He would need to scratch his own coals in the grate, pour his own thin wine, master of a house where no men lived. I feared that not even his own hounds would follow him.

Why had she come? It was not Thigg. She had no awe of men. Biting back false tears, she ruled the barons. Whether by a woman's or a witch's wiles, she had her way.

Tabak knew. I turned to ask him, but the doors of my father's hall flew open with a bang. The great host of men swarmed through it, bearing me along.

The night was cool and bright. We had no need of torches, for it was Beltane. The lower sky was red behind the houses, lit up with fires as though each hillside burned. Red shadows danced before the blazing logs, lithe and pale as Duinn's dead come back from their gray land. But these were not the ghosts of men but men themselves. Seeing the crowd that spilled from the hall, they followed, filling the alleys and the street. In their number I found myself cut off from Tabak and our company. I was pushed against a kitchen thrall.

"Lord," he said, "I saw you climb up from the river. For the peace of the land, this night I wish you well." He stammered something more but I did not hear it. I bent down, waiting, till he added, "My dad said once it was a sea king that would save us."

His voice was thin and reedy but it was edged with wonder. I doubted he had ever spoken unbidden to a lord. I did not tell him I was mountain-born and not the lord he looked for. For some moments the crowds pushed us along together.

"Have you seen the witch?" I asked.

He flushed. "No," he said, "I've naught to do with that."

"But others have?"

Feebly he shook his head. "Who is to say?" Horror rode his voice. I saw that he had only meant to wish me well, never thinking that a highborn man would answer back. But still I pressed him.

"Yet there are some," I said, "who've seen her."

"No, lord," he answered bitterly. "I cannot tell. It is said there always was a witch upon the Mound. But some say she is young and others that she is old, old even as the Mound itself. My dad, to tell the truth, never said either."

"But did he say what she did to the kings she met?"

His small eyes darted. "Aye, that he said," he whispered hoarsely. "Not that I would be forgetting it. Tore out their very hearts, he said. Tore them out with her own teeth." His nervous glance fell on me once more. But the crush of men pulled him away. I looked after him till he was lost.

By now, as word of my claim spread, the women of

159

the city came rushing out of doors. Daughters of the houses, both proud and surly, their gowns heavy with rings, pushed out ahead, their servingwomen puffing at their heels. Churls, slaves and freemen scrambled across the stones. Before me I saw the banner of the Steward furling. At my back I heard the tread of his soldiers. Men shouted. Horsemen clattered up behind. In the cool, damp night, still but for the crackling fires, it was as though the people of the city had become a storm. The earth itself held only quiet. The wood smoke floated up, placid, drifting, the only cloud there was. On such a night the stars seem sharp and close.

If I feared this thing, yet my heart was gladdened by the sight of so many. I saw the faces of the people as one sees faces in a dream: smiles, teeth, noses and eyebrows, the backs of heads and helmets. I could not tell who was cunning and who dim-witted. Leather armor squeaked beside me. Arms, swords and banners flashed in and out of view. The space between the houses swirled. Caught up in the noise and stirring, I could not tell whether I was at its center or its edge. But when we reached the lower streets, the crowd drew back and gave me room.

Thigg waited up ahead, standing on the earthworks that rimmed the river, down from the wall where first I entered the city. Yllvere was beside him. Close at hand Tabak waited, ffraw and Ceorl in his shadow. The rest were barons.

The river murmured. For a moment I thought I heard Pendyved's laugh. But when I turned my ear to it, it was only the sound of the water. I took no comfort in that sound. The mindless ripples sucked the shore. No life moved upon it. In the darkness I could not see the farther side nor was there any island visible. For all I knew the river ran empty forever. Yet it was the same Undain I had seen in daylight. We are not unalike, I thought. Somewhere in the distant hills were springs from which this river also took its life. I wondered at it. The river's darkness was mirrored in my mother's eyes.

"Is this," I asked, "the legacy you give me?" I meant the river and the dark, the witch that awaited me, and never a gentle word from her that bore me.

Her hair in the firelight was red as torches. Her face was quiet, her bold eyes aloof and still. "I owed my children only life," she answered. "The rest was Anu's."

But I would not be so easily dismissed. I caught her

gown and railed at her. "Why do you shame me before my people? It needs no test. Only a word from you, no more. But you would never have it so. Quick as you could, you left Urien to his shame. And now, having seen your chance again, you turn that shame to me."

She did not falter. With stern sorrow she met my eye. "What is your complaint?" she asked. "If you are that child, but for that shame, you never were."

I shivered. "It is the king's shame too," I stammered. "My father, his people no longer serving him . . ." But I had not the words.

Thigg gave me a look past all his men. His thin lips turned, his long face unbelieving. The muscles rose on his spare jaw. "Why do we suffer such a fool?" he raged. "Does he think one bastard more or less made any difference, one ill-got child could turn the people from their king?" He looked from face to face. "Where has he been that he speaks so readily of the king's shame, of which the broad world knows, and he, it seems, knows nothing?" A scowl covered his brow. His anger shook him. "Dare he think the people turned from Ar Elon and set me, Steward, in his place because in his dotage Ar Elon fiddled with a woman and the woman bore?" He cast his angry look once more across the barons. "Where has he been that he knows so little, not the king's shame nor the land's ailing?"

Alone I should have answered him. But Tabak took my place. In his eyes was sorrow.

"That too was kept from him," he said, "and much besides. So I hid him on the mountain, hidden in the old Kell ways and among its women, away from men lest he hear how lightly a child is fathered, lest in ignorance, blind to what he was, he give his seed." Then he looked long into the faces of the men about him. When he had spoken his voice was like the darkness itself. Those who had been stirred by Thigg's anger grew still again. Now Tabak's silence made them uneasy. They felt lessened. Beyond Ar Elon and myself, in all their lives they had not seen so tall a man nor heard words that came so hot from the heart's core. Then he laughed at them, a great laugh that blew away the night.

"You that know the High King's shame must know also why I kept it from his heir," he said. "The world's not changed." He paused. His black hair shone; his face was vast. In his huge hands they saw he held an ax. They wanted desperately to look away, their small necks like twisted ropes above their shoulders.

"Death comes after life," he said. "You know that. The best kings have one season." Yllvere frowned, but he would not look at her. Her white hands dropped from her gown. "Like breeds like," he said. "Our kings are year-wood, their lives a summer. We cut them down to feed the fire. They warm our winter and keep the dark at bay. That is their gift." He laughed again, the wolf's grin that I knew. But then he seemed to tire, his fury spent.

He looked off into the darkness of the river. "You are wise as well as foolish, Finn," he said. "I trust one or the other will save you. Sure enough it is that a little of both you owe to me. But what service I had to give I gave you. I can do no more. Others, more than you know, conspired to bring you to this place. They, not I, will have to see you through it." He smiled, yet before I found my voice, he walked away along a path that went among the river stones. Living, I never saw him more, though it was years, long after I rode east and in the way of things came back to rule, before I stopped half-expecting him. Even then, the men who knew me best, the barons who shared my table, were never fools enough to ask of it when they saw me start, the roast uncut before me, my great jaw slack and listening to a laugh that boomed outside the door. It was always someone else. Still, on dreary winter evenings, the snow piled high outside the door, the hounds about my feet and nodding by the hearth, my thoughts would often turn and fill with memories and doubt.

For all I loved him I never knew with surety whether his service, woven of all its threads, did me at the last more good than ill. The good I knew, or did when I stopped hating him. That too was long ago. Dazed and burned, my mother's curses ringing in my ears, I knew the thick brown arms that bore me up the winding stair, out of the oven fires that roared beneath the house. He kept my life then. But it was he as well who brought me to the river and there delivered me to the greater fire, hotter than ovens though it had no flame.

But he, who had been my voice when I had none, was gone. My good eye raked the empty space where he had been. The white faces of the barons stared, waiting to see what I would do. My heart drove fast against my ribs.

For a moment I mourned him. But his words, grown huge, broke in my mind and blasted all the rest. I felt them move there, fierce, secret, invading the places I never looked.

I had been kept, he said, lest I spill my seed. It was not, he said, what I had thought. The mountain and the women were meant to hide my manhood, not my name. When I thought of it, I gasped. The color rose about my eyes. But the people of the city, crowded close, saw only the shudder of my breath. I wheeled around.

Truly, too long I had been a child, looking backward, puzzling over roots and stones, old books and older names, seeking only what came before. I thought of Ar Elon and pitied him. He had never known his son.

Startled, Yllvere looked away. The blood beat in her face. I felt its warmth. I saw the muscles moving soundlessly within her throat.

I raised my head, ignoring her. Out of my own flesh would come an heir. Kings make kings. Tabak had said it a hundred times before I heard. Like breeds like, both oaks and kings. I had to lose him before I heard.

It was Thigg I turned to, waiting behind his eyes.

"Where is the island?" I said. "For I shall meet the witch and, mastering whatever death she offers, come back to rule."

The old Steward was still a moment, his gray eyes flickering back and forth among the faces of his men.

"A true king need only enter the river," he answered softly. "For it is said the waters of the earth will bear him safe enough and he will find its shore." He stopped, restless and unsure, a smaller shadow against the shadows of his soldiers.

Ceorl came silently beside me and, at his shoulder, ffraw. Their brows were drawn.

"If it is your wish, I will go with you," said Ceorl. He was the only one of Bede who had not deserted me. But for his deep voice and the murmur, deeper than any man sound, of the river all was quiet.

I found that I could smile. I looked at him. I knew he feared to go with me.

"Who is it that you serve?" I asked.

"You, my lord."

"And you, my brave ffraw?"

His mouth twisted, stilled. "As I was your father's man, so I am yours."

"That is enough," I said and did not wait to see if they

would answer more but turned from them and went down among the stones that made the shore.

A thin breeze blew off the water. The cold had gone from it. Above me, without looking, I could feel the people looking down. I saw no island, only the black water like a rimless floor beneath the stars. It was not a floor a man could walk upon. I knew that I would sink beneath it, the black water sucking at my life.

The people wondered what I would do as much as I. Over my shoulder I saw them nudging and whispering. Some had come down and perched on the nearer stones. Thigg followed, his retinue about him. I saw their armor glittering and the flash of their swords beneath the stars. Thigg was of no mind to see me turn from this. I saw clearly enough why he had laughed when in the high hall I had claimed the test.

"The water is deep here, Finn," he said. "Even for such as you." He shifted his darting eyes and smiled. "Or did you think you would wade out to find the isle?"

"How deep?" I asked.

His old brows flickered a little, drawing together, pleased. "Too deep for giant kind," he said. "So deep that even the greatest ship might moor here."

It was then I saw my way.

I drew a breath and pulled my longshirt from my neck and shoulders. Even as I lifted it I felt the weight of the thing I kept there. My fingers touched it. It warmed my palm. I cried out.

"Even you, Thigg, shall see now what I am." Then I cast the thing before me. At once the dark air shook; the water boiled. Out of the foam the bright hull rose, the wood of its sides golden, its sails like sheets of flame.

It is the one marvel the *filidh* always sing of, the one that marked me because it happened in the people's eyes. They could not speak. Awe held them even as I climbed upon its deck.

Like a crown it rested on the water, trembling in the buzzing air as though it lived. Yet to the dead I owed it, to Pendyved, who, called from the earth where his bones were scattered, rose and dared to cut godwood.

Only for a moment it seemed to rest. Then a great wind where there was no wind sprang up. The charmed wood creaked. The ghost sails filled, and, tugging at their stays, the great ship moved. The people of the city, all of Ormkill down from my father's hall, watched it from the bank. An apparition of crystal light, it filled their eyes when it was near them like the sun itself at midday. But it dwindled quickly as it moved, free of them, out into the blackened river. Until, in the farthest darkness, it seemed but a distant star, glittering, faint, removed. It vanished when they blinked.

Then, like Tabak, I was gone.

16.

I DID NOT SAIL THE SHIP. WITH ITS OWN EYES IT found its way past towns and villages, the lights of men. Then there was only wilderness. Some hours before I heard the wind waves break on its rough shore, I smelled the salt and felt the sea tide fight the river's current. The island, I decided, if I had not missed it in the dark, lay close to the river's mouth. Little I knew in those years how far inland the vast sea reaches with its briny tongue, bearing the whirling gulls above its flood, stiff ocean gales blowing at its head.

But at dawn I came to it and in the fresh light saw that it was many leagues farther to the headlands and the sea. The island, when I saw it, was greater than any of the river islands I had seen. A massive tract of forest, its roots and stones together, torn from the bank where it had grown, it floated until long after in the south it snagged and held. The bald rocks at its northern edge parted the water, which boiled on to either side. But for the rest the tall old trees came close to the shore, their black thick roots splayed and dug into the bank like fingers trying to hold on, as though they feared the island, never belonging where it was, might yet move on and find some other place.

The wood itself was wild, thick almost to choking. Woven among themselves, only the highest branches held a few bare patches on which the circling crows could perch. They were the first crows I had seen since the ship I rode had taken me from Stephen's Well. I thought of

Ninmir. But these were fish crows and too small. Yet their hollow coughs reminded me of how I had thought to send her, black, forbidding, speaking human speech, to sit upon Thigg's chair and name me king. I saw once more, though often I had fought it, how seldom the world moved as I willed but as it must.

As I sailed nearer, I looked for a place to put ashore. There were no easy moorings. No hand, it seemed, had delved among those rocks. If ever there had been a wooden pier it had rotted long ago. Indeed, though those of Ormkill knew it, it seemed unlikely that they had walked here or that their fathers had. It was a place they held in memory, passed down in *filidhes'* songs from a time so long before only the kings' names were kept and the memory of the witch upon the Mound, a few bright stones, the treasure lost. Or so it seemed. And yet I knew that here my father raised the godshrine. I doubted that, whatever he was, with his own hands he had laid the stone.

The great ship rolled along the island's western side. Close in toward the shore, the high trees stole the wind. I heard the deep keel scrape on gravel. The wide hull shook and turned until at last it came to rest, stuck fast on a bar. It was safe here near the bank. I might leave it and come back, though how I would float it once more I could not tell. Yet I knew the fell ship saw to itself.

With no more thought to it, I let myself down into the river. There I hung, waiting for the voices. Deep among its stones the river moaned. I listened, but there were no words. I had feared the river mage. Though once already I had beaten him, the memory of his whispers still hissed in my ears promising the cool green dark and palaces undersea. I would have rather then that his slippery arm reached out to pull me down. That was a better fight. For words weigh heavier than the press of arms, and the memory of words, more bitter still, I took a breath. There was no sound but the water and the crows.

After a time I ceased to listen. With some struggling I found my feet among the stones. The bar was piled up high beneath, though not so high that any of Ormkill's small folk might walk, their heads above water. I did, but to my neck in places, ill-footed, poking out for buried logs and holes, mindful still of anything that lurked. Yet nothing came snorting up or slipped between my legs.

A dozen elhws from the shore the bar gave out. As

best I could I swam, my heart quaking until I touched the sand. I drew myself up, shivering, in the dim light beneath the trees. There I sprawled among the stones, not caring where they stuck me. Thus in daylight and good weather I came to Tinkern. And there, since I had not dared to sleep an hour of the night upon the river and as the wood was hushed, I laid my head in the crook of my arm and closed my eye.

A bird kept calling. Its low song drifted through the wood, a gentle song rising and falling softly as smoke in air. I thought it kept me awake. Yet when I raised my head, no longer hearing it, it was already evening. The river, swollen with the tide, lapped gently near my feet. Farther off, where I had left it, the great ship waited, immobile on the bar. The dying sun behind it, its masts and rigging etched a fretwork of shadows across the river's back. Even as I watched, the shadows deepened. I felt the evening come. From pools among the roots the gray fine mist curled high to meet it. There was no wind to tear at it. I yawned.

Not a few elhws from the bank the wood was thick and dark. The dripping branches, deep with the richness of new leaves, rose like a wall. I felt better where I was, only needing a few dry sticks to scratch a fire. I would wait, I thought, till morning, pleased still to linger. For I was not eager to try the wood at night, less eager to find the sacred place or what it held. Not yet. Oh, I did not run from it. Whatever wills that breathed in the world and those other things, unbreathing—Pendyved and the speaking stone, whatever else that bent me to this—for myself I claimed it. I would feel them sometimes, edging near, invisible, eager as hounds for the hunt. Yet I would keep them back and would often go for days on end without their notice. But at other times, when I would feel them most, their buzz about my ears like the sea-hum of a shell, even then my own need would run ahead of theirs. For was I not the king's true son and they, bloodless and unreal, his servants only?

I built a fire. I made it from the scattered roots of a windfall and banked it high against the dark. I have no love of fires. Yet then my skin did not blister before the fire's warmth as it does now. These last years I have kept one for the men who serve me. For, being men, they do not know the dark and they fear it, thinking the cold is bitter. And when the *filidh* sing, as I have taught them, of the crystal halls on the deep sea floor and of the sea-green silver horses that I rode beneath the foam, they only mutter in the dry hair of their beards and stare. But on Tinkern that night long ago I built a fire. High against the trees I made it, that though I did not seek her yet, the witch of the Mound would know that I had come.

Under the arch of leaves the air was gentle. It was summer and I was farther south and west than I had ever been. Deep and still as they stood, here the trees grew broad as well as high, not spare and spidery like the mountain oaks I knew. Godwood they were, wheresoever they were rooted. Yet I felt that the god of this place must be an easier, wiser lord, more like his trees. He gave them fuller life.

Later, east of the island, the summer moon rose yellow in the sky. Its pale light drifted through the branches. I walked to the river's edge where I could look out. The moon's eye floated in the ripples. You and I, I told it, are pulled from the same dark womb. For a long time I stood watching. The river scrubbed at the moon like a smooth white-yellow stone lodged in its throat. The river could not wash it from its place. But it was no company. I wandered back and lay beside the dying fire, scraping ashes over the red coals until, but for the moon, the world was dark again.

There were owls in the wood. I heard one screech just before the kill. Toward midnight the bird whose song I had listened to the day I landed began its call again. I thought it odd. I knew no creature with both a morning and a midnight song. It was likely, I thought, that the moon had wakened it. But with nothing else to keep my mind, I listened. Mostly it came from far back in the tract. Then it seemed lost and trembling, high as a child's wail but not as shrill. It touched me. I knew not why. I must find words for it, I thought, and give it to the *filidh*. But on my tongue it sounded thick and cold. Thereafter I let it be.

For some time it was still. I dozed. When it came again, the song was from the nearer wood. Then I could almost hear the words. But, lulled by its gentle music as a feather is lifted by the wind, I climbed toward sleep.

It was morning when I woke. By my right hand, when I moved, I found a broad new leaf. Wrapped within it lay a dozen blue mussels. They were still wet where they had been cut from the river stones. I had been left an offering. I smiled. There were people here. I looked out. But I saw only my own deep marks upon the bank. It would wait. I cracked the mussels on a stone and ate each one. Perhaps, I thought, there is a village on the island or at least a priest to keep the shrine. The day was clear again. I felt lucky and full of the god. Whether priest or bogie, the wood had welcomed me. I went to the river and washed, knowing I must do then the thing for which I had come.

When I entered under the trees, I remembered Anu's wood and the great gore crow that ruled it. I thought, have I not stolen the children of the air? Surely then, I can take a thing that's mine.

There was no path. Yet I found my way, keeping the sound of the river at my back until its murmur faded like a breath of air. I was in the deep wood then, green with ferns and black with the great boles of old trees. But it was not like Anu's wood. Here no sad quiet lay like stone upon the earth. Rather, wood doves bickered continually overhead. Squirrels trooped through the branches squeaking with a sound like rubbing sticks. Once, when I had crossed a deer track, a gray old boar with yellow tusks came blundering out to charge me till I raised my hand and laughed. All around I could feel the wood swarming and crowding. And in those few tight places where a slim ray of sun slid through, faint starry flowers grew. Still there were no gaping holes, rising tier on tier within the canopy of leaves, where one could truly see the sky. What light there was seemed green and pale, though here no gloom was mixed with it.

After several hours I knew I was lost. On an island, I thought, you need only walk to come to water. But I could not make a straight path through the trees. No streams crossed my wanderings. I waded some time through a low black marsh and found a lightning-blasted oak uprooted. But other trees had shouldered in its place. I tramped the margins of the swamp. No brook fed it. After that I kept to higher ground. Still the way grew no easier.

There is no village here, I thought, no priest, no god-shrine. To raise monuments one needs first to break a road on which to drag the stone. Even if it were now overgrown, there would be signs. But, looking down, I should have watched the trees. Heedless, I lumbered through the undergrowth. Roped with wild grape and bound with creepers, the branches above me let in no more light. Yet I should have noticed that lately I had no need to swerve to pass the knees and roots of trees. No longer did they stand within my path but off to either side. Angry and unseeing, I called on the names of power that I knew. As if to challenge heaven, I threw back my head, my voice already lifted. But then my hot breath caught within my throat.

Before my swimming eye a blaze of whiteness flashed. Ahead of me at the end of a narrow avenue of trees the old wood opened like a door. I saw a wide green glade. About its rim in a mighty circle stood a ring of stones, each massive, twice the height and more of a man. At its center, piled higher even than the towers of Morrigan, there rose a grassy mound. I stopped.

I had wandered, I knew, much of the island. Surely, I thought, I have already tramped through this place and did not find it. Then, slowly, as I looked, I came to see the wonder of the place, that a man might not come to it until the god was willing.

The sun's full light poured through the opening in the trees. For a hundred elhws it fell straight to the earth. It seemed a golden pillar set upon the ground. Crows were rising and falling in its light. I watched them. But when they dropped, I saw, they never touched the Mound, though more than once they lit on the ring of stones. Yet I did not feel any dread in that bright air and wondered. The glade was green, the sweet air gentle.

This place is blessed, I thought. Why then do the birds so fear it? I looked some time and thought. The Mound was old, so Tabak said, compounded of the ancient earth when men had not yet walked upon the land. Perhaps, I mused, the world as it was then cannot mix with what came after. Yet how then should a king of later days find grace to walk upon its back? So I debated with myself. It may be that I said my thoughts aloud.

The voice fell out of the air. Soft as the rain it was, but there was laughter at the back of it. "The blood of kings comes down from those first things," it said. "There is no wonder when like will mix with like."

I looked up sharply. There were only trees above. One, an oak, was unmatched among the rest. Its great branches twisted in a maze of wood. Its green-black leaves lay thick as birds upon a new-sown hill. I stood beneath it rubbing the chin beneath my beard.

"Never before this have I talked with trees," I said.

"Nor have you yet," it answered back, even more like laughter than before. "Their voices are gruff and deep and hard to hear. Nor do they lightly speak with kings who ride in ships cut from their kin."

I stopped and thought before I spoke. I said, "You know then what I am?"

"None but kings and giants ever come," it said. "And you, my lord, I see are both."

I cast my eye once more through all the branches. Only the oak itself looked back at me. "Have you seen so many kings," I asked, "that you are certain of the look of them?"

I heard it laugh again. "You are the first, my lord," it said. "But the old woman who has sat upon that hill since first the sun looked down on it has marked each one. At night, when she and I grow weary looking at each other and the dark, she takes the shapes they had and speaks the lovely words they spoke to her. So I have learned the look of kings and all their talk from the first that ever walked upon the land, the salt still wet upon his arms."

I heard but puzzled at the words. The grim heights of the mountain rose, troubling my thought. Huddled beneath its double crag, I saw once more the house where I was born. It takes me for what I am not, I thought. "I am no sea king," I answered, almost sad it was not so.

"Your hair's as black," it laughed. "Near black as mine. The old woman says that I am water-spawn. It cannot be that you are other than you seem."

My eye wide open, I stared hard as I might at nothing I could see. "Come down," I said, "and let me look at you."

It did not answer.

"Perhaps you fear me."

The laugh came quickly then, but it had darkened before it stilled. "Do not yet go upon the Mound," it said.

It made me angry. I turned as if I meant to walk away, then changed my mind, more angry than before. "Come down if you would have me do your bidding," I shouted up to it. My voice rang cold beneath the tree. But its echo brought back only silence. No leaf moved. It is a bogie, I decided. I thought, it is a foolish thing to quarrel with what can't be seen. I turned once more.

"Do not go," it pleaded softly.

"Then will you come to me?"

I waited. The silence went on as though I had not

spoken. Whether a bogie or the witch's drab, it would not give me what I asked. As I listened more I thought I heard a cry, blade-sharp then muffled, sobbed back with straining breath. Something wept within the twisted wood, quietly as though it hated to be heard. I could not give a reason. Yet it stung me. I thought, I have my own grief. Still, I could not get free of it.

Perplexed, I laid my back against the oak. I let my shoulder dig into the bark, something nagging in my memory, something—though I reached for it—I could not touch. Casting my thoughts as nets to catch at it, I forgot to move.

The day wore on. I watched the lordling crows rising and falling above the Mound. They wait as well, I thought, hungry for king's flesh.

The evening came. The trees reached up and caught the sun. I watched it die. I saw the darkness come swarming up from underground and the mists come stalking through the aisles of trees, long-fingered, stooped, like heavy headless men, their beating hearts ripped from their chests.

Perhaps, I thought, it cries because it dare not show itself. And I imagined it, both furred and scaled, misshaped, ugly, drooling foam. Or else, I thought, the witch has swallowed what it was and left but a scrap of voice unchewed. It made no difference. Knowing there was another, whatever shape it had, I longed for company. The night wore on. Yet no sleep came.

I saw her early, walking slowly among the trees. Her shift was green and shining as the oak. The new sun at her back, I saw the lithe long shadow of her calves within the cloth. She laughed to see that I had noticed her.

I had no need to question who she was. Her hair, as she had said, was black as mine. She wore it parted from her face, then loose upon her shoulders. She looked younger than my sisters but to my eye more fair. In her white hands she bore a fresh-killed hare, its bloody legs twitching with remembered life.

"You brought me mussels when I came," I said, "and now a hare."

The eyes that looked in mine were large, brown-black as the aurochs', flecked with gold. I could not read them.

"This is the old woman's wood," she said. "You dare eat only what I bring you."

172

She held the hare out like an offering. Reaching, I took it. My clutching hands slid vainly over fur.

Its blood was black and dried upon my hands when I awoke. Scattered at my feet I saw its bones, cracked through, the marrow gone. A gray light welled up from the ground. It was not yet morning. I did not remember if I slept.

"Drink," she said, already near me. The word quivered in the air like a plucked string of a harp. I felt her breath. Prodding, she nestled the bowl within my hands. I felt the weight of it, unable to decide.

"Drink deep, my lord. From the well beneath the Mound I drew it, the world's own blood. It never fell as rain."

Uncertain, I pushed my fevered lips to touch the rim. Cool as the earth it seemed, cold as the old stones underground. I drank. But in my throat the water turned to ash.

I woke again. I did not hunger. In the red and seeming dawn I stood out from the tree. Among the roots I found a broken bowl. I did not thirst.

In the red light I heard her laughter.

"Will you come to me?" I asked.

Her laughter answered, gentle and amused. "Lord, you are slow to learn," she whispered. "Twice I came to you and twice you let me go."

I heard the rustle of her shift behind me and did not turn. "Three times," I said. "Each a dream."

"But I am here, my lord. You need only turn to look at me."

Still I was afraid.

"My lord?"

I set me teeth. "I will not watch you shrink to dust and bone."

I heard her move, her shoulders at my back. I felt the softness of her breasts against me. But I had no word for her. Her laugh was bitter then.

"Go without my help," she said, her voice already cold. "Meet the old woman on the Mound. And may you live. But surely then, even as now I breathe, I shall turn to dust and bone and all the nights I waited for you be for nothing." Her breath caught and she stopped.

Morning came. The red light paled, turned white

173

against the trees. Green and empty in the meadow the high Mound shone. Bright even as the sun it seemed. Yet I knew it was a tomb. She is the same, I thought, and yet I heard her weep. She laid her trembling head against my back.

"You are the only king who came to me," she said. "For the old woman there were others. For me you were the only one who was to come."

But the taste of ashes was in my mouth. I thought of the broken bowl and scattered bones. My memories came down like hail upon my head. I thought of Grieve and all the women of the Kell waiting for what never came. I pitied her, half-knowing she was my imagining and in that same moment certain she. was not. The *filidh* say that I was steadfast then. But they only repeat the lies I told them. I was young and had never had a woman. The sound of her breath flamed in my lungs, the shape of her small hands seared like coals against my back. With brown-black hungry eyes I knew she watched me.

"You are the witch," I cried. But the shout I gave came out a moan.

"No," she said. "I would have told you."

I did not answer. There was no more I could do. I turned, expecting emptiness. I touched her face. The flesh beneath my hand was warm.

She stared at me as though she cast out all her soul through her dark eyes. She said, "So at the end you find me, lord."

"As I have dreamed you."

She shook her head. "No, as I am."

I reached for her with both my hands. At once her flesh went up like husks in flames. In her place I felt the fissured oak, its old bark split and cold against my face. A great wind rocked the branches overhead and drove the swirling leaves that filled the wood and fell on me like cataracts of fire until, at last, they closed my eye.

The storm, if that it was, had vanished when I woke. I found her seated near me on the ground. The line of her neck was tilted like a swan's. Her lips were parted, amused but not surprised. In her tangled hair she wore a crown of braided twigs and leaves. The sun, now truly risen, rode at her back. In her lap she cradled a small hare, its dead eyes blank, and in her white hands a bowl. She smiled at me.

174

"You are the first man I have served," she said.

The memory of the night came back. A lightness filled my head. She is a tree in woman's shape, I thought. The soles of her feet are black and splayed beneath her gown. If I lifted it I would find her legs were rooted in the earth. But her face was rapt and tranquil. A patch of sunlight fell against her cheek.

Taking up a silver knife, she skinned the hare. To keep from watching her I set a flame. When I had done, she laid the hare's white body in the hottest part and after it had roasted, cut the joint.

A great emptiness hung around me. The wood, the fire, the bowl were mere pictures painted in the air. I did not know what time had passed. Yet because I hungered I took the flesh and tore it with my teeth. Her deep eyes smiled.

She held the bowl out to me. It was in my mind to dash it to the ground. Yet, thirsting, I put it to my lips. The breath of the water felt cool against my face. I drank it to the bottom. Her black eyes danced.

"The old woman does not eat or drink," she said. "All that I have made for her she turns away."

I raised my brows. I had not meant to speak, but I remembered what was said of her, how the witch tore out and ate the hearts of kings. It rose unbidden to my lips. "I have heard she dines on other fare," I said.

Her small mouth twisted at the edge. "Who is to say? Since I lived, you are the first who came."

"And yet you speak to her."

"My lord, we are two women by ourselves. The nights are long. I have heard her say a thousand times what each king said and all she answered, word by word. Only I do not know the end."

But I meant to have the truth of it and said, "But you have surely guessed, and still you stay with her."

She dropped her eyes. "This is an island, lord. Nowhere does it touch the land."

"Ships pass."

"And do not stop." Her crow-black hair hung at her cheek. She lifted it as if it were a wing till her deep sad eyes had found my face. "I have stood upon the rocks myself and called to them. But they are little men and much afraid. I have watched them screw up their little faces and stick their little trembling fingers in their ears."

Her mouth was set. "You may keep such men as that," she said. "Myself, I would not lick their bones."

I tried to read her countenance, but it was closed.

"Ar Elon came," I cried, "and by the stones he left I judge he did not fear the witch."

She laughed. "Like you he was no little man."

My backbone shivered. "You saw him, then?" I asked.

"I have watched the old woman walk the meadow's rim, changed, like his own shadow, chanting, as she remembered them, the holy words that raised the stones. I have watched her pull down branches of the deepest wood, whispering to herself, to make his arms and whole great trees to compound his legs." Her mouth worked oddly yet she smiled. "Lord, I have stood as close to his shape as I stand to you." She took a breath. "And seeing him, I knew what you must be."

I tried the meaning of her words and did not like them. I was not my father's mirror. Suddenly it became important that she not find me so. I turned so she could see me fully, my hair still wild, my blasted eye, my clothes that would have shamed a beggar, never mind a king.

It was my bitterness that spoke. "He was two-eyed like any man," I said. "And king already when he came."

She had bitten the inside of her lip. I saw blood. "What do I care of that?" she asked. It troubled me.

"Was it not a king you sought?"

At once the sight went from her eyes. "There are kings enough," she said defiantly.

I did not follow her.

She wheeled around. "Can you not see that I have guessed? Have I not seen you walk up from the river's edge, taller than ever were the men who lived on land? In truth, whatever you say to me, I saw it. Your black hair, sea-made, was shining in the air."

Her bright eyes shone beneath her tears. She shivered though the wind was warm. Mute before her, I touched her hair, then took her small white shoulders inside my hands.

"Long have I watched and counted, lord," she said. "Now you have come again as ever it was promised." She wept. Yet even as she spoke her voice was not one but many. Within each word a thousand voices rose, each old and sharp with longing. I turned aside. Too well I knew the words and cursed them. Even in this I could not be parted from the Kell. I felt my face grow white and still.

For a breath's space she looked up at me. I felt her push her hands to find my back.

"Who is it that you say I am?" I asked.

She made no sound but drew me to herself. She did not fade. Meeting those still, dark eyes, I knew only that she waited me. I found the strings that held her gown. When I had seen her nakedness, she laughed outright. Somewhere within the oak a bird began its song.

17.

WHEN WE WERE STILL, SHE KEPT HER ARMS around my neck. Her breasts were warm against my skin, her thick hair spread upon my shoulder like a fan. She touched my face.

I never knew the ease of love as on that morning. When in my bed in the empty place far back in the hall—the candles guttered, the barons gone—I have lain against the body of my queen and heard the wind wail as it willed along the hill, her bold eyes would catch the candles' fire and, watching me, she would know some other face had disturbed my sleep. I was blessed that she was wise. She never spoke of it. She had her sons and my ear when it was needed. As much as man and woman may, we had made our peace. But on that morning I could not see so far ahead. The bird, perhaps dreaming itself, had quit its song.

She sat up at last, the leaves still clinging to her hair.

"You cannot meet the old woman as you are," she said.

I smiled, looking down at my own nakedness. "Will I too greatly frighten her as I am?" I asked, but got up afterward and pulled my longshirt over me.

The small lines of her mouth drew back. "Nor is that enough, I think," she said. "You will need both arms and armor, lord."

I looked her up and down. She had not bothered yet to cover herself. My heart was light. But I caught the solemnity within her eyes.

"The sword that I had I left at Stephen's Well," I said. "And even that was borrowed. As to armor, there was never a ring shirt made that I could wear."

She drew her shift over her head, then raked out her long hair with her fingers. "I have not wasted the years I awaited you," she answered. At once she turned toward the path that ran deep into the wood. "Come," she said, not looking back. "Such as will be needed I have made."

I followed her into the greenwood. But the path had known only her feet. Scarcely a leaf was turned and nowhere was it worn. I trailed her around ivy-covered trunks, through hedges that brushed and scraped my thighs and soaked my skin with dew. When I was slow, she called to me. But as quickly as I went, she kept ahead. The sun slowly faded, then disappeared, though in a moment it showed in another place.

The way descended into a valley of grim oaks. Their enormous branches erupted close to the ground. Their leaves were thick and green and blocked my going. Heedless, I lumbered into them. But there were times I lost sight of her. Then all at once I would see her hair, like something winged, darting among the trees. Already short of breath, I followed after. The black shadow kept a girl's height as it fled. But suddenly it rose like smoke into the trees. I stopped before it. Formless, just at the edge of sight, a broad black wing unfolded from a branch.

The great crow shivered. It cracked its dry red mouth and hissed. "You delay," it said, its old voice harsh as wind on stones. "Already ships have moored off this island's shore. Thigg comes, his barons with him, to see with his own eyes if you are a corpse."

The eye it had was gray with age.

"You are neither crow of mine," I said. I did not breathe.

Its great eye glittered. "Mine they were till you stole them. My life's last children, though you took them early."

I felt a ghostly run of fire branch through my skull. "It was not without cost to me," I murmured. "Since you took the other, I have looked out on but half the world."

The old eye blinked.

"We shall be even, you and I," it rasped.

In the upper branches a sad wind moaned. Moving, it tore a hole through which a single shaft of sunlight fell like a sword. For a moment I saw her as she was. Her bony neck was bare and eaten, the immense wings spare and thick with lice. She turned her mangled head that I might see it. A gray hole swam before me where her eye had been. Horror crept over me. There was a feel of sickness in my head. But I felt my anger more.

"I never bartered eyes with you," I cried. "How shall we be even, then? It was Ar Elon who cast the stone at you. I was not asked. When he did it, I was not born."

Her glazed eye, fixed on mine, seemed indifferent.

"Nor did you ask when you took from me the last children of the air," she rasped. "No more than shall be asked of you when the final price is paid."

I stared, knowing it was Anu's crow. But suddenly it was Yllvere's face that rose before me, both bird and woman. Huge wings outspread, no longer bare but bright as gold, outreached till they had filled the wood. A brightness fell from them. They stunned my sight. But though I stared in wonder, my heart was cold.

"I do not serve the Crow of Death," I said.

Her smooth white face showed no surprise, no hurt. "Anu has many daughters," she answered softly. "But each one is Herself. It has not changed. She only takes what I have given. Life for life."

I felt her arms as though she held me, white, enfolding, warm as wool, her peace I had never known. My own arms ached for it. Still, I stiffened.

"Lady," I asked her roughly, "why have you sent me here to die upon the Mound?"

The shining head was bowed. Black feathers sprouted from her throat. The brightness went. In its place I felt the rotting dark.

"How shall you die," it hissed, "when I can see but half of you?" Opening wide its fleshless beak, it jeered, "Fool, half-blind, how shall you live?" The old head sank back into the gloom and grinned. "Deceived, this night already you have eaten bones for flesh and taken dust for drink. Bitter will that be to you. More bitter still the bride you took."

It laughed a laugh that made no sound.

I closed my ears. But the stench of death blew in my nostrils, pushed into my skull and crushed my thought. Already the trees were gone, sunk down to choking dust. The bare sloping hills beneath were crumbling. I caught the last rough glimpse of stones that fell, shrunken into flaming cinders, lost as sparks, snuffed out. A blind wind nosed across the waste that was the earth, till ragged,

179

mortal, even that was gone. For an awful moment I was alone.

Lady, in that darkness it was your face I met. Where nothing else was, your soft eyes followed me, held me, frightened and amazed, as if we touched. If bitterness would come of you, it was not yet. If you were false, I would not know of it before I must. Your warm breath moved beneath my heart. It was your smile that turned my lips. Then, before you had a name, I was at peace. Your eyes were shining. In that darkness they leapt like fires.

I felt my legs again. I stood once more at the border of the wood, the treeless glade in front of me. Where her eyes had been, the light still was, paired stars glittering in the evening sky, the Mound beneath. In time I went toward it.

Grief comes soon enough to men. Yet whatever else would come, I knew that I had met the dark, Death's worst, and was not betrayed. Now the shadows lay where they belonged. I smiled.

Presently I came within the ring of upright stones. The tall gray rock was almost even with my head. Marked with lichen, scarred with runes and carvings, the stones seemed older than my father's time. Yet I knew that it was he who had set them there. Perhaps even then he was condemned, shamed though I did not know the cause, abandoned by the folk he ruled. But this was his work; his word had lifted them.

Even as men are, so each stone was different—some long or burly, others smooth or grizzled, though all were huge. They were not quarried here, I thought, nor any two in one place. But where they had been dug I could not guess. Silently, I went among them, squinting at the shapes. The gray rock shone beneath the stars. Proud as kings they were, but their sides were cold as winter earth.

I stopped. Among them one stood taller than the rest. Yet even though the rock was worn, I read among the scoured lines the faded glory of a lordlike face. A strangeness came over me. I spoke to it. It took no notice but kept its narrowed eyes fixed on the Mound.

At its knees, where the stone had sunk into the ground, I found a ring shirt of a size that I might wear and at its side a sword so huge that I alone might carry it. The blade was one clear piece of metal, but the hilt was carved. Wrought amid the twisted gold I saw a man shape, naked, the face in pain. In his arms, contending with him, Death's crow outspread her terrible wings. Their warring hung in balance, the victory in doubt. By that I knew the sword was mine, newmade, with no history but the one that I would write with it. I took it in my hand. Feeling the weight of it. I smiled.

Surely, I thought, she would not arm me against herself. She is no witch, then, but what she seems.

Comforted, I took the ring shirt and put it on. The links were burnished gold, yet there was no softness in the metal. Pleased, I thought, never has a king gone so richly armed as this. And still I knew this was no maiden craft. But in truth, I thought, neither is this any black art but only what it seems. Gladdened, I lifted the sword once more. The starlight glittered on the blade. Each link of the heavy mail shone back the light in turn. I thought, now I will do what I have promised.

The glade was empty. Because I was too young to try so great a thing unnoticed, I cried out to the stone, "This I swear and you are witness. I shall not leave this place until I have wrung from her who rules it the right of kings."

When I had spoken, I went out from the stones. The way was short. It was not long before I stood within the shadow of the Mound. I scaled its far height with my eye. There was no mark or stone upon its back, only one great hill grown thick with grass. Since the world was new, it is said, men never built so near to heaven.

Yet it was a hill like other hills, not crystal, as the harpers tell it. Once before the meat I heard a *filidh*, whose song men swore went lighter to their heads than wine, plucking at the strings and calling out how I had seen the starlight shining through the Mound. Before my chair where all could see it, I had him whipped. My smallest son sat blubbering from his mother's lap that I was cruel. But the man knew what I meant. When the people will hear foolishness, no king can give the law.

The edges of the Mound rose gently. At first I climbed as easily as I walked the high meadows above Morrigan. The grass was deep, but not so that it mattered. A light wind came ruffling from the east, caught the grass and set it rolling like the sea. So easeful did it seem that had I kept my eye to it my thoughts would have deepened and I might have slept. But mostly I listened. The wind sighed. Soft it was as the breath of a man who dreams.

I climbed a long time. Though I was wary, my hand gripped the great sword lightly. On the stair road before Gwen Gildrun I had clutched fast the sword I borrowed, like my own life, fearing that should I let one go I would surely lose the other. I was bolder now. In truth, perhaps, the dark was not so thick as it had seemed beneath the Tree, though it was queerer. The sky was deep and high. In the vault of heaven two stars shone. The heavens were but one more hill above the one I climbed.

At that same moment a long, low roll of thunder broke above the Mound. I heard it echo back against the wood. Dully, I went on. I yearned then only to be done with it, to meet the witch and, if I lived, to rule. I sought no truth, no reasons. I longed only for a night's peace, for sleep and, when I woke, the girl beside me in my bed. The air was soft, the long grass whispering. What did I care, I thought, to argue with the dark. It struck without pain, was gentle, gave no lasting dreams. It is said the gods do not over a quiet man, yet I knew they let him be. There is some good in that, I thought. The Mound was empty. The wind blew softly over the edges of the hill and then was lost.

It seemed that all I did was climb. I gave my thoughts to nothing else. My knees bent and one foot came down after another. I was no longer certain where I went. There were moments when I thought I climbed the rough tower to Urien's chamber and others when I was as certain I descended the narrow steps to Yllvere's cell. Only there was no end.

The mail shirt grew heavy; the great sword weighed upon my hand. I was of half a mind to cast them off. No dark shapes rose snarling in my path. No serpents pressed about my legs. I thought of what I did. Was this the test that made the men of Ormkill tremble? Made Thigg, imagining it, smile? I shivered. Though for a time I had forgotten everything, I remembered then I would be king. In a sudden great revulsion I felt my whole life clamoring through my veins, bitter and uunused. Despairing, I remembered what ffraw had said the night he swore his life to me: A king must have blood on him if he would make his own men brave. When I go down to them, I thought, what will I say? Shamed, I cried out to the dark.

"Dagda," I shouted, "was I given arms to walk an empty hill?"

"Come, my lord," she answered even as I saw her. "Do not be angry. You will find use enough for your sword when you go down again."

She was all in green and shining. A pale light came out of the ground on which she stood. At first I did not see the trouble in her look. It was the Mound I saw. The grass was parted and in its place a bed of scented fern, woven with the living leaves of oak and hazel. The pillows were of twisted grass, shaped into the form but growing still. I watched but could not hold her eyes. It seemed that I had stepped outside the earth. In some lost part of me I knew it was high summer then. But without the stars I had no sure sense of the season. The air was flecked with light and shadow, nor was one marked from the other. It seemed I stood within some holy place before time ran.

I rubbed my eye. For a brief moment I felt her gaze and then it fled.

"Where is the witch you serve?" I asked.

She trembled. Her lips moved before she had her voice. "She was old, as I have told you." I saw she meant to look at me, but her eyes kept slipping past. She sighed, her fingers twisting through her hair. Her face seemed paler than it was. "She would have met you as she met the others," she said, looking off. "She would have found some shape to come at you. You know, she could be anything she pleased, an ox with iron horns so wide the moon might fall between; or, if she wished, small and unnoticed as a wasp. Barely would you have heard its buzzing. But the poison in its sting would have made your king's blood boil, even your great shoulders slump and tear." Her body stiffened. "Lord," she whispered, "can you not see I feared for you?" Seeing her anguish, I moved beside her. She leaned against me, nestling in the shadow beneath my arm. She looked up, seeming smaller than she was.

"Where is she gone?" I said.

There was a sadness in her eyes I could not read. "Lord——," she answered faintly, "it is already done."

I drew back, not knowing what she meant. To hold me she put her hands up to my chest.

"We were two women by ourselves," she said. "Ever she knew my thoughts. And when she looked into them she saw what I must do to save you. Knowing it, she fled. But more I knew her wiles." She was silent then, staring at the bed of fern and hazel growing at her feet. She gripped her hands as often I had seen Yllvere do, twisting each finger. Even then a smile played at her lips. So her mood swung back and forth from grief to pride and back to grief again. She said, "In a barrow on the Mound I found her hiding. By her long ears I pulled her out. She it was I brought to you. She it was, when you had roasted it, you ate."

She watched me, helpless, pleased. Tall as a spear she was, upright and about to fall.

"But even as you took the flesh, she turned herself to hare's blood. But then I ran and found a bowl and caught each drop." She lay back her head to watch me. "And that," she said, "you drank."

Something broke in me. I stared. But still I would not believe.

"It was a dream," I choked.

"Lord," she answered, "so first it was. So are all great spells at first." A flush had deepened around her eyes. "But not at the end. Nor was it all my dreaming by itself. Standing beneath the oak you joined it. Our dreams together whispered in her mind. Always she was drawn to power. How then could she help it? Our dreaming called to her. And it was a king who dreamed with me, striding through the dark. What could she do? Her soul slipped out beyond her reach. Already dreaming, she closed her night-black eyes. Then she was a black-eyed hare running on the hill. I ran behind her. I saw where she had dug beneath the ground."

She smiled slowly, letting her strong voice fade. Once more she put her arms around my neck.

"So it is done, my lord," she murmured. "Now is the end of it and you are king."

I felt my face grow white and still.

"If this is so," I stammered, my small voice sharp with fear. "If this," I halted, knowing the thought and hating it. I felt the witch's blood grow thick and sticky in my throat. She saw my thoughts. A fool might have seen them. Yet she smiled.

"You won," she cried. "What does it matter how? Always it was one life against another. So even among the gods it is. Need we be other than they are? She would have taken your own flesh within her mouth. She meant to. There were, you know, so many kings that came before."

184

Sweat thick as blood poured from my forehead. "No!" I raged. "They met her as she met them. She won or they did." I stopped, my hands clenched, my thick arms lifted. Before all of Ormkill I had claimed this thing; more, I had sworn it to myself. "It was you," I shouted. "I came to face her. But you have done it in my place."

She stood, unafraid, but swaying, her hands clasped tightly to my side. She raised her head. It tilted like a crow's. "Lord," she whispered, "was it not promised from the start that I should help you? In truth, you know it. I at least have not forgotten it." She sighed. Turning a rueful look at me she sang:

> *"Sea-made, the last of giants*
> *Shall meet the maid on Tinkern Hill*
> *There what was broken shall be mended*
> *On Tinkern, above the bones of kings.*

The old woman sang it. I learned it on her lap. I had scarcely walked before she saw I knew the words."

There was a blankness in her eyes. The wind blew harder. A wing of her raven hair was lifted across her face. I pulled it back and laid my great hands over hers. They burned.

"Who is it that you say I am?"

"A giant, lord." Her pale chin trembled. "He that the old woman said would come once more, bearing a likeness of Ar Elon, but not him." She paused. In the light that came out of the ground I saw her blush. "He that first carried me to this place," she said, "that left me here a babe with that old woman." Her dark brows were knit and troubled. Yet she laughed. "So ever as I dreamed you, so you are."

I turned my head. So she had laughed and wept when I had lain with her. I felt my heart grow still.

"How old do you say I am?"

"Lord, I have watched and counted—," she began. But I knew it. For so the Kell have always counted, careless of the stars. Her deep black eyes, so like my own, gazed at me shamelessly.

"Lord," she asked, as though the thought had only come to her, "when I was delivered to your care, was not my true name given you? For the old woman, though she had many names for me, had not the one that I was born with."

I looked into her yearning face, a child's face, wild as it was grave. Her passions, both fears and smiles together, changed her features as the weather changes, both bright and shadow. I knew then why men lie, even the best of men. In that at least I might have been the old dark man she dreamed I was. I thought, what good will knowing do her? But the name I would not keep. From the first it had only half been mine.

"Géar," I whispered though the name was blood and ashes in my mouth.

"Géar," she whispered back. Then in joy she shouted it. It was the wind that found it and blew it round the hill.

Away in the east among the gray shapes of the wood I saw a ruddy glow. For a moment I confused it with the rising sun. But as I watched, it broke and spread into a hundred tiny flames. Slowly the lights crept out beyond the trees. Twisting in ragged lines, they climbed among the stones. The lights grew stronger until, as they drew nearer, they had become flaming branches lifted in men's hands. Mail-clad with painted shields I saw them, a host of soldiers, red cloaks on their shoulders, proud men with burnished helms. At the head of each cohort walked a herald, a stave in his hand and on each pole a banner, bright in the torchlight with Thigg's colors.

A smile spread nimbly on her lips. "See, my lord," she cried, "the men of Ormkill come to claim their king."

And, High King of all the lands between the seas, I watched them come, bitterly, for then I knew the cost. Seeing me, that I was whole, not slaughtered, they raised a cry. But I saw as clearly that there were many, rising at their backs, who were not men at all, though those of Ormkill, their faces on me, saw them not. Yet for a moment I put it by.

When I had come down she was beside me, close at my heels, inside my shadow. Yet when I stepped upon the level ground, before the soldiers, she would not follow. Without a word or cry she halted. Her gown was shining. I saw the wonder that filled men's eyes. Seeing it, I turned. I thought, no man need know that I have slept with her nor who she is.

"Come," I said so all men heard it. "Among my people you shall be an honored guest. With your hand you gave them to me. Where I rule, no hand shall be raised except to give you welcome."

There was silence, for suddenly all the torches gave little light. The wood beyond had crowded closer to their backs. The Mound rose brooding over them. Uneasy, the soldiers would not look at one another. I looked and saw Thigg standing by himself, his barons far from him. His eyes were hollow. Where once there had been cleverness, now there was only fear.

"Will you not welcome her?" I said aloud to him.

I did not wait to hear him answer but turned once more to Géar, my sister. "Why do you wait?" I asked.

Keeping my eye between her and the soldiers, I saw too late that Thigg was not alone. A woman stepped out from behind his back. I knew her. Her gray eyes looked straight into mine.

"Where is the old woman, lord?" she asked. She had not used the word before. By her look I saw that she acknowledged me, flesh of her flesh, now lord of all these lands. But what else she saw in me I could not tell.

"Dead," I answered.

She watched me with her gray-green silent eyes. There were no tears on her lashes, yet it seemed she pitied me and perhaps herself as well. If fate had been my master, it was hers. Bound with oaths to him that fathered me, she had severed her last children. Unmoved, even then, she sent one child away to keep the other, though both were crying in her ears. So she had cast lots and bartered with her gods. When the lots fell, she did what they decreed. And now we met. Tabak had said it. What was taken away now came back. Though when he spoke, it had not seemed a curse.

"Dead," I answered back once more.

Her face was quiet. She said, "Then she is bound to stay on this same hill."

I would not have it so. "What is the cause?" I shouted.

It was Géar that answered, dry-eyed, one woman like another. "There has always been a witch upon the Mound. It cannot change." Her face was fixed and proud, red where the sun's first rays had touched it. The dawn wind played in her raven hair.

"Lord," she added softly, "when I took her life I knew I traded mine. To keep your life I bartered it, one life for another. I knew when it was done I would wait upon the Mound. I do not fear it now." Looking down at me

187

she smiled. "Nor will I be alone. Autumn will turn this island's wood to flame when you are gone. Yet though I burn with it, I know the winter comes. It is a sea wind that blows the snow. So I shall think of you. And when the winter's over, I shall have a son. Only you must not come for him. But I shall send him to you when he is grown. In all things save only one he will be your equal. So among all men you will know him."

She turned her head, her crow's hair drifting behind her like a cloak. A red line traced the rim of the wood. The new sun, lifted above the trees, fell red upon the great stones that ringed the Mound. Her head raised, her eyes unblinking, she saw what I alone had seen and beyond that something more. Her face changed then.

"One thing you must promise me," she said, her voice made cold. "You must tell him that he may never rule upon the land. It is only you I love, even to the world's end. For should our son, seeking to be king, come here to meet the witch upon the Mound, in truth, my fair lord, our son will find her."

Her shoulders, strained taut, fell suddenly. She closed her eyes. Already there were feathers sprouting in her hair.

"Even in the sun," she murmured, "this day is cold." Her head dropped to her knees. When once more she lifted it, I saw the flashing beak, the eyes that were no longer woman's eyes. The Mound was still. The soldiers sank away, afraid to move.

"Géar," I whispered.

It was a crow's fierce cry that answered me. For one brief moment I caught her mind, felt before I lost her the sudden sweep of earth beneath her wings.

From the host of men there came a roar. Now that she who frightened them was gone, they surged forward, terrible and brave. I would not look at them.

"Woman," I cried above their shouting, "from the first you knew, even as Tabak did. Together, knowing, you sent me here to lie with her."

Even above the noise she heard me. Though the men shrieked I heard her sigh. "Who would you be mated with?" she cried. "Never since the world was young were any born upon the land as both you are, sea-made and of the ancient blood. Would you have squandered your seed on some land wife, made more brats whose only life was scratching ground and breaking stone?"

She stared up at my sun-racked face. She drew a long, slow breath and loosed it. "On land, my lord, there was no other fit to bear your son."

I spat, angered again to hear the lie. "I was born upon the land," I cried. "On a mountain, the land about me everywhere I looked."

Yllvere unlaced her knotted hands, quietly as though some old worry had been put aside. "You are your father's son," she said. There was a kind of triumph in her sea-gray eyes, a look that only women have, holy, deeper than her single life, as though a patience, old before her birth but passed to her, had born its fruit at last. "And he the last great Selchie of the Western Sea, found when we had thought that all were lost. Found though he was dying even then and may be dying still. (For the wild old seamen went ever slow to death.) But it was I that found him while life he had. I bore him children, the old blood in me yet. Though lessened, it had come down from my mother, when it was stronger, and from my mother's mother, when it was whole, unmixed with the coarse blood of the little men who live on land. Now our children will bear a son, the old blood new in him. Now the sea road that was closed shall open and my son's son shall walk the green halls undersea."

Amazed, my eye fixed on her slender hands hanging free outside her gown. Long I had wished those hands had held me. I would not wish it more. I lifted my eye to meet her own.

"Your son's son," I murmured, the sound of my voice grown bitter in my ears. "Not who I was, nor what I did, nor whether I'd be king."

"King?" she echoed as though the word had caught her by surprise. She stared beyond me to the summit of the Mound, as though she struggled to recall what happened there. "Are there not kings enough?" she asked. Her voice was low.

"He you treasured above all else was king," I said. "High King over all these lands."

She broke in, puzzled, uncertain, it seemed, of what I guessed or knew. Doubtless she had thought I should have taken more from what she said. "He was only king a little while," she said. "Soon enough they drove him from the hall he raised, contemptuous little men not knowing what they saw. An army he had never sought to gather traveled at his back. Though he never looked for them, they followed him, an immense black-whiskered mighty man, the sea mist still steaming from his hair. All spring and summer they tramped behind him. They were gleeful when he murdered barons, thankful when he made the laws. Though he barely gave a thought to them.

"But winter came. Indoors they saw he would not sit before the heat of their bright fires nor eat their cooking. Instead he would have black eels and pale white squid brought up from far sea towns. When they saw his jaw had swollen and his dark eyes, wanting salt, turn yellow in the air, their welcome changed to grins of fear. Then they muttered in their dirty holes, huddled close beside their fires and thought again of the oaths they'd made. Then, in secret, the barons he had not killed plotted how to drive him forth.

"King? My lord, your father did not come ashore to rule. The last of what he was, he came ashore to breed and die. He looked for nothing else. He ruled because he found it there to do. In that only perhaps he was as other men, needful of some work to fill his days. And so he ruled, careless, but wiser than any lord that went before. But when he had fathered you, he was done with little men and done, I knew as well, with women too. He dragged himself to some high place where he could watch the ocean and the sky. There he waits, keeping to one place, that death may find him at the last."

She shook her head. "King," she cried out one last time. "My lord, do you think that such a father would leave his son so miserly an inheritance?"

And there it was.

The words that she would never say, now freely spoken, said before all the hosts of Ormkill, my father's people, though if she were to be believed, they were not his folk at all and the kingship was nothing.

The sun poured down emptily upon the world. I looked. On every side there stretched away the land, first the meadow, then the wood, an island broad enough so that I had wandered it and lost my way. Yet one bright river bounded it all. If that were so, the vast realm I sought to rule, its ranging swamps and rampart mountains, its men and cities and circling birds, what more was it but another scrap of earth between the seas? I groaned with the ache of my own smallness. I felt bereft.

I had dreamed of sitting in my father's chair in a hall he raised upon a hill, a girl with raven hair at my right hand. For all its worth I might have stayed within my room at Morrigan, walking the little space between my bed and fire. From the beginning the Kell had no patience with such little dreams. They wanted oceans and the rough wet touch of wild seamen, huge when they came to land, great-whiskered, webbed in feet and hands, large as the old gods, men whose salt blood festered in the air, whose flesh, brown and glistening beneath the waves, swelled and rotted in the sun. Such a man my father was, and I, if Yllvere at last were to be believed, the same.

Too late I knew the High King's shame and why the landsmen rose against him. Yet, I knew, these very men, their sons with them, flesh of their small flesh, would follow me unquestioningly. When I had walked from the river, new and huge upon their streets, there had been many, even then, ready to name me king. Now down from the Mound, seeing the wonder in their faces, I was king to them indeed. King at least for as long as the land shape held. Until, if I were to believe her, my smooth skin blistered, crusted over with dull scales, or sprouted tusks or whatever bogie shape fell to me. King, though it was nothing in her eyes. I sucked my wounds and lifted up my arms.

All at once I was aware of the hosts of Ormkill standing at my feet. Their bodies tense, sword bright in each small hand, they waited to see what I would do. It was clear that they made nothing of what I asked Yllvere or what she answered. To them it was all wonder and gibberish and women changing into birds. I stared out among their faces. Only two stared boldly back at me or saw my pain.

"You are faithful yet, old ffraw," I said. And to the second, "It is not yet finished, man of Bede. Though you came to me early, still you must go on waiting."

"I do not understand you, lord," Ceorl answered. His face was sad. Like ffraw he was no longer young. Together, having sworn to me, they had tramped the wilds of the realm between the seas seeking where I would be found. But when they found me, I had gone off again. A thin wind blew over the field, from behind the host where no man looked. Ceorl sniffed the air. There was something in it he did not like.

I strode forward, coming away from the Mound. The soldiers parted. I reached out my long arm to Ceorl.

"It is not yet time for me to rule," I said. "There is one thing more that I must know, one place more that I must go."

His gray lips tried to smile. But I saw he felt himself unjustly used. He had left his own folk to serve a king. So in truth had most men there, journeying from Ormkill, eager either to see my corpse or, if my claim were honest, deliver up a crown. Then seeing me whole and walking from the Mound, the kingship won, it had been in their mouths to cheer. In their hearts were great oaths ready to be sworn. Since first light they had waited. Now filled, they were about to burst. But the business with the women got in the way. Their eyes narrowed. For Ceorl it went deeper. He had waited longer, given up more. I saw him shiver. The blood drained from his face.

Once more I broke the quiet.

"Hear me, each of you," I shouted to the host. "Hear me and bring back my words to Ormkill, to Stephen's Well, to old red Hwawl, wheresoever men dwell in the land, to the greatest and the least of towns. I name my Stewards, ffraw and Ceorl of Bede, jointly in my place. Serve them. They will keep the peace. Lest any man among you grumble, know it is their word I shall hear and none beside when I come back to rule."

The soldiers stirred. There were questions in their eyes, in some bewilderment, in others fear. And none were more bewildered or afraid than the two that I put over them. Yet the eyes of the barons were empty, even as mirrors are, casting back the world they saw and nothing of themselves. But I could guess what thoughts were smoldering in their skulls.

"Two I name to hold the land," I cried. "And the third to hold the two and give them counsel, her word first, even over theirs." Then I named her, Yllvere, my mother, she who had set the order of Morrigan, its orchards and its fields, whose word in the wild North among her women was as near the law as any, whose cunning, I doubted not, was sharper than that of even the most thoughtful of the barons. The soldiers heard me. The name took all their sight. Blind and mute they stood like men who have seen the sun, bright overhead, devoured by the moon, amazed, as if a moth, instead of burning, ate the flame. Only she looked up at me.

"You dare much," she said softly, though the sound was in all men's ears.

"You care so little for the land that it is safe from you," I answered.

She drew a breath. "You go to him?"

"When you will say the place."

She smiled, though even then her mouth was frowning at the edge. I saw her longing, old and unassuageable. Much of what my father was I would never know. Yet, before the rest, it came to my mind, whether in glory or in folly, he was her lover and had lain with her. Once his heart had cried her name. And she, whatever now she had become, had answered him.

Her eyes had a strange glitter. "He has gone to Hren," she said. "Back to that high place where first he came to land." She made some motion with her slender hand, tentatively as if she meant almost to take it back. "Lord, you know it. It is the place where Urien slew Lot and won our house for thanks. Still, you dare not go there lightly or alone."

"I do not go alone," I said.

She shook her head. "There no men will follow you."

"They are not men I call," I answered. "Or do you forget, lady, what it is you made me?" She gave no answer.

I had in my hand the sword that Géar had given me. New-made, it had never gone through the belly of a man. Yet it shone red as copper when I lifted it, as though the very air could bleed.

The wind blew. And on it suddenly, when the sword was flashed, the thunder of heavy feet came to the host. The soldiers shivered when they heard the sound. Those who turned saw them first, the tall shapes black against the wood. But those too frightened to move their heads, their faces frozen, the next moment saw them nonetheless. Huge and moving from all sides, like an avalanche that walks on level ground, the stones of Ar Elon's ring tramped toward the Mound.

Gray old faces were carved and pitted in the rock. Though they were men no longer, yet they had the look of kings. Their rumbling voices were borne across the field, roaring, tongueless, without words—an empty soulless noise like gravel drawn by tides along a beach. The true men caught at their ears with the pain of it. Yllvere only did not shudder at the sound.

"These will be my companions," I said to her. Perhaps she heard me above the sound. She smiled. Years later, when I came east, inland from where I had put to shore along the coast, they told me she was dead. Nine years she had ruled the folk of Ormkill then and all the lands between the seas.

IV.
Hren

18.

THEY WERE NOT LIKE THE STONES OF MENHIR. Those stones were thrust out of the earth like crusted fingers, raised out of the grass like dead men's hands. Those stones were soldiers, but soldiers who had grown unmindful of their guard. So long had they been rooted in their place that some had fallen and all but one had forgotten speech. They were the ruin of ages already passed. If they once had had names, those were forgotten. Men had lost track of who they were. Save for the one who waited, their eyes were closed. The stones of Ar Elon's ring were not the same. Their hard eyes bright as garnets, they had kept their watch upon the Mound, tireless, one year to the next since Ar Elon set them there.

No weeds grew at their feet. The thyme and thorn grass, which throughout the field lay thick and deep, here curled back before them, the young runners trampled in the earth. Once each moon the great stones breathed. So R'gnir told me, he that was foremost of the nine who came with me. We walked beneath the oak shade, the men of Ormkill already at our backs. His voice was gentle, like a mist escaping from the ground.

"Long we had been dead when Ar Elon called us forth," he said. "Even our bones were cracked and gone. Still we remembered our own names, for the earth remembers when even men forget. But he, though ocean born, had heard them. Night after night he called to us until we could not keep from listening. For, know this, lord, the dead are sad and long to be remembered. Hearing our own names again, his voice insistent, still warm with life, though there was nothing left of us, we came. He remade us then of what we had become, with arms of granite, nails of slate. From the mountain's core he cut our hearts. Speaking to the stone, he quickened it."

Remembering, he sighed. He was old. He set down his broad rough furrowed feet, one after the other, sluggishly. He compelled each to move. The land shook under him like the beat of his slow heart. Yet in all this neither pain nor bitterness rose to his thick face. Anger leaches from the oldest dead, I thought, till they are free.

Behind us I heard the men of Ormkill shouting, a storm of anger broken out among them. Already several of the barons were barking orders of their own. I heard Thigg call his name, then Yllvere's voice lifted over it. My heart was too full of other things. I was glad I could not hear her words. The tumult rose. It would be no easy thing to master those of Ormkill. Yet at the start, the sight of walking stones would linger in their eyes. I trusted to their fear, that with the strands of it she might weave her rule.

This time I did not lose my way within the wood. The road I had come to last through wandering I followed now. The nine, advancing slowly with their heavy gait, swept the low scrub before them and trampled the smaller trees. Nine came. The rest, many times that number—for among them were all the generations of kings since men first walked on land—still kept their watch upon the Mound. The old witch was gone, but they knew another had taken her place. I thought of the black-eyed girl who had walked beside me through the wood. Her neck was white as the inside of a shell. What filled her head, I wondered, when she saw me go?

The sun stood fully overhead when we came out from beneath the trees. We found the shore and there the great ship as I had left it, rocking in the current. A crowd of lesser boats were drawn up on the stony edge of land. So the soldiers and their barons had come to the place. Scarcely a dozen men had been left behind to guard the craft. They fell back groaning when they saw what moved among them, their mouths gaping, drooling in their beards with fear. I forgot them as soon as they had slunk from sight. The river knocked at the great ship's hull.

"Great as that ship is," I said, "it will not carry you."

R'gnir turned his gray face from the water. "You are still thinking like a man," he said. With a long unwinking stare he watched me. It may be that he laughed, but it was hard to tell. "We shall walk beneath the river, lord. And when we have made the other bank we shall walk beside you as you said. Though we are slow of step, we do not tire. When you must sleep, we shall not stop to rest." He stood a moment. "Together we shall come to rocky Hren. That much was promised. It cannot be forsworn."

Too many oaths had been sworn this day, I thought. Some must break or, if not, their keeping was beyond my understanding. "Men lie," I answered him. "I have seen great oaths melt before a moment's anger."

R'gnir grumbled. "The oaths men make have only a man's strength in them. He that swore we would go down to Hren was not a man. His oath will hold."

That was the last speech I had with him before he set his feet within the river. The water lapped about his knees. He walked. The river leapt up to his chest. The other kings went after; their going lashed the water into foam. Then I was left alone upon the bank.

Shortly, I knew that I must go myself. For a moment, unhurriedly, I stood gazing out across the world. The wind was blowing upriver, from the south. There was a breath of salt upon it. Behind me the greenwood was still. Beyond the trees, hidden at the island's heart, I knew the little men of Ormkill still argued about the stewards I had put over them. In my mind's eye I saw Yllvere, her hair like white gold lifted in the wind, her gray eyes terrible and deep. ffraw and Ceorl were with her, the last of the me I knew. I feared for them and for the promises I had made. More I feared the child, growing in the belly of a woman I barely knew, my sister. Her dark eyes stared at me, her lips moved faintly with words I could not hear. The women of the world are one, I thought, all born of the same dark womb. How then, I wondered, are all their children strangers? I had come to the river's edge, alone.

The Undain groaned. Feeling the sandy bottom with my feet, I waded into the black water. I walked as the kings had walked before me. The cold rose through my loins and clamped a ring around my heart. The bottom fell away. Nor shall I touch the land again, I thought, until I rest on rocky Hren. To no man I swore it, but to myself. I floated from the land, a disembodied head. The river murmured. A tender, agitating scent rose to my nostrils. Shivering with the cold, I knew it, crow-black anl streaming, the scent of sea hair shining on my shoulders. I dropped my head beneath the waves. Huge before me, the hull of that great ship rocked overhead.

She bore me.

The river wound through the glad green heart of the land. The hedgerows at the river's edge were rife with birds. Deer drank in the shallows. The soft wind rippled the face of the water, then, unthinking, lost its breath, stilled by the long green summer's peace. The sails hung slack. I drifted south, my only work as steersman at the oar. One day yielded to the next. Each nightfall was pierced with brilliant stars, each morning fair, the great sun golden at its height.

When I hungered, I moored the ship north of some neck of land or cast the anchor in the stillness of a wooded cove, a green bluff over me. There in cold pools I dove for eels and dug blue mussels with my fingers from the rock. At night I stared hard across the shadows to the beach. Before dawn the old kings passed, their shields and armor of rough stone, glittering dully in the moon's eye. Steathfully they went, keeping to the thick, dripping grayness of the trees lest they raise alarm among the farms. Yet men could not help but hear the terror of their passing—the shaking earth, the thunder of old trees uprooted on their way. Afraid, none ventured forth. But in the day they went and found the tall hills beaten down. Along the river the deep old wood was tossed to either side and splintered, the very earth stones crushed. So a way was cleared between Tinkern and the sea. The King's Road, it was named in later days when I sent my *filidh* out to spread the tale. But the hearts of the farmers could not be moved. To them and to their children it was the Witch's Walk, for the marvel fell in the first year when Yllvere was mistress of the land. So even to this day the wrong name is better known, though I have taken care to mention it before the court. Even there I have seen the younger barons smile behind their hands. The king grows old, they say among themselves. You little men. I whisper in my beard, you would have crawled back screaming to your mothers' wombs rather than see what I have seen. The young men and I watch each other uneasily across the floor stones of my hall. Yet when rain drums hard against the roof and thunder growls outside the doors, they are quick enough to look and see whether it is the gods or else their king whose anger shakes the earth.

If there is weather for sails, it is not over far from Tinkern to the sea. But there was no wind. The great ship, that which was sent, Pendyved boasted, so as to hurry me, lagged in the south's damp bottom lands where the banks are leagues to either side. The moon pared down. I grew uneasy with hunting eels or sitting the sunlong on the golden deck with only the phantoms of my thoughts for company. Yet each day I felt the tides' tug more. I learned t o count the hours till it turned and marked how it advanced. All day the water sucked at the hollow weeds along the shore. Then there was nothing but myself and the lonely piping of white birds. Seeming incorporeal and bleached of life, like nothing I had seen before, they wheeled and cried above the marshes at the river's edge. I thought them souls of drowned men come upriver from their deaths, drifting back from the immense oceans of the South and West, the seas too huge to ease their pain. At night my dreams were haunted by the bark of seals.

With each day I thought of Ar Elon more. I am the seed, I thought, that he left growing in a woman while he wandered. I winced, a coldness creeping toward my heart. Even so I abandoned Géar, my sister, and the child she carried. A bastard and a bastard's son. So the threads of the weave are drawn together on the loom. In my anger I clawed a sign in the empty air. The sickly yellow flame rained down upon the deck. It reminded me only that I was as much Kell as I was his. I swore, crying out to Duinn, he that rules the dead. My words fled out across the water's waste. The smudge of far hills did not send them back. The river kept them. Together we fell toward the gulf.

One night there was a squall. In the morning the river had turned more green and salt than I had seen. The tide ran fuller at the flood. Now the banks rose boldly in the west. There old towers leered from promontories, a line along the rock like broken teeth. At the mouths of creeks that fed the wash I saw small boats pulled up along the stones. But no men came. If the villages had dogs, the men killed them or drove them to safety in the wood. At night there were no fires. That year the herring tax went unpaid, for the sailors let their pitched keels dry upon the banks and stayed at home, idle and afraid to follow in my path. The sea was cursed, they said, wheresoever I had passed. It may have been so. Either way their children starved for it.

When next I woke I heard the sea waves crashing on

the shore. Sitting up, I saw the brave wide ocean fill my sight. I rubbed my eye. It was not a thing I knew. Huge, it rolled in from the world's end or beyond. Panting with exhausted breath, it heaved its thousand torpid arms against the coast, went slack and, groaning, heaved itself again. Yet away from the land it seemed unmoved. My eye sought its farthest boundary. With nothing to contain it, I wondered why it did not drain away. Resting on nothing, yet it held—vast and unsupported, the heaven's mirror. Before it I felt poor and fugitive, no better than those small men who fled from me, leaving their houses in order to hide among the stones. When I breathed again, my breath rasped in my ears like something tearing.

In the afternoon the sky turned heavy, battered by the wind. I kept the great ship moored in the lee of an island at the river's mouth. There all day I sat and watched the harbor town, empty of its folk. Hren was north along the coast, no river journey. In truth, I feared the passage on the open sea, feared it as any man will fear a great thing which he has never done. Then I cursed the river folk. Had they not fled, I would have walked among them and bidden the bravest come with me and man the sails. It was many days since I had seen the shapes of R'gnir and the kings tramping the hills west of the river. By then, I judged, they had turned north themselves. No counsel would I have from them, nor comfort either.

Unsettled, I saw to some small matters on the ship, for I had taught myself to keep the sail lines free and the great ropes coiled. The day wore on. I looked up when I had done. A line of thunderheads had massed above the town, casting purple shadows on the rock. Lightning leapt among the clouds; thunder bellowed but there was no rain. Still the water foamed, churned white as milk within a pail. It was while I was watching, impatient to be setting out, afraid to go, that I saw the webbed brown fingers reach out of the spray, become whole hands with shining nails, reaching because they did not need to grope, knowing from the first where they would find the mooring line. The head came after, old and ugly, pointed, as if pressing against the tide had narrowed it. Its rough blunt teeth were bared. Its harsh breath sucked the air. Sea hair, black and green, clung to its shoulders. Fixed on where I stood, it gave me as deep a glance as I have ever had from beast or man. Then, throwing back its head, it climbed the rope effortlessly and in a moment flung itself upon the deck. I saw then what it was.

He smiled.

"Well met again, my lord," he said.

But it was not that the beast knew man speech that astounded me. Crows talk and even boulders grumble. It was that he had smiled. Black leather lips pulled back from yellow teeth. The fierce lips turned. So now and then, when I most hated her, Yllvere had smiled. It was nothing I understood. I would not have been more amazed if at the earth's deep core, beneath the bones of mountains, I had found a stone that bore my name.

The arms were short. Still I took care to stay beyond their reach. The mad wild eyes, like the teeth, were yellow.

"If we have met," I said, "I do not know it."

"Lord, the moon long I swam beneath the river's roof, and now at the sea edge the salt has tangled all my hair. For, lord, until I spied your ship I had not tasted the sweet air since I leapt the wall that rings that city where Ar Elon ruled." He turned his whiskered head. Where the hair was pulled back and plastered wet against his neck, I saw no ear but only a knob of darkened flesh, much like a seal's. He scratched the place with his shining nails.

"You are . . . ," I started, "or were," I stammered, "Fyris, whose song brought the Steward's anger. Once a man . . ." But seeing it was so, I stopped.

His sly mouth crooked. "Who drowned?" The clever undead eyes looked deep into mine. "The sea knows what shape best suits the things that dwell in it," he said. "For myself, as the sea willed, I am what pleases me."

I shook my head. My pulse beat strangely and my long face burned. I said, "I have not found that a man might be what he desires."

Absently he found another place to scratch along his flank. "Lord," he barked, the words whistling through his teeth, "you have forgotten how the gods first pitied Tân and changed him. He was fire and the maid he wanted mist and ice. You know they did not leave him as he was for all men now alive come down from him. We are not pitied less because we are his sons. There is a vessel for all that burns. Out of Dagda's pity. Else the world long since would have gone up in flames." An old gentle laugh came from his lips. "Even the heart of Ar Elon's son, cursed as it was blessed, was not made too small to beat."

Out of the cramped space in the clouded sky a rain-washed moon gazed down.

"Mark," he said. "The moon long I have waited under-sea, the wide ocean rotting the shape I wore till I had found another. For I meant to be here when you came, to sail this ship, as you could not, that at the last you should come to Hren."

From off his shoulder he drew a satchel. With care he opened the flap that sealed it from the sea. I saw the carved neck of a harp. He drew it out and laid it on his knees.

A shadow gathered in his face. The lips, that at first had been open as he thought, now came together in a line, haggard, bloodless. I had seen that look before but could not place it. He shifted restlessly. When he had drawn a breath, he ran a thumb softly across the strings. And then he played, the harp notes wheeling into the night like birds.

Listening, I drew the anchor. He played the song again. Unslackened, persistent, its music filled the bay. The song was as wind to the sails. Like cool air out of the north it filled them. The bow nosed out beyond the skerry, free of the harbor and the empty town. Beyond the headlands the moon rode to our left, silver in the heaven's darkness, green silver in the darkness of the sea.

My life was still. It was the sea that held it, not myself. I had known such times before, when Pendyved took me, when I had looked into the fire. Surely, I felt some piece of my life was coming to a close. I felt it gathering at my back, ready to be cast behind. Yet I was helpless to send it on its way. I studied the *filidh*'s face, a man's no longer, trying to guess where his mind was when he played. But he had little time for me. His song consumed him. When he stopped, the great ship floundered. So morning and evening he played upon the strings.

The second day we went beyond the sight of land. I had slept beneath an awning on the deck. When I woke and looked there was nothing but low clouds far off to show where land had been. The third day the sea was all around.

"Why do we come out so far?" I asked. "Hren lies north and close upon the shore."

The *filidh* stared out to things I could not see. For a moment he ceased his song. "If you would live, you must come on it from the west, even as Ar Elon did," he said.

"The stone kings come by land," I answered.

"They are already dead," he replied and went back to his song.

The fourth day he did not play at all. The wind that was not heaven's wind died out. He took my place beneath the awning. Long into the day he slept. Asleep, I grew less certain of the shape of him. A mist had risen about the ship and mantled his features. He was not so small as he had seemed, I thought. From behind the blankness of the mist I heard the droning labor of his breath. Once, when he had turned, an arm fell long across the deck. But of his head, laid back against the mast, whether it too was changed, I could see nothing. The mist withheld it. It was as though I looked into a wall of vaporous wool.

For a long time there was silence. The sea lay sleek and flat as any mountain pond. I ranged the ship. The fifth day dawned without the sun. I leaned, exhausted, against the rail. The eye that I had lost was sick with pain.

Soft drops, thickened from the fog, fell from the rigging. It was so still I heard them splash into the sea. I heard them sink, one drop among the million, one lucid sound in the huge monotonous quiet of the deep.

I was never certain when I slept. Waking, I would pretend that I was backing into sleep once more. The sky held the same gray emptiness whenever I awoke. I prayed for rain, for sun, for darkness, for the whales that lived beneath to rise and batter the great hull with their looming heads.

I reckoned it was three days more.

The first sound cracked the stillness like a goblet broken by a stone. It was distant, yet it seemed to roar. In time it grew still louder in my ears, until I knew it was the crash of waves upon a beach.

The great wave bore me up along the wall and then fell back. The ship ran down into the dip between the water hills. I cried out. For when it rose again—the great mist shredded like a cloth—I saw the rough blue stones of Morrigan. Tall elms ringed the yard. Grieve stood among the others, my sisters, aunts, Vydd bent upon her staff. Yllvere came walking from among the trees, her deep eyes distant and chill as stars. The red gates of morning opened. I looked upon the women of the house.

"Where is Géar?" I asked them.

But when I had said her name she came. Her black hair drifted behind her like a cloak. I held my hands to her but, the sea between us, we could not touch. All I had known of her came back and so I yearned for her. She would not meet my eye. Cradled in her arms she carried a dark-haired quiet child. For a moment, the silence between us hung like a wave.

No, I thought, there is yet no child. It is not long since I left her.

"The water brings me dreams," I said aloud.

From behind, the brown hand with its black nails had clasped my shoulders, and I turned. The ambiguity of his shape and features had gone, had settled back into the form I had seen on him when first he sprang out of the sea.

"Not dreams, lord," he said. "The sea is too big to care about your life or mine. You cannot scar it like the land. Your dreams are lost in it."

Still I looked straight across to the women, cool under the trees, standing on the emerald grass and looking back. The child woke. I heard him cry.

"Do you not see?" I asked.

He answered bluntly. "Each man licks the wounds he has," he said. "So the tongue comes back to what it cannot cure."

I waited till the wave had borne me up once more along the wall. The house was so near to me I might have knocked upon the doors. For a moment I came level with her eyes. For that instant I looked into their depths.

"What will you name the child?" I said.

Behind her, small beside my sisters, Vydd, old and bent and leaning on her stick, had parted her dry lips. But only the gray smoke of her pipe came through her teeth. I knew then I would have no answer. She had kept such a secret once before. The deep fevered current of her blood she shared with Géar. I felt my own shared blood grow cold. For if the women of the house were one, so were the men. I had begun to shiver. I knew, like Urien, that now for long years I must seek a name that would not be given. For all it changes, the wise *filidh* only know one song. All men must sing it. I thought of Ar Elon then, for that once without bitterness, knowing at the last that the fathers are as much cursed as their sons.

Beside me the seaman hunched his shoulders,

coughed. I pulled my eye away from her. I watched. He waited. The wind was fitful between the rough sea hills.

"We have stayed too long," I said. "Take up your harp."

He had it waiting.

So out of the west, the open sea, where nothing is but mist and water hills, I came to Hren. So Ar Elon came to shore, over the long blank sea to that same place, though no ship carried him.

19.

THE AIR WAS STILL. THE GRAY SEA WAS QUIET as an old woman. Softly, it muttered half-remembered grudges to itself, grudges so old that no man has heard of them.

In the light of morning the walls of the island rose above the sea, a hundred elhws of blue-gray stone. At its crown the oak wood, lifted high from the sea edge, blazed red with autumn. I stared at it with a half-lidded, exhausted eye. The tide was sliding in. I had not slept. The long way in, I had stayed awake listening to the ocean's old complaint and with it, in even measure, the *filidh*'s song till they rose and fell together and I scarcely parted them. Yet I knew that gaunt old seaman sang his own deep grief and not the sea's. Drab he seemed and sullen as his song was sad, like some cross and jilted lover. Yet at the last I knew all grief was one. It is the same bare cup whether it had been spilled or never held the wine.

He paused in his thumbing. His forehead wrinkled. He seemed to examine the wedge of land thrust up from the sea. "That island stood before the land beyond it rose," he said. "The trees that grow there grew in the world's first light. Their roots reach down to the oldest darkness that was before."

The crease in his eyelids pulled as though with some

subtle pain. "Under those old trees, knowing that the darkness gnaws them both, Ar Elon waits and listens."

The west wind rose as though it meant to drive us on the shore. It stung my cheek. It angered me.

"What does he think to hear?" I scoffed. He felt it in my look. I had heard too many tales and was tired of riddling. Inside each shell was always another shell, no kernel. I had come myself. I meant no more to listen to what any man or bogie guessed or thought. I spat into the sea.

The seaman grunted and looked up at the sky.

"I will put you ashore beneath the wood," he said. "There a path leads from the beach. If you can follow it, in time you will find a wall. Within the wall there is a gate such as a man might pass through, though I never heard that any man came back again. If you pass it, you will find a beast your father keeps but which, in his keeping it, keeps him. It is this beast that you must come to, if ever you will look on him or see Ar Elon as he is."

The seaman hesitated, peering into my face as if only then a thought had come to him. "Lord," he said, "you have lost an eye."

The old itch welled up in my throat. "It was my father bartered it," I said, the old anger new again. "What was never his he gave to buy his glory."

There were white birds above the island, crying out. If he answered, the words were lost beneath their cries.

The swells were heavy. Rushing in, they roared when we came near the rocks. A great wave broke above the bow. It swung the ship. The seaman put his hand behind my back.

"Jump," he shouted and with one motion pushed me. Too startled to take a breath, I fell. The green-black water hissed about my head. Yet my first thought was not for air. Franzied, I clutched my belt to feel the new-made sword that Géar had given me. At last I felt the pommel in my hand. Smiling then, I gave a mighty kick and rose through spray and bubbled foam.

All was quiet but for the water and the wind. The great ship rested idle beyond the breakers; light as a cork it took the swells. Already its sails were down upon the deck. But the seaman whose work that was had gone. I called to him. No answer came.

Wet and steaming, I walked out on the beach. Sitting

on the stony shore where once Urien slew Lot and won
his house and all that followed, I emptied my boots. It
was not a triumphant coming. Yet there were none to
see how the king of the lands between the seas stripped
the tangled waterweed out of the greater tangle of his
hair. I dug a little yellow crab out of my beard. Sharp as
the crab's pinch, a thought came back to me. Even as I
came to Hren, so I had entered my father's city, looking
more like a crowned sailor than his heir. But then I
thought, my rightful inheritance never was the land but
rather the whale's deep, weed and yellow crabs. I laughed.

Above the cliff edge, sharp against the heavens, the
island's ancient wood reared over me. From those trees,
I knew, the charmed wood of the ship was cut. There
Lord Ar Elon waited, he that had waked Pendyved from
the dead, that had set the stone kings around the Mound
at Tinkern, slaughtered barons and built a hall greater
than any in the land, its corners posted with the hearts
of those that hated him. Along the deeds, remembered
and forgotten, both great and small, he found a woman,
already wife of a man who followed him, and lay with
her. When he had done with her, he never saw her more.
I wondered. She herself had said his kingdom on the
land was nothing in his mind. Had she been more? By
what they were, the Kell would take such matters seri-
ously. Yet I could not think what pressed his thoughts
that night he took what gladly she had given him. My
heart beat thickly. I wondered if, when I had seen him,
I would know his mind. I rose. Standing by the sea edge,
I looked toward the wood.

A path ran clearly from the upper beach, winding back
and forth into the rock. Well worn it seemed, great boulders cast aside, the sand scraped down to the rock beneath. I thought, they were not men who passed here.
For I knew the track of R'gnir and the kings. I did not
wait for the sun to dry me, but went then as I was and
with some effort came up at last upon the headlands.

Beyond the rock, the air was filled with the whisper
of the leaves. Yet this was but the lesser wood, where
saplings grew beside great oaks. Whatever grew here,
from the first green shoot, was gnarled in the sea wind
as the slow years turned. In time each rotted through
and fell. Here as in the towns of men were birth and ruin,
both gathered in one place. Had I stayed at Morrigan, I
would have lived just such a life and gone to death at last

like any man. One day I would have dug a pit for Urien's bones. In turn, others, my sons if I had had them there, would have opened up the earth for me. There is no small comfort in that, men say, old men who have learned to smile on Death as women smile at infants in their arms. So I might have been, content to watch my short life measured out. Perhaps it might have suited me had I not, so early, stood above the heads of other men or had there never been in Anu's wood above the house a tree whose black leaves whispered, though never one leaf, not in the world's time, fell.

I left the little mortal wood behind.

Now the bodies of the trees grew thick. Their gray unchanging trunks were hung with tendrils, roped with vines. The path I followed twisted as though it meant to keep out of their reach. No small things grew up beneath their shade. What sunlight filtered through was soft as moonlight, changed. The shifting colors of the earth were muted, silvered, hid. Then even they were gone. I sensed, more than I saw, the steep land rise ahead of me.

When at last I came to it, the wall loomed up like a piece of the dark itself. It gathered there as evening gathers, not built stone by stone; but, rising, it was everywhere at once. Even as I watched it seemed to grow, a high shadow without cleft or stairs, running over the back of the earth to either side. I had no doubt it was the wall the seaman spoke of. Yet he had said a man might find his way beyond it. But everywhere its outward face was sheer, too high to scale. Alone I had no hope to cross it. My eye ran over it but found no end. A man might as well assault the night. For some time I walked along its length. The more I walked, the higher still it reached.

"Though I have sworn it, I see no way to enter here," I said aloud.

"You have done well enough to come," a voice beside me said.

R'gnir pulled his rough shape from the wall. The bare earth buckled as he moved. The stone kings followed at his back. Even in the darkness their shadows fell upon my face. Yet little comfort I took from seeing them.

"What good to come at all if it is closed to me?" I said.

R'gnir answered. "You need only look," he said and pointed.

In truth at that same moment I made out the two great pillars of a gate. A massive lintel lay above. I skirted the shoulders of the wall and went to it. The gate was ancient, black as iron. It shone as of itself. But some strange cunning had fitted it to the wall. There was no handle nor was there any way I could see to enter it. I turned away.

"It has no latch," I said. "Nor are there hinges."

"Nor need it have," he said. "It is Death's gate and so not hard to pass. Since men first lived, more skill was needed to keep this side of it."

I saw the watchful silence of the kings and was not satisfied. Close by me they muttered to themselves, softly, in a language of their own. "How may I know?" I said.

R'gnir answered. "All this day we waited for you," he said. "From the morning, as we stood our watch, a thousand passed. You traveled your own way or you would have met them in the wood, lame men and whole, mere girls limping from their beds. Out of Tyre and Imradis they came. From all the broad lands of the earth they found their way. Not an hour gone, the folk of one great town went on before us. The battle at their gates had passed inside. Their blood had not yet dried upon their necks." His thick old face was sad. "Fear not, lord," he said, "if a man bleeds, he will find a way to enter here."

"And live?" I said. "And still come back?"

He dropped his eyes. "You are in peril. Who is to say that you are not? And yet the one you seek there lives."

My own eye turned from him. It is said a strange stern look had come into my face. But it was only the cold I felt. Though the day was windless, I knew the leaves were falling in the world I had left. At Ormkill now, men sat inside before the fires, their meat in front of them, their great cups filled. But I remembered then, though it was nothing, that I was king. In truth that old woman's flesh still lingered in my mouth. I thought, the price is paid. If I call them, they may not turn aside.

"Who then will come with me?" I said.

R'gnir moved. His face was troubled. "Lord," he said, "you do not know how great a thing you ask. For should we cross, our almost-lives would fade, our grisly breath forever locked within this stone."

The old kings stirred. I heard their grating breath. I

saw on them the ancient wounds that Ar Elon had healed, and their old majesty. They were not men. The swords men wielded would only blunt against their sides. Yet in the thing I asked they saw their doom. Their voices gathered. Though I had never heard them, now they spoke.

"Lord," they said, "when we first walked the earth, the land was wet from being undersea. An age has come and gone since then. Now the grass is not so green nor is the moon as bright. But it is grass and nightly there is a moon that rides the air. Lord, there were women in the towns we passed. Though seeing us, they fled; still one looked back, her bare arms tight against her breasts. Her yellow hair was flying as she ran. Lord, you know our hearts are stone. They do not ache to hold our wives as once they did. Our kin and all our gold are gone and we are less. This earth is not the earth we knew. But though it is diminished, it is not the grave." Their icy breath went out of them, rose silently once more and fell.

I searched the troubled shadows of their eyes, grim eyes that still drank in the wonder of the earth. Brave lords they were, not lacking valor, tall as any men that ever walked on land. Yet their dread beat hard against me; like bitter smoke it piled before my eye.

I waited. But now each moment lay like a sword within my hand.

He is so king, the *filidh* say, who cannot send a man to ruin. Yet at the river I sent Ceorl back and old ffraw with him, though they had sworn their lives to me, because I saw they were afraid. These others, I knew, already dead, could not leave their blood upon my hands. I smiled then, a smile that froze my jaw. It is my right, I thought, and raised my head.

But in the wood about the hill I saw once more the darkness of the earth, all the green of it gone, the great sun guttered out. It was R'gnir who saw the turning of my heart. The rest were still; but he stepped out from where they stood. A faint glow of old manhood warmed his face. And yet he was no gentle, easy man. The earth where his old bones had lain still clung to him. The other kings were crowned. Their cloaks, though cut of stone, still shone with gold. His head was bare; his cloak, ill fitted, seemed no more than the stone that fashioned it. His eyes that had seemed to wait behind their lids now smiled.

"Go where you will," I said. "I do not bind you. Let him who wakened you say when you sleep again."

He moved, and it was as though a hill had changed its place, had come to rest before the gate and rooted there. I felt his gaze. His old eyes burned, yet with such a fire as sucks light to itself.

"Though I would not gladly lose this life," he said, "I know there is no way out of dying. So this I promise you. Though I may not follow, I will stand between this world and the next, fast between those posts, so when they open, Death's gate shall not close till you are back again."

I thought to answer but he went on.

"But one thing in return you must promise me. Swear it now, or I shall keep you where you are." The odd fire in his eyes had grown; his beard stood out stiff from his face. It was a shelf of stone. When he stirred, sparks fell from it. I feared him then.

"I will hear the bargain first," I said.

The old king laughed. "Hear it then," he boomed. "Between those gates I am only half my own; the rest is Duinn's. Going, you shall pass the man I am. But coming back you shall not find the man you left."

"What is the price?"

"Returning, you must kill the thing that holds the gate for you."

"I see not what is served by it."

The old eyes had not changed. "We must be even, you and I," he said.

I shook my head. "Between us there is nothing sworn. How can you speak of what is owed?"

"Lord, there are oaths that no man swore and yet they must be kept. Before men lived, Life bargained long with Death. What man, though he is king, can know that price? You, of all men, shall not be free of it."

He closed his eyes. Only then I saw that the length of his great brow was carved with runes and stones of many colors were set in his flesh. Half-seen faces looked out from his hair. Dim with years, they crawled out on his arms. Their hair was braided back for war. Their arms were lifted with bright swords. Jewel-like, each blade dripped blood. Amazed, I looked at him.

His eyes flashed open. I saw the anger gathered at their backs. "There is the gate before you, lord," he said.

Across the space between us I felt his sudden anger

move, unchecked and howling. "Go," he said. "But you must swear to kill me when you are done. Swear it or I shall stalk you through the living world. Nor shall I rest until I eat you whole. Nor shall I stop until I've found your heart's deep stem."

He finished. But there was no stillness. The creatures of his flesh peered out at me. I could not guess the cause. I knew only that it was not just. What was the good of killing him? Had I not seen it? Death never gave back life.

I cried at him, "How can you give and take away at once?"

His gaze fell hard against my face.

"Who shall ever answer you?" he said. "There were never answers to the things you ask. At least no answers that a man will listen to."

"Not everything," I shouted. "Just this thing between us: why should I swear to take your life?"

"What would you hear?" he shouted back. "You take from me that only which I gave."

But I heard him dimly. There was a roaring in my head. I knew only that I must see my father, that R'gnir, whether dead or living, said he was the way to him. Beyond that little, I could work nothing out.

"Swear," he cried.

The faces in the stone king's flesh were screaming in my ears. Still R'gnir's voice roared over them.

"I have not promised to go mildly to my death. Your life, like mine, hangs in the balance. Though I am slow to move, my flesh is stone and you will have to sweat to cut my heart." He laughed. "What after all is the quickness of a boy to me, a boy but scarcely bloodied and half blind? I at least shall fight with two good eyes."

Thus Urien had mocked me.

It was his face I saw among the hundred that haunted R'gnir's flesh. His twisted beard was laid like yellow snow upon his knees. Still his eyes were bright. Their hard gaze had not softened. They mocked me yet.

My anger filled me and I swore.

The stone king moved.

In an instant he had placed himself between the posts. The dread dark gate split wide. Then one last time old R'gnir looked on me. The thin, haggard line of his cold lips was parted. Perhaps he smiled. I took no notice. There was a land beyond the darkness of the wall.

20.

THE GREAT OAKS STOOD APART. THEIR TRUNKS were huge, but their height, crowned with many boughs, could not be judged. If the wind rocked their summits, I could not see it from the ground. It may be that in the upper air they whispered, but the words, whether senseless or deep with cunning, could not be heard. Old beyond the world, what they were men little knew. Such wood had Pendyved cut to build my ship. So old they were, men said, that they had learned to listen to the thoughts of men. Who is to say? It may be that they heard the Kell when the shore folk cursed Pendyved for his work. I did not doubt the Kell had seen the huge trees falling.

The land was high. To the east across the strait, the small towns of the Kell lay huddled on the shore. Beyond them, like an outstretched arm, the cloven mountains that I knew fled north as far as sight could reach. Set somewhere among their piled blue stones was Morrigan; above the house another wood. There I had climbed to see the place where now I stood, not knowing then what place this was, nor the long way I would come to it.

I felt the wind upon my face. Sharp as the world's wind, it brought no peace. I waited. If the dead had walked here, as R'gnir said, their dragging feet should have trampled the heather black and cracked the stone. Yet they left no sign. If they had come, they had walked off in the air. I thought, the dead are so many their kingdom must be broader than the lands of earth. It may be that each man has his own place and this is mine.

I walked beneath the trees. No leaf had fallen, but what had not turned gold was red. Late flowers bloomed in the deep spaces between the trees, a few blue spikes, the rest gray bracken. Already the thistles had had their heads blown off.

It is written that I found the oak wood red as blood as though the island were a corpse I had come to hack. The *filidh* make much of that. They would have it that my thoughts were bloody when I first walked beneath the trees.

The *filidh* never thought ill of a man for murder. In truth, death was their trade and murder what they bartered most. Whether in the narrow gloom of a crofter's hut or in a wide king's hall, it earned their ale. Yet, so often told, it may be that mere death grew tame to them, that the old lord slept and the women went about their work unless the tale was warmed with wonders and the cold moon spouted gore.

But that was not the way of it. The corpse I made there was not for the sake of the year's cold turning, nor the color of the oaks. No unexpected frenzy stirred my blood. I killed for the sake of what I was, had always been. No more. We knew it, he and I. The marvels were a part of it, not added on. It is said the oldest wounds lie nearest the heart. I knew the truth of it. The blood I spilled had been running from my birth.

Where the hill rose steeply I found a path. Old work it was, like the roads that crossed our mountain. It ran due west. Although here and there thick roots had broken through the plates of stone, I made my way. It is not for nothing this is made, I thought. The wind trod with me.

Soon, to either side huge chimneys of blue stone rose up. Close to the track the trees were less, but beyond the stone, dark with ivy on their sides, the ridges rose again, and there the oaks held on against the wind.

I listened. There were birds within the rock. In great ragged flocks they had settled there, clambering in each other's way, squawking and fighting for a place to stand. Their rusty voices scraped the air. Indignant, bitter, their cries were filled with old complaints, old oaths against the wind and rock. Their pale beaks shone, quarrelsome and sharp as knives. I bowed my head, meaning not to look at them. Still I could not keep my eye away. The rock was like the rock that made the walls of Morrigan, its harsh stone blue as the very stone that made the stable wall beside the mews. Leather reins were hanging from the wall, saddles piled up in orderly fashion on the floor. I could not think.

"Do you not know us, brother?" the birds called out to me.

My eye turned back to them. Their feathers were grim and black as holes between the stars. Brokenly they rose and beat the air. I knew them not.

"Brother," they called to me.

I set my teeth and answered stubbornly. "The crows I knew were women and the women crows. Each one was Anu's and none of mine."

Two laughed together, set apart. They flew and hisseed about my head.

"You named me Ninguh," the first crow rasped. "When the snow lay deep upon Géar Finn, I tapped the window till you woke. Cruel the winter was, yet crueler the spell fire was that filled your head."

I knew him then and stiffened. The other flew up by my ear.

"Ninmir you named me. Before you came to Stephen's Well, I went to it, that ffraw would hear your name. For Ar Elon's sake, he swore to you."

Once more I stiffened, for my sight had cleared. The shafts of chimneys grew up with the trees so, when I looked, I saw that the towers and the wood were one. Already doors had opened in the oaks. It would not be strange, I thought, to see the cook, her red cheeks puffing, wrapped against the cold, come ambling into the frozen yard to scatter crumbs, the great birds falling to her feet. I sniffed the air. It seemed dark as the deep kitchens beneath the house, thick with the smell of onions, dried cod and oil. Like salt in wounds the memories of Morrigan washed back on me. I turned away.

"Long has it been since last you came to me," I said.

"Brother, we are dead," they answered.

The air itself was darkening, closing without a flaw upon itself until the oaks, the towers and the sky that held them all were one. I looked into the dark.

"This is not the place I sought," I told them. "Where are the holy wood of Hren and he that rules it?"

The crows came out of the air and sat upon my shoulders. I felt their careful talons on my flesh. Ninmir nuzzled her old beak beside my ear.

"Brother, you have forgotten all you knew," she hissed. "Death walks only where the living went. From the hour of your birth His hounds have licked your heels. How could they follow except where you had gone? It is not otherwise. There is but one earth under heaven, whether the sun has risen or the light has gone from it."

I did not answer. The uselessness of remembering held my tongue. I sought a stranger, Ar Elon, whom I had never seen, not someone I had lost. But this wood was not his wood but Morrigan. These trees were not his trees but towers, their blue stone barren but for the excrement of birds.

"Only tell me where he is," I said.

Her faint breath rattled. "You have had my counsel. The dead have no wisdom for a living man."

I ground my teeth. Like all the Kell, they gave no finished answers but only half-said things that were worse for knowing.

The old anger filled my heart. "Where?" I cried.

She drew a final breath. "Upon the hill there is a mere," she rasped. "There is a beast that waits you there, that beast he keeps. It has not changed. It may be you can make him answer. Yet, brother, how shall you find what you have sought unless, before you looked, you knew what it could be?"

I swore, but she was done. Her drab wing she had folded across her eyes. She shrank away. So I left her, her scaly head tucked deep beneath her wing so that I would not see the look in her sad eyes nor what they held.

Above the island a huge moon rose. Its rim was broken at the edge, horned and shining. Its lights fell cold upon the wood until, the uplands ashen, near white as though with early snow, I could not tell what was moon-silvered and what was frost. The track wound slowly. Comfortless, in my cold hand I grasped the untried sword that Géar had given me.

Sometimes in the silence I fancied I heard a moaning at my back. But when I stopped to listen, it was only the night wind prowling the island from the west. It was gentle but enough, I thought, to fill a sail. I remembered the golden ship that waited on the shore. Tomorrow I would feel that same wind on my neck. Tomorrow, if that is given me, I thought.

In time the trees came to an end. Gaunt and bitten by the wind, but a few bare stumps were left to straggle into the open field. A gray waste stretched before my sight. Scarred and weathered, it hung above the sea. Yet I was relieved. From its borders I saw the shores of all the western lands, the mountains and the mouths of rivers where they poured into the gulf. If the wood below were Morrigan, these at least were not the fields above the house. Truly, I thought, I have not seem such lands before. I did not wait to see if they would change but stretched out my legs as far as they would go.

The land still rose. I climbed the hill until I thought I would come out on the stars, until in the great open places I grew afraid and walked with caution, looking for shadows where I might be hidden. There was a sullen feeling in the air. I shuddered. The hill seemed long as the night itself.

Long after, when the quiet and the blackness lay heaviest upon the hill, I came at last to the high mere's edge. Alone I stood on the stones that ringed its banks. The wind was still. No breath stirred on its waters and yet it shone, pale with its own grim light, as though foul candles burned beneath its depths. The *filidh* say it is no proper mere but a fragment of the ancient sea, left rotting in that place. So it had been, they judged, and would be long after I had gone, the home of churning sea worms and krakens tangled in their silver hair. But when I looked, I saw only that the mere was shining, pitiless and cold beneath the moon.

I was alone. Men I might have brought with me. Yet, knowing them, I did not hold them to their promises. Those oaths were hollow. It was my father's blood they swore to. I had my own. Ar Elon. My heart cried out to him, not as a lost child cries for home but as a man, weary with the day, will snuff the candle, daring the darkness, ready at any cost for dreams. But cursed by my half-blindness, so destined always to be surprised, I found its eyes already set upon my face.

It waited in the mere, quiet as the stone that bore it or like a snake upon a stone, scaled, huge, like a thing already dead. And yet it lived, arrogant to hold to life where death had taken all the rest. Slime dripped from its night-black hair. Its flesh was blistered, the thick arms rotting where they sank into the mere, the hands longfingered, bent, unlike a man's. It had a fish half-eaten in its jaws.

"So we are met," it called out thickly, my father's beast but not my father. The crows spoke gibberish. The thing that was not a man stared back at me. There was weariness in its old face, and pain. But its mockery was more.

"Fool," it wailed, "none passes me. These years I

waited, I met the little men that came. One last game they had with me. Now their heads rot separate from the rest." Then it laughed, its rank head lifted, grinning at the moon. "Can you tell me you are different from them?"

I did not answer. The hands of all the men I knew had blood on them. I might have said it, but I felt my silence like a nut between my jaws.

"Fool!" it whined and, though it laughed again, it saw my longing. With all my might I pushed the knowledge back. My heart pounded. But my thoughts were lead. Yet even them I must have known. For that brief space it looked at me, something more than hatred or even laughter in its swollen eyes. Then darkness filled them and it sprang.

Like a striking snake it flashed across the mere, its black hands flying to my throat. I felt the hot blood on my neck. In the tail of my eye I saw the white bone sticking out. But when it lunged again I caught the thrust against my sword. Where I hacked it, the old flesh burned, red flames licking out from the wounds. The black flesh fell away like burning rags. There was stone beneath. Then, as I watched, the great black fingers hardened, thickened with its chest and arms until it rose, one thick pillar out of rock. My breath lay indrawn in my mouth. It was Lord R'gnir's face it wore. It was the old king's eyes that glittered, cold and red as garnets in its head.

"An oath you swore to kill me, Finn," it cried and swung its heavy sword across my knees. But, falling, I pulled its craglike shoulder after me. I wrenched it down and slammed my own blade hard against its ribs. The sword recoiled. I heard it fall among the stones. The old king laughed.

"There was never a sword fashioned that would cut cold stone," it roared. My face white as my knuckles, I turned away.

But it was there.

It edged around, moving like a cat before it springs. It had no ears. Sea hair, black and green, clung to its shoulders. Its rough blunt yellow teeth were bared. He snarled, my father's harper. He smelled of weed and crabs. It seared my thoughts. Amazed, unthinking, I circled with him until against my foot, unlooked-for, I felt the heavy metal of my blade. I stooped to lift it. He seemed surprised.

"What man has given you a sword to murder me?" he barked.

I felt the burning metal that was no gift from him that fathered me. It was a flame that ran beneath my skin, into the roots of my hair, and filled my brain. I sucked the air.

"No man," I cried, and all at once I felt the darkness, a hardness in me melt. "She gave it who had no gift from him nor saw his face. No more she had from him than I did."

My anger, remembered, was like a flame. I would have done with this and all the changing shapes he flung at me, both men and beasts, things already dead, not him I sought.

The seaman sneered. "Ever there were too many women in this, Finn. The first death was for that. The others followed."

I meant to speak no more but only to stick my blade in him. Yet I found the words already in my mouth. "What death?" I said.

"Lot's, whom Urien slew, because his tongue was loose within his head."

It was one door I had not opened. But it was Urien's, no use to me. He never was my father. When I left the mountain, I was free of him. And yet I raised my head. "I never heard," I said, "the words that got his dying."

"That thing is done."

"Yet I would hear them."

The seaman's eyes were strange and restless in his head. "Lot swore Lord Ar Elon never came ashore to rule, that he cared nothing for the lives of men."

My heart was still. "What made him come?"

"That which brought the ancient Selchie, though the stones of the land are dry and the sun is cruel."

I shook my head. "That does not answer what Lot said nor why Urien slew him."

"He said the truth."

"What cause is that?"

"Urien did not know that it was so."

I saw him smile. "What were the words?" I said.

His eyes were quiet. "Lot was a little man and often drunk. For three days as they rode toward Hren he had been muttering in his cup. He was of Twyw, his folk the Kell. His wife had left him. That last day, when they reached the island, his cup was filled and so he emptied it.

He told the king to crawl back to the rotting sea, to rut with squid and whales or whatever godless thing would have him, only he must leave the women of the land to such as were true men. Himself, he was a little man. But his voice was loud. The people heard him. It was to this that Urien took offense and so—his head."

The seaman laughed, yet his eyes were cold and sad as the darkness undersea. A blackness twisted in their depths. I do not think he knew me when he sprang. His eyes had yet to find me when he leapt, fixed as they were on the murderous edges of the thing he flung at me. With one great stroke I drove my sword up through his throat and on, deep into the dreadful head. It passed his eyes. But when he fell, I caught him in my arms.

His head, which needed no jaws to speak or eyes to look at me, turned at last to meet my face. The wisps of Pendyved's hair were blowing from his skull. Like leaves before a wind they fell away. My strange thoughts raced. But already the skull had changed, grown flesh again. Wondering, I saw the old bent head of the mage who bore the wood up Ormkill's hill. I felt his gaze. A spasm ran across his lips. Gray and haggard, they pulled back in a smile. So enemy and friend had smiled at me. His breath blew out of him. And still he spoke.

"Now, a little while you shall be free of it," he sighed. "Yet you must know the wood grows year by year. When you have grown too huge and black for what springs up beneath, a woodsman . . ."

But after that he did not move. It may be that his life was already gone from him, though it seemed he barely noticed it.

I dragged the corpse up from the mere. The flesh, no mind to rule it, squirmed upon its rack of bones. A new face gathered on the skull, peered out, curious and troubled to be awake, then, vague, slid sideways, fell. But then another took its place. Men I saw, great kings with distant burning looks, and squinting fools, and sometimes, roused within the graying flesh, the heads of beasts, a sadness in them, gazing out with desperate, cunning eyes. They shifted as I watched them, fretfully, as clouds change in a gale. A few, before their dying took them, I had known.

In death he had my size, the same black hair. I lugged the corpse, the soles of his great feet scoring the ground we crossed, until I had him on a stone. On the high place of the island, the sea at every side, I built a cairn. From the legs I built it, setting each stone with care. Before I placed the last, I looked once more at what lay dead. The flesh was still. I saw at last the years on him, the creases of his neck, the cold gray cheeks. The wind blew from the west and tore his hair, tormenting it as though unsatisfied. Uncertain, it blew into his eyes. But if it found one last spark there, it blew it out.

The dawn came quietly, red above the land. Soon, I thought, I shall go down and close the gate the stone kings watch. But I did not go, and long I sat with quiet, bloody hands. At last, in the stillness, I lifted the ax where he had dropped it and, grieving, set it down upon the face I knew.

Thus ends the first book of the FINNBRANCH, which is called *Yearwood*. The second is called *Undersea*.

ON THE
OTHER SIDE
OF TIME
AND SPACE

Stories of
Fantastic, Futuristic Worlds
That Illuminate Universes

Pocket Books offers the best in Science Fiction—
a genre whose time has come.